FAMILY TIES ON BEAMER STREET

SHEILA RILEY

B

Boldwood

First published in Great Britain in 2025 by Boldwood Books Ltd.

Copyright © Sheila Riley, 2025

Cover Design by Colin Thomas

Cover Images: Colin Thomas

The moral right of Sheila Riley to be identified as the author of this work has been asserted in accordance with the Copyright, Designs and Patents Act 1988.

Every effort has been made to obtain the necessary permissions with reference to copyright material, both illustrative and quoted. We apologise for any omissions in this respect and will be pleased to make the appropriate acknowledgements in any future edition.

A CIP catalogue record for this book is available from the British Library.

Paperback ISBN 978-1-80483-297-4

Large Print ISBN 978-1-80483-298-1

Hardback ISBN 978-1-80483-299-8

Ebook ISBN 978-1-80483-295-0

Kindle ISBN 978-1-80483-296-7

Audio CD ISBN 978-1-80483-304-9

MP3 CD ISBN 978-1-80483-303-2

Digital audio download ISBN 978-1-80483-300-1

This book is printed on certified sustainable paper. Boldwood Books is dedicated to putting sustainability at the heart of our business. For more information please visit https://www.boldwoodbooks.com/about-us/sustainability/

Boldwood Books Ltd, 23 Bowerdean Street, London, SW6 3TN

www.boldwoodbooks.com

*Family Ties on Beamer Street is dedicated to my beautiful
granddaughter, Abi, and her partner Dylan, who gave us the precious
gift of Darci Mai to love and to cherish.
Ain't life wonderful. xx*

PROLOGUE
LIVERPOOL, 1894

'What's this?' Maggie O'Day's Irish lilt was tinged with surprise and ever-growing dread. Her voice quivered when she saw her sixteen-year-old daughter Violet dragging herself up the three concrete steps towards the open front door.

Maggie could not help but notice the heavy woollen shawl around her daughter's slight shoulders. In the cloying heat of a summer's day, it was concealing something she dared not even contemplate.

'Why aren't you at work?' Maggie asked Violet, who was employed as a maidservant in the large house of a prosperous businessman in Southport, twenty miles away. Maggie depended on the wages Violet sent home every week. For her to be here at this time of day could only mean one thing. 'Have they let you go?'

Violet's eyes, wide with a mixture of fear and desperation, darted around the small room, as she entered the narrow back-to-back house. In the heart of Liverpool's dockland, her mother had raised eight children – the youngest of whom was Violet – and lost five more after coming to No. 2 Rose Court Cottages as a young bride thirty years ago with Seamus, her seafaring husband. Seamus was rarely home for more than a few days at a time, but when he was, the whole parish knew about it.

'Don't tell me you've walked out of another job?' Maggie wagged her finger in her daughter's face. They desperately needed the money she earned. 'You won't get another one that pays better!' Her admonishment brought a powerful sense of foreboding. Although, when she saw the look of wretched fear in Violet's pale blue eyes, Maggie's stern words softened. She could not ignore the nagging feeling deep within her that told her this visit would bring forth findings beyond her control.

'Is he home?' Violet's trembling voice betrayed the fear in her words, as she let the shawl fall open to show her swollen belly.

'Jays, Mair and Joe Bloggs,' Maggie breathed, not allowing herself to take the names of holy saints in vain. 'He'll skull-drag you, so he will.' Maggie, knowing her husband's unbending views on how a God-fearing woman should behave, closed her eyes, trying to deny the sight before her, an invisible hand squeezing her heart and pushing precious air out of her body. Then, as the enormous realisation dawned, one hand flew to her gaping lips to suppress the agonised cry. With the other hand, she blessed herself.

'Ma, will you help me?' Violet gasped as the ticking of the grandfather clock filled the room, punctuating her terrified words and amplifying the terror she knew her father would create when he came home and discovered her *condition*.

'He'll not be home until tomorrow,' Maggie whispered, dragging the shawl around her daughter to cover the unholy sight.

Violet's eyes filled with tears as she mouthed a heartfelt plea. 'Holy Mary, mother of God, pray for me!'

'It's a bit late for that.' Maggie spat the words as her eyes shot a venomous glare towards Violet's swollen abdomen. 'I suspect there's a streak of something dark inside you, my girl. Something wilful and unrestrained. Isn't that the reason the Church sent you to Southport in the first place?'

'It wasn't my fault, Ma!' Violet's voice trembled. 'You have to believe me.'

'Get out of my sight!' Maggie shouted, unable to cope with the sight of her daughter, who had brought her nothing but trouble. 'Go next door to Aunt Biddy.' Then, watching as the young girl turned and swiftly left the house, Maggie's icy tone melted, and softened. 'Biddy will know what to do.'

1

LIVERPOOL, MAY 1926

Thirty-two-year-old Peggy Tenant hurried along the cobbled streets of Liverpool's dock road towards the bank. She would be late visiting her mother this morning, because she had to press her husband's suit ready for this afternoon. Her lateness would put her mother in a foul mood, but it couldn't be helped. She had to make an appointment at the bank for herself and her husband, Dar, as they needed to see the manager today, and the bank hadn't opened until ten o'clock.

Looking up to the Victorian clock hanging on an iron chain above the door of the bank, she could see it was already ten thirty. Ma would be livid she was late bringing the milk for her morning cup of tea. Peggy felt a zing of apprehension shoot through her body like one of those whiz-bangs on bonfire night and hoped her mother wouldn't be as difficult today as she could be, especially when she heard her news.

Today was Peggy's seventeenth wedding anniversary. The day she and Dar had promised themselves since they married all those years ago. Today was the day their life would change for the better.

Peggy had also ironed Dar's best white shirt and laid out his only suit on the bed next to the suitcase, which usually lay hidden under the bed. She would have his dinner waiting for him when he came home from working on the docks at one o'clock. Only then, when they were both dressed in their Sunday best, would they take the suitcase and deposit every penny they had saved, since the day they married, and put it into the bank, before signing the papers that would make their rented house at No. 3 Beamer Street their own.

Lost in thought, Peggy deftly navigated the cobbled road that snaked alongside the bustling docks, defining Liverpool's maritime industry and hosting some of the world's biggest ships. Although she knew there would be no ships docking in this part of the port today.

As she headed to the newsagent to get her mother a morning paper, she realised she had never known the road to be so quiet. Not even on a Sunday, before the local church bells rang out, calling everybody to mass.

Her smart, highly polished Louis-heeled leather lace-up shoes skimmed the pavement, and she longed to undo the single hip-button of her loose-fitting coat or remove her brown cloche hat in the heat of the morning, but she wouldn't. It would not be proper, and Peggy, being a proud woman, lived her life by propriety and respectability.

Dark Marcel waves peeped out from under the turned-up rim of the hat, casting a faint shadow over her determined face, when Peggy noticed a young boy moving from the newsagent's wooden counter, a stick of orange barley sugar in his grimy hands, and she gave a little shudder.

Grimacing, she watched him wipe a trail of thick mucus from his nose onto the frayed sleeve of his woollen jerkin, and she quickly reached into her pocket to take out a clean white hand-kerchief.

'Here, mucky boy,' Peggy said impatiently. 'Don't wipe your nose on your sleeve.' She clicked her tongue against the roof of her mouth, tutting as the boy took the pristine cotton square and gave a colossal blow. Then, to her disgust, he held the handkerchief towards her, offering it back.

'I don't want it. You've used it.' Peggy's lips turned down at the corners, her eyebrows pleating in horror. 'Take it home and get your mother to wash it.' Stepping aside, she held open the door to let the ragged boy duck under her arm, leaving just enough room so the barley sugar did not meet her best coat.

'There's only two papers being printed until the strike is over,' said the newsagent, when Peggy enquired as to why her mother's usual morning paper was not available, knowing that from the fourth of May, the whole country had come to a virtual standstill. Workers all over Britain had put down their tools and walked off their jobs in a show of camaraderie for their fellow workers in the coal industry, when the Trade Union Congress had called the strike to try to force the government to step in and put a stop to the loss of pay and longer working hours of coal miners.

'*The British Worker*,' said the newsagent, pointing to a pleated row of folded newspapers on the counter, 'they're the ones supporting the general strike, and then there's *The British Gazette*, supported by Mister Churchill—' he pointed to the other row '— who is soundly condemning the withdrawal of labour.'

'Aye—' Peggy rolled her shoulders and lifted her chin, a sure sign she was not in agreement with Mister Churchill '—but he doesn't have to make do on a pittance, does he?'

'I don't suppose he does,' said the newsagent, knowing that martial law had been introduced on the ninth of May, which meant the temporary suspension of civil law, allowing the military to keep order and swiftly address threats to national security during the strike.

'And what about us poor women who have to keep body and soul together, whether our husband is working or not?' Peggy was indignant. 'We don't have the luxury of going on strike, do we? Even though we're the ones that keep the home fires burning,' she said, reminding the newsagent of the patriotic wartime song composed by Ivor Novello in 1914. Not that any of this political stuff troubled Peggy, except when it meant her own family had to go without – only then did it become a matter of concern. A political newspaper, such as those on offer, would be of little interest to her mother, either. 'Mam won't be best pleased when she can't read her morning paper at luncheon.'

The newsagent offered no comment but raised an eyebrow. His half-shrug told Peggy that his usual patrons never used the word 'luncheon', unless they were part of the upper classes or employed in service. Neither of which concerned her. She was never going to be in service, she was going up in the world. Today she was going to the bank to buy her own house and was entitled to use words like luncheon, as most rate-paying property owners did.

'I suspect you are as fed up with the strike as everybody else?' Peggy continued, ignoring his indifference. She decided to buy the newspapers for Dar. 'My husband likes a quiet read after a long day's graft.'

'I agree with you, missus,' the newsagent held out his hand for the money and gave a patient sigh. 'So do millions of other men, that's why they're out on strike. But I can't magic up the usual newspapers. Unlike your *working husband*, the printers are also on strike.' Peggy detected a note of scorn in his voice. 'They're forgoing their wages in support of the miners, who also graft for long hours.' There was no denying the implication that her husband was a money-grabbing blackleg.

Peggy could not ignore his obvious contempt. 'I take it *you* didn't feel inclined to support the miners either,' she retorted, handing over the money for both newspapers.

'It is my job to sell the news, not to make it,' he said.

Peggy tucked the papers into her basket, and she too raised a scornful eyebrow, satisfied some people, like the newsagent, had elasticated principles that only stretched so far. If the strike did not impinge his own well-being, he would talk about supporting the strikers all day long. Peggy said nothing. Dar would want to keep up with both sides of the story. Although, she thought as she left the shop, she had a sneaking suspicion her husband wanted to strike in support of the miners as much as any man, but he and the other workers employed at Hutton Logistics had no choice but to heed the ultimatum they had been given. 'Work or want!' Henry Hutton had told his workforce. Dar, being one of the best master stevedores on the dock, feared not only for his job, but also that of their eldest lad, Jack, who was a can-lad at Hutton's. Losing one wage would be bad enough in this poor financial situation, but her family could not afford to lose two pay packets, even if the wages were a pittance.

Dar and Jack had no choice but to work, and Peggy was glad. She couldn't be doing with two of them hanging around the house all day. Jobs were not easy to come by. And she had no compunction in voicing her thoughts. 'If you have no work there will be no pay,' she had told Dar, reminding him she was just looking out for her family, ignoring those who crossed the street to avoid her and those who shouted out, calling Dar a money-grabbing blackleg for not uniting with the rest of the strikers. But those people did not know how hard Dar had worked to accumulate their precious savings, nor the sacrifices she had made to allow their house fund to grow over the years.

Her eldest lad, Jack, was not of the same mind these days, though. He had gone on strike, believing that if men did not stand

together, then where would they be? 'Out of a job,' Peggy had told
him, and warned him not to come running to her when he was
short. Dar was more forgiving and told her that the lad had to make
up his own mind. Even when she reminded her husband they had
saved long and hard to buy their house in Beamer Street. That
house would be her security from the hunger she had known as a
child.

Nipping in and out of the few shops that were still open opposite the great, smoke-blackened dock walls looming over Regent
Road, the warm air was heavy with the smell of curling smoke from
domestic chimneys. The only way some women could cook was on
the open fire, and even though it was a bright May day, the
sunshine rarely penetrated the back-to-back courts. Peggy knew
she would have to get her skates on if she was to meet Dar when he
knocked off work from Hutton's – the only firm working on the
docks. He was taking a rare few hours off to complete the purchase
at the bank.

She also knew he too would have to run the gauntlet of striking
men who had no hesitation in showing their fury for a strike-
breaker. And even though the whole country was on strike, Henry
Hutton had warned his workers they would be sacked if they did
not turn up for work. Dar told her he suspected Hutton was getting
more than a handshake for threatening his own workers, so she
knew Dar had no choice, although Peggy was secretly pleased.
Going on strike would delay the purchase of owning their own
home which they so desperately wanted, and with it the security
such a possession offered. Something neither of them had known
before.

Peggy was proud her husband continued to work, even though
he had been threatened with violence by the strikers, who believed
the government would try to reduce their wages too, if the miners
caved in. Even so, she had little sympathy for the striking men,

who, in their fury, would have attacked Dar had it not been for the presence of the military. She suspected their fight was futile and did not agree with taking bread from the mouths of children, knowing the powers-that-be would do as they pleased, and the workers would be starved into submission.

Peggy eyed the street plaque, high on the rough red-brick wall, which pointed the way to Rose Cottages, the back-to-back court name, where her family had lived for donkey's years. It was barely visible through the grime of the surrounding port of Liverpool dockyards opposite.

The home port for vast numbers of British overseas shipping companies, with direct sailings to every major world port, but Peggy had never known it to be so quiet. She knew the wealth and prosperity, so near, was as far as earth from heaven to the people who lived in these cramped courts overlooking the dock's enormous warehouses. And she could not get out of here fast enough, when she married Dar seventeen years ago, today.

2

Peggy shook her head at the audacity of the town planners who gave the dilapidated dwellings such a sweet, perfumed name as Rose Cottages when they hastily threw up the cramped houses for Irish immigrants during the *great hunger*. She felt ashamed of the pretty name that made a mockery of the run-down buildings, which signalled the hardship faced by the relentless drudgery of working-class families. The families who lived hand to mouth most of the time.

Peggy, deep in thought, nearly jumped out of her skin when a fishwife bellowed the contents of her basket less than a couple of feet from her ear.

'Jays, Mair and Jo Blogs,' exclaimed Peggy, her hand splayed across her chest, 'you nearly frightened the life out of me!'

'Sorry, girl.' The fishwife, known in these parts as a *shawlie* or a *Mary Ellen*, threw back her head and set free a loud, raucous cackle that carried along the Dock Road. Peggy grimaced when the cavernous mouth displayed two rows of shiny gums as pink as Dublin Bay prawns. 'It's been dead slow down the market since the strike. I thought I'd chance me luck along here, door to door.'

These women, known for their resilience, and their formidable nature, at once made Peggy feel sorry for the hard-working woman's plight.

Her toil was physically demanding while carrying heavy baskets of fish, which she would have helped her husband or brother land, and only then, after gutting the fish, would she be able to trawl the market, barking out the price of her produce. Peggy knew she would have spent many a long hour trying to sell the catch – no easy task in these straitened times.

Peggy also knew these women were well known for their sense of community and support, often working in familiar groups, helping each other with selling. Sometimes even pooling their resources to get better prices from suppliers and noted for using a unique slang that set them apart from other market traders.

'I've got a nice piece of *finny haddy* for you, girl,' said the fishwife, already taking a decent-sized piece of smoked haddock from her basket. 'Your family will think it's their birthday when you give 'em this.'

'How can I resist,' Peggy said, shuddering as she paid for the fish she loathed so much. 'I can't stand the smell of it, meself, but me mam loves it.' Something about the smell reminded her of her childhood, when her father was home from sea, and an uneasy cloud hovered over her, but she was forever at a loss to explain why.

'I 'eard the strike can't last much longer,' said the fishwife. 'People are going hungry, and shops can't afford to trade on *tick* no more.' *Tick* was the system whereby goods were bought on credit. The customer's name went into a ledger, and they paid the money due to the shopkeeper when their husband received his wages.

The practice worked well, usually, and was the only way some families survived from one pay packet to the next, while keeping traders in business. But, with no financial support from anywhere else, even the merchants were falling on challenging times.

'I agree with every man getting a fair day's pay for a fair day's work,' said the fishwife, 'but when the whole country downs tools, things are getting desperate.' Peggy was familiar with the fish women who played a key role in the community, which extended beyond selling in the market. They were a natural part of the area, sharing snippets of gossip and knowledge that wasn't so readily available from other quarters.

'Aye,' said Peggy, watching as she sauntered along the cobbled road with her half-filled basket of fish, calling out her wares to people who did not have the means to buy, her black shawl billowing out behind her like dark wings.

These women had no union to protect them, thought Peggy, knowing if they didn't sell their perishables early in the day, the fish wouldn't be fit to eat later. After all the hard slog, it was unfortunate to see the women sell their hard-won fish for mere farthings.

Peggy put the smoked haddock into her basket and hurried on, narrowly avoiding a collision with a gaggle of small children sitting in the gutter, poking the cobbles with a stick. Some, with dirty bare feet, were dodging stationary carts and wagons that were unusually idle at this time of day. The road should be alive with dock workers unloading ships, porters stowing merchandise into the huge warehouses and carters transporting bales of cotton, hogsheads of tobacco, drums of palm oil, sacks of sugar and all manner of cargo, which had been transferred from those self-same warehouses to their carts and pulled by the working horses plodding the cobbles.

But there were no calls from the usual crews of dock workers, save for the strikers standing around glowing braziers, still needed even in the month of May, when a keen wind blew in off the river and could make the hair on the back of the neck stand on end.

Through a fog of smoke from the matchstick-thin, hand-rolled cigarettes, dangling from food-hungry lips, they shifted from foot to foot to keep their circulation moving, while waving handwritten cardboard placards.

'Mind out me way,' Peggy called impatiently, heading towards the compact streets of back-to-back courts, towards her mother's cramped dwelling. Rose Cottages? The only smell around here was the acrid stench of smoke, grime, outside privies, rat-infested middens and poverty. She sighed heavily. There was not one single perfumed floral bud to be had, nor a charming, picturesque cottage between them.

The dim passageway, situated between the towering gable end of two houses, leading to her mother's dwelling, seemed even more oppressive under a low sky casting its gloomy pallor across the stone-flagged courtyard.

Peggy could not get away from this place fast enough seventeen years ago. This inadequate type of housing, with high walls that bellied out into the narrow corridor, blocking out any natural light even on a sunny day, was common in this part of Liverpool. Peggy thanked every angel and saint above that she had managed to turn her back on all of this and got out of here as soon as she had married Dar. Her sixteen-year-old heart had yearned for freedom and security, to escape her mother's small kitchen, overflowing with family who were always coming and going. There was no peace. No comfort. No privacy. A bed of her own and a clean chemise had been a far-off dream.

Memories of her father's sea-going absence and her mother's daily struggles of hand-to-mouth existence flooded her mind with a mixture of sadness and a lifelong determination to create a better life for her own children. That dream would come to fruition this afternoon when she would become the proud owner of her own home. She and Dar had striven for this moment since the day they married, their sacrifices proving they had achieved something their predecessors never could.

Ma was like most dockside matriarchs, always strict. Not cruel. She just didn't know any other way. Sparing the rod meant spoiling the child, and being spoiled was something Peggy would never be in danger of experiencing. Her ma's worry of putting food on the table, or a roof over her family's head, was always in evidence. Her careful planning was always accompanied by worry, not only of where the next copper was coming from, but if there was anything left to hock.

Nothing was out of bounds when the pawnshop was calling Ma. Peggy was never certain her shoes would be where she'd left them the night before. Most weeks, they would end up in Uncle's, the name commonly given to the local pawnshop where the poor women of the dock road hocked their family's shoes or clothes for a few pennies to feed their family. Or worse, sold them to a neighbour if they still had a bit more wear left in them.

Peggy had got out of here with unconcealed delight, sure her feet had left scorch marks on the cobbles in her haste to see the back of this place. Sighing, she entered the passageway, safe in the knowledge she had never missed one miserable day of living in her mother's dwelling, cramped with eight older siblings.

As soon as she found out she had 'fallen' with their Jack, Dar had got a special licence to marry. Peggy had forged her father's signature, and they had married in Brougham Terrace registry office, which neither family attended. A good-living Catholic girl, she was not considered decently married from a registry office, nor to a Protestant boy. So, none of her or Dar's family had blessed the ceremony with their presence.

The parish priest had come around to give her a telling-off she would remember for many a long day. Her mother and older sister,

Violet, had said she was a disgrace to the family and told her they would never be able to hold their heads up again.

Peggy knew it wasn't her sinful pregnancy that had got people so hot under the collar, but the fact she had married one of King Billy's, the name her Catholic mother gave to a Protestant from Netherfield Road.

Yet, the families got on well enough at the *hooley* afterwards, Peggy recalled, knowing a party was hastily arranged in the mainly Irish courtyard, where someone had brought out their piano and everybody sang their favourite rebel songs until the wee small hours. The beer had flowed, and the table was bulging with pork pies, bacon ribs, ham sandwiches and bowls of trifle. Then, when they'd had their fill of food and the alcohol had diluted their blood, all hell had broken loose, which could only be expected when two tribes of differing faiths made their true feelings known.

As Mam had explained later, a comment was made, which had upset the 'other' side, and the ensuing fisticuffs had ended what had been a memorable day all round. Not that Peggy and Dar knew much about it until a week later. They had been busy enjoying a surprise five-day honeymoon on the Isle of Man, paid for by Aunty Biddy, her father's good-natured but wizened sister, who lived next door.

Life hadn't been easy when they returned from their honeymoon. They had walked the length of the dock road. Eventually, finding a couple of rooms in a large Victorian house near Strand Road, cooking on a small fire in the narrow hearth when Dar found work on the docks.

Six months later, it was difficult trying to keep a new baby quiet when the occupants of the lodging house were night workers. They had left her under no illusion that she and her baby son were considered a nuisance. Then she was given orders from the landlord to keep the child quiet or she would have to move out.

Peggy had tramped the streets, pushing a second-hand pram in freezing fog looking for accommodation, while Dar was out working all the hours he could. She was barely seventeen and so lonely it physically hurt. She had longed to greet Dar with the good news that she had found them a house of their own, when he came home from a hard day's graft. But she never did. Instead, she had to walk the streets during the day, so the working men could get their sleep. Coming home, frozen to the bone, Peggy soon realised she was just a young girl with unreachable dreams, but still she had strived to save every penny to give them something better.

When Dar was called up to fight in France, she had two babies. Two-year-old Millie was in the pram, while four-year-old Jack sat on the apron as, once more, she tramped the streets, desperate to find somewhere they could finally call home.

Eventually, her fortitude had vanished to nothing, she was at the end of her tether. Tears had rolled down her face as her teething baby had bawled, fit to wake the dead. Then, when all seemed lost, a gentle old woman, brushing rainwater from her step in Beamer Street, had asked her if she would like to come in for a cup of tea.

Usually so private, Peggy was grateful for someone to talk to, and she had let the whole sorry tale pour from her lips like a running tap. She needed to find a better place to live. She needed somewhere she could raise her children in comfort and safety. She needed the security her family was reluctant to offer.

'There's always my parlour and the middle bedroom, if it'll suit,' said Mrs Jenson in that softly spoken way she had about her. Peggy smiled at the memory now, knowing Mrs Jenson was kindness personified. Her guardian angel in human form. They kept each other company during the war and Peggy missed her so much. In November 1918, just as the armistice was called, the old woman had died. It seemed she just couldn't hang on any longer.

Then Dar was discharged from the navy and successfully applied to take over the tenancy. Only days later, he had found secure work on the docks.

Molly Haywood, a friend to all, especially Mrs Jenson, had given her and Dar a good reference, saying they were just the type of people who deserved a house in Beamer Street, and the money Peggy had saved from Dar's very first wage packet went to pay key money on the house, proving that they were worthy of such a solid abode.

They could not have been happier. All thanks to Mrs Jenson, who had once told Peggy that her home had always been a happy one, and although she had never been blessed with her own offspring, she knew number three was meant to be filled with children and laughter.

Every week she paid her rent on the nail, never missed. Then her housekeeping was shared between various empty cocoa tins – the rent, gas and food. Dar would have his weekly 'baccy' money, and, unbeknown to him, Peggy would slope half-a-crown into the back of her purse for her mother, before putting the rest away in the cardboard suitcase under the bed to buy the house.

She didn't care if they had to save for half a lifetime, determined that one day, the house in Beamer Street would be theirs. And only then would she and her children be secure. The thought gave her peace of mind, and she soon got into a comfortable little rhythm, knowing each week they were a few shillings closer to owning their own home.

Even now, she still gave thanks to the good Lord above for allowing her to meet such a wonderful woman as Mrs Jenson and a hard-working man like Dar, who shared her hopes and dreams. A good provider who cared for his family, Dar did his best for all of them.

Her life, after she had married him, had turned from a reality of want to the dream of *maybe one day*. And that day was going to be today, because of Dar – one of the few men who did not go on strike like the rest of the country.

Being a good provider, and doing his best, meant everything to Peggy, even if Ma, and her older sister, Violet, could not bear the sight of him. Dar, unlike her sister's husband, tipped every penny out of his wage packet each week. She managed a clean and tidy house, and they were happy being careful, as well as determined.

* * *

Dar Tenant had experience of loading and unloading ships' cargo, the only method of training for head stevedores, or blocker men as they were known on the docks. He decided where goods of varying shapes and sizes needed to be positioned for maximum efficiency and being a fair-minded man, he was a friend to many.

Pushing back the customary bowler hat that showed his superior standing on the dock, Dar motioned to the crane driver to lower the huge rope sling of hessian sugar sacks, which were being unloaded from the hold of the ship. An expert in gauging the many weights and sizes of valuable merchandise, he knew the cargo must be loaded and unloaded in such a way that there would be no danger of damage, especially to outgoing cargo, during transit.

His job on the dock was vital to the smooth turnaround of the ship leaving port on time. Under his expert guidance, goods would be packed in a way that would enable the ship to still be stable. Also, as the vessel would be calling at several ports, Dar knew it was his job to ensure the gang of men packed the merchandise in the correct order for discharge.

This ship was sailing on the midday tide, and then he and his Peggy would be off to the bank to deposit the money he had worked so hard for since he'd married her seventeen years ago and sign the deeds to his own house.

Although, that was not the end of his working day, he would return later, on the twilight shift, to oversee the unloading of incoming coal directly into railway wagons at Herculaneum Dock. In normal times, coal would be exported through the port, but with a reduced labour force because of the miners' strike, coal was having to be imported from outside the country.

But those were thoughts for later. Right now, he could see the sling of hessian sacks of sugar was swinging closer towards the head of one of the younger, less experienced lads working on the dock. The thick rope creaked and groaned under the strain of the huge sacks, and Dar's heart pounded in his chest, his breathing coming in rapid, shallow bursts, imagining what was about to happen if the lad didn't move out of the way.

'Stop! Move out of the way!' Dar yelled to Miles Houseman, who was working the crane. Houseman was the nephew of Henry Hutton who owned the firm of men loading and unloading ships.

Dar's hand shot up in the salty air to warn Miles to slow the rope sling swinging like a pendulum across the deck of the ship and heading straight for the young lad, waiting to unload the contents of the hold onto the quay.

'Slow down on the winch!' Dar's hands waved high in the air, a sign to slow down even if Miles couldn't hear him over the dock-side cacophony. Dar knew any sensible crane driver would be alert to his warning, but Houseman seemed oblivious. Some said he was drunk after only just getting back from the local alehouse, where he'd been since opening time. 'Get back!' Dar called to the young lad, as the rest of the working men stopped what they were doing to see what all the shouting was, the older men knew the dangers of the docks extremely well. 'I said get back, that sling's gonna go!'

Soon, most of the men had stopped work and were shouting, warning, creating a chaos of noise enough to waken the dead. But the crane driver still did not slow down.

Cal Everdine, an extremely qualified engineer, who was part of the team in charge of building the new Gladstone wet dock, was heading along the quayside. When he heard the commotion, he quickened his step. One of the first men to respond, he skidded alongside the ship, frantically trying to catch the attention of the crane driver and regain some control of the desperate situation. But there was no time to reach the lad. Nor warn him about the danger overhead.

At the same time, Cal saw Dar hurling himself forward, his legs moving but not seeming to get far on the wet quayside, slippery beneath his heavy boots. He had seen this kind of accident happen once before and he knew, if the lad didn't move out of the way now, he would end up in the dock and probably suffer fatal consequences.

Dar hurled himself forward and pushed the young lad out of the way. The sling turned, swinging closer. Closer. Dar's heart was pounding. His breathing shallow. Time was running out. What was that fool, Houseman, thinking of?!

Dar didn't feel a thing when he pushed the young lad clear and the sling caught him on the back of his head. All he knew was that one minute he was on the deck of the ship and the next he was looking down into the hold, watching himself being held down. He was lashing out with his arms, his body jerking. Dar could see his own body fighting with all its might. He was struggling to get up. Why wouldn't they let him get up? Anger spiralled from the pit of his stomach as a huge crowd of men slid down into the hold and gathered around him. They were loudly demanding he keep still. Not struggle. The ambulance was still minutes away.

'Keep him still, it's too dangerous to let him move!' someone shouted. That was when Dar looked into the terrified eyes of the man struggling to stay alive and realised it was he who needed to get to his feet, otherwise this might be the last job he ever did.

3

Old memories caused small currents of excitement to run through Peggy's veins, pushing down the claustrophobia she usually felt as the high red-brick walls of her former home closed in on her. She couldn't wait to tell her ma the good news that she and Dar were going to become the proud owners of their very own house.

The thought put wings on her heels and, hurrying now, she entered the courtyard, where tall skinny dwellings, almost within touching distance, faced one another. The middle of the smooth flagstones was interrupted by a narrow gulley, along which rainwater, domestic liquids and other pestiferous slops were evacuated into the sewers beneath.

Peggy shuddered as the pungent smell of the nearby privy hit her, her brow furrowing at the stench of an overflowing midden, which was only a few feet from the nearest, poorly ventilated house whose inhabitants had to put up with the almost certainly poisonous gases.

She felt sick when she saw the children, their feet bare, drinking water from the standpipe near the grid in the middle of the courtyard. Peggy's observation was interrupted when she was sent stumbling, almost knocked on her backside, by a heavy-set woman in a dark shawl, who had elbowed her way through a throng of children sitting on the worn steps of her mother's house, before disappearing into the gloom of the passageway and out onto the main road.

'Don't mind me, missus!' Peggy, not one to hold her tongue when the need arose, called angrily. Her breath coming in short quick bursts, it was only when the woman reached the end of the passageway, Peggy realised the barging woman was her sister, Violet. 'I might ha' bliddy known,' Peggy shouted, balling her fist in the air, before continuing to climb the worn steps up to her ma's dwelling.

Reaching the half-open, paint-chipped front door that revealed layers of colours beneath, she took a deep breath and braced herself.

'I've brought your rations, Ma,' Peggy called as she walked through the front door of the dwelling, entering the kitchen that was separated from the street by a threadbare curtain hanging on a taut wire, which was secured by a nail either side of the door. She forced down the gag-inducing smell of stale kippers – a local favourite sold cheaply from the nearby market. Peggy could not bear the lingering smell, refusing to cook them in her own house, no matter how many times Dar pleaded.

She hadn't noticed the different local smells when she had lived here, but the evil-smelling pong of the docks, the gasworks, not to mention the surrounding warehouses, factories and shops selling produce connected to the port, hit her like a barn door these days.

This was where her mother had raised every one of her children alone, since her father was away at sea for months on end, like so many Liverpool men. And, although there were good and bad in every area, Peggy knew that no stranger would ever walk around here alone at nightfall if they knew what was good for them.

A massive influx of Irish immigrants had descended, back in the 1840s, her own family included. Having been forced to leave their homeland, they had helped to build the surrounding docks, and needed somewhere for their family to live. So, the money men threw up as many defective dwellings as they could fit into the unthinkably small spaces, and soon the overcrowded houses became squalid and difficult to keep in an orderly fashion.

'I managed to get you a small loaf from Mary Jane's bakery,' said Peggy, hoping the news would please her mother as she opened the near-empty cupboard in the recess at the side of the black polished range. Bread had become as precious as gold during the strike, due to the lack of flour and yeast, not to mention all the other supplies needed to keep body and soul together.

'Yer didn't have to do that.' Maggie O'Day's voice sounded weary as her small beady eyes gobbled up the contents of the basket in one sweeping glance when Peggy placed it on the oilcloth-covered table. She'd just had their Violet in here asking if Peggy had been yet? Since the strike had started, Violet had no money coming in from her job as a ship's cleaner. She was wanting to borrow the money Peggy always left for her. Money that would go behind the bar of the local alehouse and straight down her husband's gullet, no doubt.

Peggy knew her mother would have enough provisions to see her through until her next visit. Unless Violet came scrounging around, that is.

Sighing patiently, she never voiced her thoughts where their Violet was concerned, knowing one minute she and her mother would be at each other's throats and the next they would be remarkably close, whispering to each other behind their hands.

'You still look a bit peaky, Ma,' said Peggy, full of concern.

'Aye, well I'm not as young as I used to be,' said Maggie. The ruck had taken it out of her, and she had even considered giving Violet a few home truths. But she managed to keep her tongue civil. There was nothing to be gained by going over old ground.

Peggy wrinkled her nose in dismay to see the congealed remains of her mother's last meal sticking to a cracked plate situated near two mismatched pots of salt and pepper, a cold teapot, an empty sugar basin and a sticky tin of *conny-onny*. The thick, condensed milk used to lighten and sweeten the stewed tea, which was always kept warm on the hob and grew stronger and more bitter as the day went on.

This kitchen was vastly different from her own spotlessly clean home back in Beamer Street, even though Peggy scrubbed the place from top to bottom every week. At first, her mother wouldn't hear of somebody else cleaning up after her. 'What's the point in titivating the place when it needs to be demolished?' Ma would say with scathing accuracy. But Peggy could not stand filth and grime and set to cleaning with a block of green soap, a bottle of Aunt Sally disinfectant and a scrubbing brush.

'Aren't you cold, Ma?' Peggy asked, picking up the dirty plate, knowing it was warmer on the street than it was in here, and decided the best way to keep warm was by keeping busy. So, lifting the kettle from the black range, she took both out to the tiny windowless scullery at the back, put the plate into the deep brownstone sink and filled the black-bottomed kettle with freezing water from a single copper tap.

The only other conveniences in the scullery were a couple of orderly shelves on the opposite wall and a rickety old chair. All cooking was done on the range in the other room from which her mother rarely ventured, and she wondered if the fire in the next room would be strong enough to bring the kettle of water to the boil.

'I saw our Vi on the way in,' Peggy called, reluctantly removing her coat and hanging it on the back of the scullery door, feeling her mother's chilly mood wrap itself around her.

'Did she say anything?' Maggie asked, her monotone voice dull, and Peggy heeded the advice she'd had drummed into her as a child, to mind her own business.

'What about?' Peggy was always cautious, knowing Ma and Vi had secrets they didn't care to share with her. So, Peggy knew she had to choose her words carefully.

'Oh, nothing.' Her mother was giving nothing away either, having brought Peggy up to *ask no questions and you'll be told no lies*.

'She seemed to be in a hurry. Come for a borrow again, did she?' Peggy asked, not expecting an answer, as she looked around for a clean cloth to wipe down the table. She saw the only thing available was a damp rag, which smelled to high heaven.

Peggy couldn't understand why her mother wanted to live in this overcrowded part of Liverpool, when she had offered her parlour to her mother, who could so easily live with her. But Peggy knew Ma was still waiting in vain for the return of her seafaring husband. And if it wasn't for her dutiful visit, she would never step foot in the place ever again. Her disgust at the living conditions of these poor people burned with passion inside her, but there was nothing she could do about the situation. And she knew the best thing she had ever done was marry Dar and move as far away as they could.

I'm not a toffee-nosed cow, Peggy thought, recalling her sister's words last time they spoke, *but I do have standards*. Tomorrow would be a better day for her, Peggy thought, unlike their Vi who was stuck in this hellhole with a gang of kids and a husband who hadn't done a full day's work since God knew when.

'Your fella still workin', I take it?' Her mother's surly question sounded more like an accusation, as if Dar was doing something illegal instead of looking out for his family during the strike. She barely looked up from the dying embers of the coke fire when Peggy placed the kettle of water on the range.

'He's always working, Ma,' Peggy answered brightly, proud of the fact her husband's job on the docks meant he was always in demand. His job supervising the loading and discharge of cargo by firms like Hutton's was something Dar had worked hard for.

'He must have had a word with the divil himself to have landed a steady job on the docks.' Maggie O'Day's disdain was caustic, and Peggy, knowing her mother's goading of old, tried to ignore the biting description of her husband.

Ma liked the thrust and parry of words when they were about Dar. She had never known the security of a regular wage until her sons had grown and got work on the docks or followed their father out to sea, before they all got married and left her.

Nor did she have the regular company of a loving husband, like she did, Peggy thought. Her seafaring father left a small allotment, which Ma collected from the post office every Saturday morning. The money enabled her rarely seen husband to have a room to come back to – if he ever deigned to come home from his sea-going travels.

'Too good to be true, Dar Tenant,' Maggie sneered under her breath.

'I don't know why you can't be happy for us, Ma,' Peggy tried to disguise the tinge of hurt and defeat in her voice, desperate as always for her mother's approval.

'You used to say that finding a decent man, who didn't spend his hard-earned wages in the alehouse and keep his wife so short of money she had to go hocking, was what you wanted for your daughters.' Peggy felt sorry for those women she'd seen sloping into the pawn shop when they thought nobody was looking. 'A good man was all you wished for your daughters, and Dar's a good man.'

'Aye. A good Catholic lad would have been nice,' Maggie said grudgingly, 'not one of King Billy's.' King Billy's were Protestants who lived mostly around Netherfield Road and proudly marched to Southport every twelfth of July. A march that usually ended up with fists flying as denominational violence between the two major religions inevitably broke out.

'Is our Violet's husband not working, even when there isn't a strike on?' Peggy asked pointedly, ignoring her mother's scathing remark. 'Mind you, I shouldn't skit the afflicted. Not with him being too scared to bend his back in case it breaks.' Peggy was sure Violet's husband had some kind of disorder that kept him in bed most of the day and in the alehouse every night. He had it bad, apparently. And as far as Peggy could tell, there was no cure.

'He can't get a start anywhere because of his bad back.' Her mother ignored Peggy's sarcastic retort. 'He couldn't get a job even before the strike.'

'That's what comes of being a troublemaker.' Peggy's words were critical. 'He ruffles too many feathers with his forthright opinions. He'd cause a war in an empty house.'

'It's not his fault he's got a bad back... And don't mention the strike, the whole country is on strike – except your husband.'

'I bet a pound to a pinch of horse muck Violet's husband would be first in the queue to down tools and throw his hand in,' Peggy said. 'He should be flogged for letting his wife go out cleaning ships. You wouldn't catch me doing that kind of work.' Dar would never allow it, she thought, as her sharp features writhed in disgust. Screwing the remains of an old newspaper, with which she had just polished the windows, Peggy threw it on the miserly fire. 'D'you have any more paper, Ma?'

'There's no papers to be had. Like you said, they're on strike, and I'm not buying the information the government are trying to shove down our throats.' Her mother continued glaring into the grate and Peggy chided herself for her direct opinion of her sister, who was only trying to make ends meet in dire circumstances, and tried to cover her impulsive retort. 'Dar wouldn't allow me to work among foul-mouthed men, who don't even want women on their ships, doing their best to make life as unpleasant as they can.'

'How do you know?' Maggie asked, her voice sullen.

'Everybody knows sailors don't like redheads like our Vi on their ships; they think they're bad luck.'

'My husband's a red-haired sailor; the whole family's got red hair!' Her mother's voice held a warning note, and Peggy sighed, not dwelling on the fact she was the only one in the O'Day family with hair as black as coal. She was too busy wondering why Ma still defended such a feckless man after all these years, knowing her father had kissed her mother's cheek one day, went back to sea and had not been seen or heard of since.

'You only know he's still alive by the pittance of an allotment he sends to the post office each week.'

'Don't speak of him like that,' Maggie said, 'have some respect.'

Peggy couldn't understand why she should respect a man she hardly knew, who had only shown his face for a couple of days a month, if that, and not at all for the last twenty-odd years. But there was no point in arguing the point with her mother, who wouldn't have a wrong word spoken about her disappearing husband.

'Did I tell you we're going to the bank to buy our house this afternoon?'

Peggy hadn't said a word to anybody, not even her mother. She knew Ma would tell Violet, and her sister would be knocking on her door, day and night, wanting to borrow money. Over the past seventeen years, she had longed to tell her mother she was saving to buy her own house. But Peggy had kept the revelation secret, knowing her mother would think she was getting above herself, especially after she had left the courts, and her suspicions were proven by her mother's terse reply.

'I hope it stays fine for yer—' Maggie shifted in her chair '—and there's your poor sister, not a pot to piss in, while you go all la-di-da, buying your own house, no less.'

Peggy had no intentions of getting caught up in another argument about their Vi, who, fifteen years older, was married to a lazy ha'porth, who usually got himself carted off in a paddy wagon after a Saturday-night skinful, putting her sister in dire straits when she had to find the bail money to get him out of the assizes on Monday morning.

'I got you a nice bit of finny-haddy for your tea,' Peggy said, showing her mother the flat package of smoked haddock, hoping to appease her.

'I bet you forgot the milk.'

Ma could not sound less grateful, Peggy thought.

'I got the milk.' Peggy lifted the bottle from her basket and placed it on the table, next to the sugar basin, which she had filled from the dark blue paper packet before putting the rest in the cupboard. 'I also got us a fruity Eccles cake from Mary Jane's. We can have it with a cup of tea, later.' There was many a body who would give their eye teeth for a fruity Eccles cake from Mary Jane's shop, the best bakery for miles.

Mary Jane was one of her best friends, who knew what it was like to feel the wrath of some of the less sharp inhabitants of Beamer Street, like Ina King, the mother of a large, sometimes unruly family, who never kept her opinions to herself, especially where Dar's refusal to strike was concerned.

'I don't know why you bother,' said her ungrateful mother. 'I'm not fussy on them.'

Peggy knew that wasn't true, her mother usually devoured the treats she brought from the bakery.

'Well, maybe you could save it and give it to our Violet, next time she brings her hungry kids over.' Peggy was running out of patience. No matter what she did, no matter how hard she tried, her efforts were never good enough. Yet Violet expected her self-absorbed mother to look after her children, because the slob of a so-called husband lay on the couch and moaned about the noise they made.

'You know how your sister's placed,' her mother said, still staring into the dying embers. 'It can't be easy for her, having to leave her children with an old woman who can't get around as well as she used to, while she's out cleaning the ships.'

'Mam, you're not on your last legs yet, you've got plenty of life left in you.' Peggy tried to reassure her mother, who, for some strange reason, expected every day to be her last. She wished her mother's belligerent carping would cease, even though it came as natural as breathing.

When the kettle boiled, Peggy made her mother a fresh cup of tea before filling a bucket with hot water, mixed with a thick gloop of Aunt Sally disinfectant, and took her scrubbing brush out of her basket. This was the only thing that relieved the frustration building up inside her, knowing every time she came to visit her mother, Maggie O'Day made it plain she didn't have time for her youngest offspring, no matter how hard Peggy tried to please her.

Anger swelled in Peggy's gut as she got down on her hands and knees to scrub the kitchen floor. Only then, when the floor was spotlessly clean and her annoyance spent, did she feel, as always, the stabbing pangs of remorse rear up inside her.

Mam wasn't a bad old stick. She'd had a hard life, that was all. Like every other dockside matriarch, whose existence depended on the ebb and flow of the tide, or the whim of a chargehand. 'You won't ever catch me cleaning ships,' she vowed under her breath. 'Never in a thousand years.'

'Well, some women have no choice,' said her sharp-eared mother, waving a dismissive hand. 'But let me tell you, Peggy, you have turned into a snooty little madam since you moved into that stuck-up Beamer Street.'

'I have not!' Peggy was shocked. She was the same person she had always been. 'Many's the time I've suggested you move into our parlour.' Granted, there was a streak of selfishness on her part, Peggy thought begrudgingly. Life would be much easier if she didn't have to traipse all the way down here with a heavy shopping bag every few days. 'I've asked you a hundred times, I've had a word with Dar, and he agreed you can move in with us. You'd even have your own privy and not have to share with the rest of the street, how's that for a bit of luxury.'

'Oh, he agreed, did he?' Maggie O'Day's lips curled in disgust. 'Well, I'll have you know, lady, I will not be beholden to an eejit like him!'

Peggy watched her mother roll her shoulders and expel a loud, forceful irate breath. He was not an eejit, thought Peggy. Dar was a good man who provided well for his family. Ma was just annoyed that he wasn't of her faith. Although, nor was he one who marched along Netherfield Road on the twelfth of July, in commemoration of King William of Orange, a Protestant king, who won the Battle of the Boyne in 1690. Ma, and many like her, had never forgiven King Billy for capturing the Catholic cities of Dublin and Cork from King James.

'You would be more comfortable living with me than living here,' Peggy said, quickly changing the subject. She didn't want to go into the whys and wherefores' of religion with her mother.

'It's not good enough for you here, any more, is that it?' Mam always had a way of twisting her words, so Peggy said nothing for the time being. 'This is where I've lived since the day I married, and this is where I'll stay.' Her mother said the brusque words with a finality that allowed no argument. 'What if Pop comes home?'

Oh look, a pig with wings! Peggy would never dare voice her cynical manner, but she knew her father could not wait to see the back of this place either. 'He's been gone over twenty years, Ma, why would he come back now?'

Somewhere in the recess of her mind there was a vague notion, which Peggy could not address. How could she possibly when she didn't even know what the question was, having tried to grasp a tenuous feeling of anxiety that had haunted her for years.

The memory, always just out of reach, was there. Real. Alive. Unforgiving. Yet intense, dark and so deeply buried she could not ever put the gossamer recollection into words. The unexplained notion made her feel different from other members of her family. Apart. Other. An inborn sense of... what? But the *thing*, whatever it may be, was the reason her father was never going to come home again, she was certain of that.

'Pop might be a smooth-talking chancer, given to flights of fancy,' said Ma, 'but he's my husband and I'll not have anybody say a bad word against him.' Maggie had a sob in her voice.

Peggy sighed, knowing every conversation ended up with the subject of her father's abandonment. 'He was an impetuous roamer who gave no thought to how his family would fare in his absence,' Peggy said, feeling unusually numb to her mother's distress; she barely remembered what he looked like.

He had said before his ship had sailed that he was never coming back to the courts of Liverpool. Or was that something she had heard being said by her family repeatedly? Maybe she didn't remember it at all.

Nevertheless, the weekly allotment from Pop's seafaring wages, which Ma was always first in the queue to collect each Saturday morning, was the hope her mother always clung to for his return.

'So, you look after Vi's kids while she's working?' Peggy asked, changing the subject again, in the hope her mother wouldn't ruin her happy day.

'They always come over here after school, I told you.' Ma sounded surprised. 'They come here for their tea. That's what I expect them to do when their mother is out working every hour God sends.' Violet lived in a two-storey, flat-fronted building just across the flagstones, barely twelve feet away. 'They're in and out all the time. You can't expect a man to look after young children, it's unheard of.'

'Dar looked after my children when I wasn't able,' said Peggy, trying to paint Dar in a better light in her mother's eyes. But she was wasting her breath, she knew. Nothing would convince her mother that her husband was a decent working man who obviously loved his family and worked extremely hard to provide for them.

'I don't see your little ones much, but that'll be his doing, I suppose.' Her mother's words were like salt in an open wound, and Peggy flinched, knowing the hurt was intentional.

'Has *Our Lady of Sorrows* handed over any money since she started work?' Peggy asked, deflecting the hurtful comment. 'Has she even offered a loaf of bread to feed her tribe? Treated you to something nice?' Peggy doubted it, knowing her sister's husband watched where every farthing was spent. 'Her husband is so tight he could make a penny scream.'

'We can't all be married to plaster saints who tip up every penny.'

Her mother's words hit the spot and Peggy bit her tongue, refusing to get into a slanging match about husbands. They had a comfortable life, not lavish by any means. But not as poor as those who lived from hand to mouth along the streets and wharves of Liverpool. Dock work, casual though it might be, was not always easy to come by. Although Dar, being a competent and capable worker, was luckier than most. He had a first-class work ethic, he was strong and had never missed a single day's work, ensuring his rise to foreman. Although, his work ethic was another fault in her mother's eyes, even calling him a brown-nose – one of her milder insults.

'He's always been a good provider, and that's all that matters to me. We've never asked anybody for a halfpenny,' Peggy said, knowing she still hadn't been forgiven for marrying out of the faith, blaming Dar and his lofty ideas for moving her away from her family. In their eyes, moving away from your own area was tantamount to emigrating to another country. 'I didn't notice Violet's husband refusing the price of a pint last time Dar put his hand in his pocket.' Peggy was not afraid to let Mam know what she thought.

'Those nets could do with a wash,' her mother said, knowing how quickly words could get out of hand in the volatile O'Day family.

Peggy, recognising the tactic, climbed onto a straight-backed chair by the table and slipped the net curtain off the wire. Then, climbing down, she said, 'I've brought a Dolly Blue to steep them while I clean the windows.'

Living so near the docks, the industrial smoke and grime soon yellowed the nets and the only thing that housewives could do to restore the whiteness was to soak them in a bucket of Reckitt's Dolly Blue to neutralise the creamy tinge.

'Please yerself,' her mother muttered as Peggy went out to the scullery to fill a bucket with water.

'Our Jack works with his father, but he wants a trade, an

apprenticeship,' Peggy called, trying to coax a civil conversation out of her mother, 'he wants to better himself, too.'

'What work is he doing now?' asked her mother, and Peggy knew her answer was not going to please her.

'He's a can-lad at Hutton's.' The ensuing silence made Peggy feel she had just lit the blue touchpaper. The indignant reply was soon forthcoming.

'Hutton! Lord, love us and save us. Hutton. Even the name makes my skin crawl.'

'Why?' asked Peggy. 'What's Hutton ever done to you?'

'It's not what he's done to me, girl,' her mother said as Peggy stood in the doorway between the kitchen and the scullery, having never heard her mother mention the name of her husband's employer before.

'Are you going to give me a clue as to what you're talking about?' Peggy, sensing a change in her mother's attitude, waited for a reply.

'It might be better to ask our Violet,' Ma said, staring into the dying embers in the grate, her voice almost a whisper, and Peggy's forehead pleated into a question, but she hesitated to ask what Ma meant by her remark. 'So, what's our Millie going to do with herself when she leaves school? Not visit her grandmother, that's for sure.' Her mother's change of attitude did not fool Peggy for an instant. Ma was hiding something, she could tell.

'I'm sure she'll be along when she's got time, Ma,' Peggy said, her eyes taking in everything in the small, cramped room, furnished with a couple of fireside chairs that did not match the horsehair sofa, the table and a scuffed sideboard that had been in the same place for as long as Peggy could remember.

'Well, she'll have to get her skates on, because I'm not long for this world. There's summat wrong, I can tell.'

'Have you seen a doctor?' Peggy asked, suddenly concerned. Maybe this was what Ma had been trying to hide?

'I've never seen a doctor in me life,' Maggie spluttered indignantly, 'and I'm not starting now. Since I'm not made of money.' Her mother suddenly came to life and Peggy realised what she was up to when Maggie said pointedly, 'Not like some I could mention.'

So that's why she was so miserable. Peggy had not yet crossed her mother's reddened palm with silver. As she did every week. Unbeknown to Dar. He would not be happy if he knew she had been subsidising her mother all these years, especially now, when there was a strike on and he was in danger of being attacked for being a blackleg.

Peggy pondered for a moment. The way her mother treated her, disapproving of her husband and family, she had every right to leave her without the half-crown she donated. Peggy sighed, knowing she never would leave her ma penniless. She didn't have it in her to be so mean.

Taking her purse from the basket, Peggy opened it and took out the silver half-crown, suspecting her mother looked forward to seeing the money more than her own daughter.

'Here you go, Ma,' Peggy said, placing the coin in her mother's hand. 'Get yourself something nice.' For the first time since she'd arrived, she saw her mother's features soften.

'You're a good girl, our Peg.' The older woman unashamedly cheered. 'I don't know what I'd do without you.'

Those few short words caused the long-awaited spark of delight and Peggy smiled too, even though she had promised herself earlier that she would not appear so in need of her mother's approval. She had never been Ma's favourite, nor the treasured confidante she had always longed to be. That prime position was held by Violet, and nothing Peggy did or said seemed good enough. Although she was satisfied she had put a smile on Ma's face, bringing her a little security, which she always seemed to need.

'You know I'd never see you go without, Ma,' Peggy said,

enjoying the limited glow of appreciation from her mother's eyes. She never begrudged the weekly money she provided to her mother's well-being, even though she knew every half-crown could have gone towards their savings to buy their house in Beamer Street. Nevertheless, Peggy had the satisfaction of knowing her father and her sister hadn't been able to bring that special look of appreciation from her mother. 'I can put that nice piece of fish on if you like.' Peggy could see the money had raised her mother's low spirits, and it was for that reason she would bring the money every week as she had done for the last seventeen years.

Ma nodded, accepting anything she had to say now.

'You need something for that cough,' Peggy said as she waited for the fish to cook. 'I'll have a word with Ellie.'

'Who's Ellie when she's at home?' her mother said, not trusting anybody she had never met.

'She's a healer, Ma.' Peggy watched with satisfaction as her mother's eyes devoured the cooking fish. 'Everyone calls her Ellie, and she's been a godsend to many poor souls who didn't have the price of a doctor. I'll bring the medicine over to you tomorrow,' Peggy said, placing the fish onto a clean plate, along with buttered bread, which she placed on the table before helping her mother across the kitchen. 'I'll be off now, Ma, have you got everything you need?'

'Aye, I suppose so,' said her mother, not looking up as she concentrated on her food.

Peggy put on her coat and hat, then bent to kiss her mother's cheek.

'I'll bring that cough medicine along tomorrow. Ta-ra, Mam.'

'Ta-ra, girl.' Maggie watched as Peggy walked out of the door with her proud back straight and her head held high, reminding her so much of the girl poor Violet had once been before life had knocked the stuffing right out of her.

No doubt Peggy felt she had done her duty for another week. Obviously, she didn't know how lucky she had been to get out of this rat-infested hole, away from the snide comments and the sidelong glances. Because she had shielded her from the truth.

Appreciating the weight of the silver coin in her palm, Maggie turned it over before dropping the precious money into her purse. Half-a-crown a week was a small price to pay for bringing up another woman's daughter.

4

Peggy walked past the striking men with her head held high. She had no time for what went on outside the docks, especially an all-out strike in support of 800,000 locked-out miners who were being asked to work longer hours for less pay, which started the general strike, the likes of which had never been seen before.

Liverpool, along with the rest of Britain, had come to a standstill. She and every other housewife she could think of had no time to sit idle, or lean against the corner wall hoping a kindly soul would take pity and drop a few coppers into their bucket.

Walking towards Gladstone dry dock, she knew Dar was working on the construction of the new wet dock on the other side of the wall, which promised to be one of the biggest, deepest docks in the world, enabling the biggest ships to dock. Dar had told her, after listening to a BBC news bulletin on the wireless, that a plan had been put in place to secure essential supplies, with the deployment of troops who would assist the police, and an extended force of special constables, to make sure work continued if the strike went on much longer.

There was also a focus on keeping transport moving on the

buses, trams, trains and lorries, said Dar, who had explained that, by recruiting volunteers through the newly formed Organisation for the Maintenance of Supplies, goods would still get through, although not at the same rate as before the strike. Volunteers, of which he was one, were also being used on the docks and in power stations, aided by senior staff.

Peggy's attention was caught by a gang of dock workers shouting and gesticulating. A large crowd had gathered. She was one of the lucky ones, Peggy thought, secure in the knowledge Dar was not among the strikers. They had saved money left over after essentials, squirrelling it away in the suitcase every Friday, so they could purchase their little terraced house in Beamer Street, which wasn't grand by any means, just a three-up-three-down, with no hot water and an outside lavatory. The terraced houses with their modest rents were always in demand and never remained unoccupied. Peggy could think of no better house she would rather live in.

Number three was their dream home, which she and Dar had made a happy household for their four children: sixteen-year-old Jack, fourteen-year-old Millie who was leaving school next Christmas, ten-year-old Jane and eight-year-old Eddy. Peggy could not wait for the day when every brick and windowpane belonged to her and Dar. Owning property was not only her security, Peggy knew, but her opportunity to show her mother that Dar was not the divil she purported him to be.

A skilled seaman during the war, his work was highly specialised, and he took exceptional pride in his craft. Often, working with men who were not so highly skilled, led outsiders to lump them together as unqualified labourers. But Dar, unlike so many other dock workers, enjoyed secure work, and a comfortable family life, allowing him to save enough money to buy the house of their dreams, situated near Saint Patrick's Catholic church, where

Peggy went to holy mass every Sunday, while Dar peeled the spuds
and vegetables for their dinner.

Peggy was glad Dar had left the sea when the war had ended,
unlike her roving seafarer of a father. She knew Dar would never
join in a dispute that would risk him not being able to bring home
his wage packet every Friday and placing it in the middle of the
kitchen table after his tea. Then, he would sort out the money for
the following week. Something very much unheard of by most
women, whose husbands took their share for beer and tobacco.
The men had the say in what was to be spent in most houses. But
not in their home, where Peggy and Dar shared the money and the
upbringing of their children.

Working conditions at Hutton's were poor, she knew, but at
least the work was steady, and the reason Dar got their sixteen-
year-old son Jack in there as a can-lad when he left school, with the
promise of an engineering apprenticeship with Cal Everdine when
he was old enough to be indentured.

Peggy was pleased her Jack had decided he wanted to become
an engineer like Mary Jane's husband, Cal. Jack certainly had the
brains, and Peggy could not be prouder. She knew Dar could have
got Jack a job loading and unloading the ships, but they both knew
Hutton's labour force had no rights. The pay was low, although
regular, which meant many workers were loath to leave and try for
better wages when work was becoming thin on the ground.

Deep in thought, Peggy gave one of her involuntary tuts. The
delivery vans had stopped running on time, and the trains along
the track high above Beamer Street were rare. Buses and trams
were manned by military troops, leaving the top road ominously
silent for much of the day. The dock police were noticeably absent,
and many shops had closed because of the lack of deliveries,
resulting in empty shelves. Peggy knew if everybody had the fore-
sight to run their business like Mary Jane Everdine, then under the

circumstances such as the strike, they would not have had to shut up shop.

Peggy gave a friendly wave to Daisy, who was busy washing the bakery windows on Beamer Terrace, adjoining Beamer Street proper.

'I see you're still open, then,' Peggy called across the cobbled road and Daisy crossed to speak to her.

'She's a shrewd businesswoman is Mary Jane,' Daisy said, enjoying the warm sun on her face. 'She had the good sense to gauge the situation by keeping her eyes to business and her ears to the grumbles of our customers.'

'Aye,' Peggy agreed, 'she said the men working on the docks and railways weren't happy. So, she ordered stock in lieu of the threatened strike.'

'We'll make sure there's no shortage of bread for our regular customers,' said Daisy, nodding to Ina King, who put her nose in the air, after calling Dar fit to burn for not taking part in the strike.

'Aye, and I can tell you who will be first in the queue,' said Peggy with a knowing smile, watching Ina scurry down the street.

'Dar managed to avoid the wrath of the strikers when Hutton's gates opened this morning,' Daisy assured her. 'I'm at the bakery before the crack of dawn, as you know, and saw the men hurrying into Hutton's without any fuss as the strikers were protesting down at the docks.'

It was common knowledge along the dockside that strikers did not like blacklegs, who broke strike conditions and continued working. Nor was it uncommon for certain workplace windows to be smashed. The strikers considered the continuation of work to be treacherous disloyalty against their fellow working man and Peggy knew blacklegs were treated no better than the conscientious objectors, who had been given a white feather of cowardice during the war. Dar had done his bit during the war, she silently reasoned, knowing he was now doing his bit for his family.

Dar had told her it was against his principles to ignore the needs of the working man and carry on working during a strike, which was why he did not blame Jack for following his own beliefs and come out of work in sympathy, even though he faced being sacked, whilst Peggy let them both know it was against her principles to sit her children down at the table to an empty plate. And that was the last time they had spoken of the matter.

'Mrs Pearce said there's been an accident down the docks,' Molly called across the cobbled road to her daughter Daisy and Peggy.

'There's always something on the docks,' said Peggy, who was not in the least bit worried.

With no traffic running, the atmosphere was a little unnerving. No horses and carts clip-clopping on the cobbles, hardly any trams or omnibuses zipping along or wagons heaving towards the dock road. Only children caught up in the excitement of running adults to shatter the quiet of the day.

'That looks serious,' said Daisy, watching people hurrying towards the docks.

'It'll be something and nothing,' said Peggy as she headed towards Ellie's herbal shop, open as always, which had become a blessing and a mainstay to the community who could not always afford the expensive services of a doctor.

Ellie owned the apothecary with her husband Aiden, and her services had proved an important part of the surrounding streets, where illness was an everyday occurrence, and Peggy was always glad of the chance to have a little natter with Ellie, the fount of all medical knowledge.

The apothecary bell gave a familiar tinkle as it opened from the street. And as she entered, Peggy took a deep, calming breath, inhaling the fresh smell of scented herbs that were in sharp contrast to the smoky soot outside and proved a pleasant sanctuary to many a mother round-about.

'Hello, Peggy. What can I do for you?' Ellie Newman asked brightly. She liked Peggy, who, although brimming with the self-pride that peeved some of the other residents of the street, always paid for her purchases at the time of buying, and never asked for credit.

'Some children need a good scrub before they're allowed out,' Peggy noted, watching through one of the small windows as a boy sauntered nonchalantly along the street. 'I'd die of shame if one of mine went out looking like that.'

Ellie didn't pass comment, nor did Peggy expect her to.

Inhaling the subtle aroma of lemon-and-beeswax polished counter, Peggy was careful not to disturb the sleeping white cat curled up like a Cossack's hat on the counter, oblivious to the antique apothecary tools, teas, tinctures, lotions and potions, which had been carefully displayed on the shelf behind Ellie. The shiny glass jars, adorned with delicate hand-painted labels displayed the names of various herbs and treatments.

'I need some more of that cough linctus you gave me last time,' Peggy said, 'it's for me mam.' She sighed, rolled her eyes, and needed no invitation to sit on the straight-backed chair near the counter, admiring the things that hinted at the rich history of her friend's profession and evoked a sense of security – something Peggy greatly admired. 'She's got this rotten chest on her again. Her voice sounds like a cinder stuck under the door. I've just been to see her, and I said I'd pop in and get another one of your special bottles. She said it did the trick last time.'

'She might have needed something a bit sooner if she's really croaky.' Ellie's finely shaped brow creased, and her kind eyes showed concern. But Peggy shook her head in that decided fashion she had about her.

'Ma doesn't like to make a fuss. Or so she says.' She gave a wry smile. 'The Spanish flu took her mother after the war, so she refuses to acknowledge her ailments for about ten minutes.' Peggy smiled as she told Ellie. 'If anybody else is feeling a bit off colour, she tells them to ignore it, and it will soon go away.'

'Sometimes that is true,' said Ellie, 'but sometimes the body needs a little helping hand.'

'If I so much as mention a doctor, she thinks her days are numbered, failing that I'm trying to cart her off to the workhouse.'

'I'm sure you'd never dream of it,' Ellie said in the soft-spoken way she had about her.

'Don't tempt me,' Peggy laughed, not really meaning what she said, but she knew her mother did have a way of rubbing her up the wrong way. 'I can't be doing with her taking to her bed, though.' She shrugged. 'I'd have to traipse along the dock road to see to her, then I'd have to traipse back again to see to my lot.' Her machine-gun delivery filled the shop. 'Then, I'd have to do the same thing all over again the next day, and the next, because sure as rain is wet, our Violet wouldn't look after her and Mam would love having me at her beck and call.'

'Violet?' asks Ellie when she could get a word in.

'Me older sister,' said Peggy, 'married to the laziest man in Christendom. And they've got a cheek to talk about Dar.' Her eyes widened, and she nodded her head as Ellie busied herself collecting the liniment from the stock cupboard under the counter.

She didn't involve herself in family lore. What might be fine for Peggy to say about her sister was not an invitation for Ellie to do the same. 'This'll do the trick,' she said, knowing her regulars around the dockside suffered with what they called bad chests.

The dockside was rife with disorders and disease, mainly caused by the many industries operating alongside the river.

'She's usually in the best of health at this time of year...' Peggy wrinkled her nose, showing her disapproval of her mother's situation, enjoying the soft crackle of a log fire near the window on the other side of the shop that added to the warmth of the room and created a cosy atmosphere. Peggy often came in just for a warm, as she didn't light her fire until much later in the day to save money on coal.

'Is your mam not from around here, then?' Ellie asked, knowing most people were extremely territorial about their own neighbourhood and rarely moved far from the place in which they grew up.

Peggy shook her head. 'No, she lives in the back-to-back courts along the dock road.' She decided not to go into detail but could not resist giving Ellie a vague sketch of the poorest area, which she had been born into. 'Terrible place. I wouldn't live there for a big clock. But I can't get Mam to budge out from there.'

Ellie nodded. She had seen the crowded abodes first-hand when she came to Beamer Street and recalled wondering how people could survive in such cramped dwellings, where space, light and fresh air were in noticeably short supply. Having spent her life in the Lancashire countryside, Ellie could think of no worse place to live. However, she did not voice her thoughts to Peggy, knowing most people rarely had a choice. 'This is the same camphorated liniment,' said Ellie.

'It certainly did the trick to ease the pain last time.'

'It might pong a bit, but it does its job.' Ellie cradled the brown ridged bottle in the palm of her hand.

'I don't care if it stinks the place out,' Peggy said, leaning back when the white cat unfurled itself and stretched. 'The smell is better than those bliddy middens.' Peggy wrinkled her nose as the cat looked in her direction. She didn't trust cats. They were far too independent for her liking. Had a mind of their own. A slave to nobody.

'Didn't you say your sister lives near your mam?'

'Aye,' said Peggy, putting her elbow back on the counter, watching Ellie pour chamomile tea into two dainty bone-china teacups, 'but she's done nothing to help our mam. She says she's too tired to do much when she gets home from cleaning the ships, yet Mam thinks the sun shines out of our Vi's backside.'

'I take it you don't get on?' Ellie could tell something was bothering Peggy, a proud woman, who, unlike the other women in the street, wasn't usually one for jangling. But she sounded like she needed to let off steam today.

'It's not that we don't get on,' said Peggy, 'she thinks I'm still a kid she can boss around. Our Violet's always been good at giving orders, but not so good at taking them.' Peggy shrugged her thin shoulders. 'And that husband of hers, take, take, take. You've never seen a body so greedy as him. He wouldn't move off the couch to mind his own kids while she goes out to work, so those poor kiddies get dumped on Ma. She must be worn out with the lot of them.'

'Children have so much energy,' said Ellie, not taking sides.

Peggy looked thoughtful. 'I suppose our Violet has her good points, but I'd have segs on me eyes looking for them.' She gave a definite nod of her head, knowing segs were areas of thickened skin caused by over-use. Ellie knew she had done the right thing not to offer an opinion of Peggy's sister, knowing it was wise to keep on the right side of her customers. Big families were usual around the dockside, but she was never sure who was related to whom. Discretion was part of her stock in trade. If the customers couldn't trust their healer, then who could they trust?

After finishing her tea, she put the liniment into a paper bag and gave Peggy a compassionate smile. 'I'm sure this will see your mam right in no time. It's a good thing she's got you, Peg,' Ellie said, and she noticed Peggy's face brighten.

'Thanks, Ellie.' Grateful for the kind words, which she would never hear from her mother or her sister, Peggy was glad she had made a friend of Ellie. One of the newest arrivals in Beamer Street, she had made her mark almost immediately when she arrived. Younger than the Beamer Street matriarchs, Ellie was wise beyond her years and the mother of six-year-old Melissa and Charlie, who would be one year old at the end of May. 'I noticed little Charlie-boy enjoying the sights from his pram.'

'He loves being outside in the sunshine watching the world go by, enjoying the attention he gets from passers-by.' Ellie missed the countryside where she grew up, but she doubted she would ever go back, knowing she had work to do here. Although she was much more content here than she had ever been at Oakland Hall.

'Like his dad,' said Peggy, 'he's an outdoors man.'

Ellie was married to Aiden, a gardener, whom she called her best friend, and they ran the business together. He did the heavy work of growing the herbs and she made up the cures and balms. The people had taken her, Aiden, Melissa and baby Charlie into their hearts and accepted Ellie for who she was, a kind-hearted healer, and not the witch Ina King, who had initially regarded her with suspicion, but was now one of her best customers, had implied. Although healing made her and Aiden a comfortable living, it would never bring them absolute wealth – but certainly made them prosperous in goodwill. 'I hope your mam's feeling better soon.'

'So do I,' said Peggy, handing over the money she knew her mother would never repay. Her eye caught the Victorian framed photograph of Ellie's late mother, which sat proudly on the counter and was silently guarded by the white cat. 'You look so much like your mother,' remarked Peggy, knowing Ellie liked to keep the photograph visible, as a constant reminder to the shop's visitors of the generations of healers who went before her.

'Thank you,' Ellie said simply, 'she had a good heart and a kind nature.'

'As do you, Ellie,' replied Peggy, who did not offer compliments lightly. 'I'd better be off.'

Peggy hurried along Beamer Street, walking a little taller as she headed towards her own house, where no speck of dust was allowed to land on her polished ledges, which displayed a healthy aspidistra in a glinting brass pot, her pride and joy. She had placed the green plant in the centre of the window, surrounded by equally gleaming brass knick-knacks, displayed for all to see against the backdrop of white, starched net curtains. But behind the show of quiet respectability, Peggy hid the truth of an empty room, reflecting the contrast between social expectations and the reality of her frugal life.

She and Dar both longed to give their family the security neither of them had known. The dream, which they had striven for since they married, would be within their grasp today. The thought filled Peggy's heart with a song, and she hummed a jaunty tune as she made her way home.

She and Dar had sacrificed so much to put a few shillings away every week, both determined to avoid going back to the courts. Their resolve, to evade the threat of eviction and escape unscrupulous landlords, gave them both an iron will to save Dar's hardearned money and Peggy's thrifty housekeeping. Where most people could save a penny, Peggy could save sixpence. They'd saved every penny, knowing the proudest day of their life was the day they moved up the ladder into Beamer Street, without having to go cap in hand to the bank for a loan.

5
___

Sixteen-year-old Jack Tenant came tearing around the corner so fast he almost knocked over his mother.

'Mam! You've got to come quick!' His words grew more frantic with each syllable. 'You've got to hurry, there's been a terrible accident!' Jack's face was pale against the ebony darkness of his hair. His large pale eyes looked frightened as his fingers raked a loose fringe. 'It's Dar, Mam! He's been hurt bad.' Everybody who knew her husband called him Dar.

'What kind of bad?' Peggy's mouth dried and, clutching the front of her coat, she followed Jack, who was already skidding along towards the dock.

He called over his shoulder, 'I don't know all the details, but it's bad... really bad!'

'No.' Peggy gasped the word and quickened her pace, her voice trembling as she repeated over and over, 'No, not Dar... please, not Dar.' Tears filled her eyes as the enormity of the situation sank in. 'I can't lose him... I can't...' She knew the dangers of the dockside, and the treacherous tidal changes, and so did her husband. The Mersey docks had claimed and maimed many working men.

Stumbling on an uneven cobblestone, her breath hitched in her throat as Peggy struggled to regain her balance, and Jack put his hand out to steady his mother, knowing he had to be strong for her.

Racing down Beamer Terrace, off the main Beamer Street, she could see the large crowd gathered by the dock wall. They were pushing and shoving, craning their necks, to peer inside the dock gates, trying to catch a glimpse of the injured man, and Peggy's heart hammered in her chest, as she neared the place where panicked voices overlapped, to a cacophony of noise, in their urgency to get the story out. Men who had seen the accident were angry, their obvious fury adding to Peggy's despair.

'Dar knows everything there is to know about his job,' she said aloud as she neared the crowd of onlookers, unable to take in what the bystanding workers were trying to tell her. The men were telling her something about a swinging rope and a young boy who was in danger. They were saying Miles Houseman was to blame but he was nowhere to be seen. Peggy tried to make sense of what was going on around her but her thoughts were jumbled and mixed up. 'How could something like this happen?'

'It wouldn't have happened if he'd been doing his duty by his striking workmates.' The snide comment came from the back of the crowd, but Peggy was far too distressed to retaliate.

'Mam, we know how careful Dar is, he's told us often enough, and I know how dangerous the docks can be.' The fear in Jack's eyes belied his brave words.

Then, as if the enormity of her son's statement hit her, Peggy's voice cracked. 'If this could happen to him, what hope is there for anybody else?' She knew her husband's work on the docks was hazardous, but Dar was always so careful, he was precise in his work and took pride in everything he did.

'Miles Houseman could no more handle that crane than a

slippy-handed five-year-old,' called a male voice from the crowd. 'He scarpered very sharpish when he realised what he'd done.'

'He's probably headed straight for the Tram Tavern,' another worker called, 'or hiding under his uncle's coattails as usual.' Houseman's uncle, Henry Hutton, had a reputation as a mean employer who got the largest amount of work for the bare minimum of pay, but the work was regular, so most were thankful.

But even now, when there was an all-out strike in sympathy with the miners, Peggy knew Hutton made sure his workers never missed a day's work, nor did he allow any of his workers to join a trade union, with the threat of being sacked if they did. His stance was probably illegal, she knew, but there weren't many who were going to argue the point when their jobs were at stake, given the state of the country and the lack of work.

'Let me through,' Peggy cried, elbowing her way through the throng of onlookers, her mind now blank except for the thought of her injured husband. *Please God*, she prayed, *don't let Dar be dead.*

Pushing her way through the concerned crowd, the strike momentarily forgotten, neighbours urged her on, making sympathetic noises, and Peggy reached her husband just as Cal Everdine got Dar onto the back of his horse-driven cart, covering him with empty sacking. Jack helped his mother to sit next to his unconscious father, before jumping up next to Cal Everdine.

'We all heard Dar, loud and clear. That young lad would have been killed if Dar hadn't pushed him out of the way. Houseman was drunk, and we all knew it,' Jack called over his shoulder to his mother, gently stroking her unconscious husband's head. 'I wasn't the only one who heard him either.'

Cal expertly steered the cart down Derby Road towards the borough hospital, known locally as the dockers hospital. 'Houseman told your man he was there to obey orders, not to give them out,' Cal informed her in his low drawl tinged with an American accent.

'Houseman's a right upstart, nobody likes him,' Jack said, 'he's too full of himself.'

Peggy was only half listening, too worried about her beloved husband to indulge in workplace talk.

When they reached the sooty red-brick hospital, Cal and Jack carried Dar through the iron gates and into the hospital, while Peggy hurried alongside them.

Once inside, a canvas stretcher on wheels was brought into the foyer and a porter took over. Meanwhile, Peggy provided Dar's details to the uniformed man behind an opaque glass window.

'I'm sure he's going to be fine, Mrs Tenant,' said Cal, a strong, upstanding member of the community. Yet, his voice, although full of compassion, did not sound so certain. 'I'll ask Mary Jane to call in on you later. Meanwhile, if I hear anything I will let you know.'

Peggy nodded as Cal turned and headed down the corridor, and it was only when he had exited the double doors, she realised she hadn't even thanked him for helping her and Jack get Dar to hospital so quickly.

The overpowering smell of antiseptic was making her feel queasy, but such strong disinfectant was crucial in keeping disease at bay. Contamination was one of the biggest killers to the patients. 'Jack, you go back and see to the little ones with Millie. Tell them I'll be home as soon as I can.'

'No, Ma,' said Jack, his dark eyes hooded, 'I'm not going to leave you on your own.' His mother was a strong capable woman, even if she didn't think she was. But nobody should be expected to face this kind of place alone. 'Our Millie's going to be just fine – she's had a good teacher.'

'Thanks, lad,' said Peggy, who tried to make her children's lives as comfortable as she could possibly make them. She squeezed

Jack's hand, glad he and Dar got on so well. Unlike some rough-and-ready fathers who resided around the tough dockside streets, Dar was a caring man who listened to his son, considered the situation, then gave Jack a thoughtful, measured reply, enabling him to grow into a confident young man with a mind and opinion of his own. Unlike her own father, who couldn't give his sons the time of day if he could help it.

Peggy didn't know how long she had been sitting in the hospital corridor but was secure in the knowledge her eldest daughter, Millie, would be looking after the younger children, Eddy and Jane, in that sensible way she had about her. Then, in the middle of a long sigh, Peggy noticed one of the double doors open and a tall, efficient-looking woman in a rustling crisp uniform came towards her.

'Your husband will be moved to another facility when he is well enough,' said Matron after she introduced herself. 'He will be taken to a rehabilitation establishment called Lavender Green, where they have specially trained doctors and nurses who are experts in the care of men who have suffered these types of injuries.'

'What type of injuries?' asked Jack, his face grave.

'Your father has a fractured skull and a broken femur.'

'Femur?' Peggy had never heard of a femur.

'His thigh bone,' answered Matron. 'He is having urgent surgery, and we expect it to take at least six months to heal. He will stay here until he is well enough to be moved to Lavender Green.'

'Where's that?' Peggy asked.

'It is out in the Lancashire countryside, part of the Kirrin Institute, a beautiful place; he will be well looked after.'

'But the countryside is miles away, there are no trains running because of the strike.' Peggy could feel the blood in her veins chill, and she shivered. 'How am I supposed to get there?'

'There will be no visiting for the first few weeks,' said Matron crisply, 'until your husband settles in.' The danger of infection was extremely high, which was one of the reasons this patient needed to be carefully moved to a countryside hospital, away from the soot and grime of the dockside. 'However,' she added in a more sympathetic manner, 'when your husband is strong enough to see visitors, you will receive a communication from the Matron at Lavender Green. He will be kept here until he is strong enough to travel, but I must warn you, the next few days will be critical.'

'You mean...?' Peggy could not bring herself to say the awful words being hinted at. She found the possibility that Dar might not survive unbearable.

Matron put a gentle hand on her arm. 'He is still unconscious. If he survives the night—'

'Survives the night?' Peggy cut off Matron's words, burying her face in her hands. She could not face a future without Dar. He was her mainstay. Her lifeline. If anything happened to Dar, she would not be able to continue. She depended on him for everything.

Peggy felt her son's hand on her arm, and she knew she had to be strong. Jack was a good lad, but he couldn't shoulder the weight of responsibility for the whole family.

'I'm fine, Jack.' Peggy straightened. 'We'll all be fine.'

'You may look through the ward window for a short while,' whispered Matron. 'But you will not be allowed onto the ward. Mr Tenant will be kept in a single room next to my office.'

'Thank you.' Peggy felt there was a huge hand gripping her throat, and it was painfully squeezing for all it was worth. Nodding her head, she lowered her burning eyes. Today was her seventeenth wedding anniversary. It should have been the happiest day of her life. But instead, with the threat of Dar dying hanging over her, it was the worst.

Looking through the window adjoining Matron's office, she

could see Dar lying unconscious in a pristine bed, the sheets of which matched his pallor. The covers were starched to a crisp and the smell of disinfectant was so overpowering, Peggy knew it would cling to her coat even when she left the hospital. What was she going to do if anything should happen to Dar? What if he died?

She shook her head as if shaking off an unlikely thought. He couldn't die! He couldn't...

'Go home and get some rest,' said a kindly nurse. 'The next few weeks are going to be testing. You will need all the strength you can get.' The nurse put a gentle hand on Peggy's shoulder, her body enveloped in the same antiseptic smell, and Peggy nodded.

She took one last look at her husband's prone body. His face, usually so rugged and weatherbeaten, was now as wan as death. Quickly, she turned from the window, unable to bear the thought of losing her precious husband, and began to walk along the silent, antiseptic corridor ahead of her. How would she cope if...

No! She must not think that way. Dar was strong. He was a fighter. He would get through this. *Please God!*

She didn't recall the silent journey she and Jack made back to Beamer Street.

'I'll go and talk to our Millie,' said Jack, when he saw the small throng of women outside the bakery. 'You speak to Molly and Mary Jane. You'll get no peace until you do.'

6

'Oh, Peggy, love, how is he?' a tight knot of neighbours chorused, their faces etched with concern for their independent friend who was more inclined to offer help than to ask for it.

Peggy wasn't in the mood for talking, she wanted to run back to the hospital and hold her husband's hand. Will him to live. But she knew she could not do that. Dar was in the hands of those who knew better than she did, and she had to trust they would make her beloved husband better.

Even though she wasn't in any mood to share her feeling with the rest of the street, she knew that their strength came from sharing. Peggy wasn't usually the kind of person who spent every minute of her day gossiping in the street like some, but she knew these women – Molly, Mary Jane, Ellie and predictably Ina King, who never missed a heartbeat of the goings-on in Beamer Street – were there if she needed them. Not that she would ever ask for help, mind. That wasn't her way.

Nevertheless, these women had seen enough life and had been through plenty of their own personal distress at one time or another, to be able to offer the support they knew she was going to need.

'Come over and have a cup of tea, you look like you could do with one,' said Molly, a motherly body who looked out for anybody who needed her help.

Peggy explained that Dar had a fractured skull as they entered Molly's large house on the other side of Beamer Street from the bakery.

'That's bad,' said Ina King and the other women gave the nosy gossip a wide-eyed look of disapproval, or maybe it was a warning not to say anything that might upset Peggy even more. But Ina ignored them, determined to air her story. 'I knew a fella down the docks who died with a fractured skull.'

'I thought you would.' Molly glared at Ina, who seemed, at times, to delight in the misfortune of others. Ina's husband, a docker, had been aggressively vocal in his opinion of what he thought of Dar and all other blacklegs.

'I can't stop long,' Peggy said, 'I've got to go and see to my little ones.' Her heart was racing in her chest, making it difficult to breathe, and Peggy felt as if she was suffocating. Trying to stay composed, she lifted a trembling hand to wipe away a stray tear.

'Come on, queen, sit down here,' said Molly, taking hold of Peggy's elbow and leading her to the sofa, 'I think what you need is a good strong cup of tea.' Molly then began edging Ina to the door. 'Come and give me a hand with the tea.'

Peggy could see there was no getting away from the anxious questions of her friends, and if truth be told, these women were doing exactly as she expected they would. They were behaving the same way she too would have reacted if one of them were in this situation. They were caring, banding together with the strength of a pride of lionesses, creating a gently nurturing shield around her.

'Jack is going to tell our Millie, and let her know where I am,'

said Peggy, 'but I don't know how I'm going to tell the little ones.'
The enormity of the situation suddenly hit Peggy, who gave vent to
a torrent of built-up tears.

She barely managed to get any words out, to explain what had
happened with Dar at the hospital, and the close-knit women, who
had become firm friends over the years, stroked and soothed and
spoke in hushed tones to Peggy.

These women had seen it all. Good, bad, and in between. There
was nothing they could not face. No hill too high to climb, no river
too deep to swim, and Peggy knew she could not be in a better
place.

'I don't know what I'll do if... If...' But Peggy could not bring
herself to say the devastating words that were searing inside her
head.

'You will do what you have to do,' said Molly, bustling into her
front parlour with a tray full of tea things, where four of them sat
and assured her they were there for her if Peggy needed any help.
They told her she would not be left alone to deal with what life
would throw at her. But none of the caring women dared broach
the subject of what would happen if Dar did not survive the night.
They had to still be positive and somehow persuade Peggy that she
had to feel the same.

'Dar also has a broken thigh bone,' said Peggy, and she heard a
small gasp from the chair near the window where Ellie was
sitting. 'Matron said the next twenty-four hours would be critical.'
Peggy was too wrapped up in her own distracted thoughts to
notice Molly place the saucer holding a cup of strong sweet tea
into her hands, or the look of sympathy that passed between the
women.

'I saw such injuries during the war, when I was nursing.' Ellie's
gentle delivery did nothing to quell the pounding of Peggy's heart.
'He will be in hospital for a long time.'

'They are going to move him to a specialist hospital in the Lancashire countryside.'

'I've never been to the countryside,' said Ina, 'is it far?'

'Far enough,' said Molly, slightly annoyed at the inane questioning.

'How will I get there?' Peggy asked. 'There's not a train running with the strike being on?'

'Aiden will take you in the wagon.' Ellie's gentle Lancastrian burr, so familiar around the street these days, was immediate and brooked no argument. She knew the place Dar would be moved to intimately, it was once her home, or rather, her prison. Lavender Green was part of the Kirrin Institute – a place of healing and well-being, named after her beloved mother, but she refused to ever go back there. 'Aiden goes to Lavender Green for herbal supplies each week, he'll be glad to take you.'

'I don't know what I'd do without you all.' Peggy felt a growing sense of their friendly compassion, which, although she would never say aloud, was beginning to make her feel a little uncomfortable. Not used to wearing her heart on her sleeve, she felt undeserving of their pity.

Nevertheless, she knew these four women would not allow the weight of her plight to hang around her neck like an anchor, threatening to drag her down into despair.

'You've four children who need you to be strong.' Mary Jane's Celtic words were blunt, but kindly meant, Peggy knew. Taking a deep breath, she put down the empty cup of tea she didn't remember drinking and stood up.

They were right, these women who strived to do their best for their family, of course they were, and she would do well to heed their abundance of common sense by putting her own feelings to one side and concentrating on looking after her children, like Dar would want.

'None of us can man the battlements alone, and I doubt you had any say in Dar's decision to work during the strike.' Ina's rare show of concern for someone other than herself and her own family made Peggy draw back, as if trying to make herself smaller, her cheeks suddenly burning with shame. She had encouraged Dar to carry on working when the other men had withdrawn their labour. This whole, terrible situation was her fault.

'We are all here when you need us,' said Ellie.

'Thank you,' Peggy whispered, knowing they all had their difficulties – more so than many, she was sure – but they had come through their hardships stronger and, some would say, feistier than ever, and she knew their caring hearts were bigger than they were. 'I'll let you know what happens,' Peggy said, 'and thank you for...' She could say no more as her throat constricted again. She wasn't used to people being kind to her, and their compassion went to the core of her. She was used to rules. Straight talking. No nonsense. Her mother had drummed it into her that showing emotion was not the done thing in the tough-talking, hard-living O'Day household. She suddenly recalled her sister, Violet, being scorned as soppy when she showed any kind of affection and was warned not to spoil Peggy. 'Please don't be nice to me any more,' she said, forcing a tight smile as her chin trembled. 'I'll end up in a pool of me own tears.'

'Away with you,' Molly said with a wave of her hard-working hands, and her eyes met Peggy's in a silent understanding of the friendly bond they had formed, through years of shared joys and sorrows, 'we'd do the same for anybody.'

Peggy knew these women meant well. She was glad of them. Even though she hadn't realised it fully before today.

A knock at the front door silenced their words and Molly popped her head out of the parlour door, looking towards the ever-open front door to see Peggy's fourteen-year-old daughter, Millie, standing on the step, her eyes red-rimmed from crying. Her voice held a quiver of apprehension when she enquired, 'Mrs Haywood, is me mam still here?'

* * *

As she entered her own house near the top end of the street, Peggy could almost hear Dar's laughter echoing through the rooms, it was a fragile sound that seemed so distant now. What was she going to do? Matron said it might be weeks before she could see Dar again, because of the risk of infection. How was she going to cope with four children, and no money coming in?

No money coming in! The thought hit her like one of those concrete wrecking balls used to knock down houses.

'Jack explained about Dar, Mam?' Millie's words broke her contemplation and gave a little warning that her children must be her first concern. 'I'll make that tea.'

They needed her to be strong, thought Peggy, keep the family together.

Coming back into the room from the back kitchen, Millie handed her mother a freshly made cup of tea, shooing the youngest two who were wrapping their arms around their mother, before sending them out to play in the street. The children unwrapped themselves and skipped outside, too young to take in the enormity of the situation.

'They don't need to know the ins and outs,' Millie said in a tone more mature than her years, and Peggy was grateful. 'They'll be better off not knowing,' Millie continued, 'they're satisfied just knowing Dar has hurt himself at work and would be in hospital for a time.'

Unknowingly, her children provided Peggy with the glimmer of solace she so desperately needed, and Millie promised to be the strongest of the lot by the way she had taken a silent control of this awful situation.

'I'll call them in for their tea when it's ready,' Millie said. 'The little ones must be fed, even if we can't stomach food right now.'

Peggy's mind raced as she held bread against the glowing fender, replaying memories of better times with Dar and the children, desperately clinging to the hope that he would pull through. And, selfish though it might seem, Peggy needed Jack and Millie to be strong. Because she was not sure she had it in her to support her children on her own.

Silently praying for strength, Peggy's thoughts were a mixed jumble of fear and sorrow as she watched the bread turn to a golden brown and handed the hot toast to Millie, who slathered it in best butter, cutting it into four squares while the next lot toasted.

Peggy had no idea what the future was going to hold for them now. Dar was her backbone, her rock, the ballast that kept her steady and chased the wolf from the door. He had given her the security she had never known before they were married.

Peggy had been just a girl of sixteen when everybody had told her she would rue the day she went over to 'his' side. Not even trying to hide their doubts the marriage of mixed religions would last. Dar was her first love. Her only love. When he showed her a little attention, she clung to his kindness like a starving girl desperate for food.

He wasn't loud or brash like some of the other cocky young lads who hung around the dockyards. He didn't drink himself incapable or gamble or mix with the wrong sort. He was just a nice lad who wanted to be with her. He was quiet and so very sure about what he wanted from the future: a wife and children, and a nice house in a nice street. Nothing fancy.

Peggy thought she had met the man of her dreams, then, terrified, she had discovered she was expecting a baby. He could have done what some less responsible men would have and run away to sea, leaving her in the lurch, but he didn't do that. Instead, he asked her to marry him, and she was more than glad to accept his proposal.

'I can't cope on my own,' Peggy muttered, 'I can't face living without him.'

'Well, you can stop that kind of talk, for a start.' Millie's words were abrupt, but she knew her mam would respond positively if she was dealt with a straightforward option, rather than being soft-soaped.

Like the women round about, Mam was the down-to-earth type who had never had it easy and dealt with life head on. She wasn't one to go tiptoeing around the mulberry bush when things got a bit rough.

'What would Dar say if he saw you pacing back and forth, frightening the little ones by crying your eyeballs out? He might not be home for a long time, but we can't wallow in self-pity.'

'You're right, love,' said Peggy and she took a deep sigh.

'And you're stronger than you think you are, Mam.' Millie's tone softened. She had never dared speak to her mother in such a direct way before. 'The thing is, you are the only one who can't see it.'

She called the children in from the street before she put their supper on the table. It had been a long, harrowing day, which none of them had expected. It was time to close the front door and try to work out what they must do next.

* * *

Later, Millie took the hot milk off the burning coals and made each of them a cup of malty Ovaltine, adding a little sugar to each one – something their mother would never allow usually. 'We've all had a big shock, Mam,' Millie said, 'but we have to look out for each other, to get through this.'

'Dar's always been here, looking after us, shielding us from life's storms,' said Jack, and his mother took a deep stuttering breath that rocked her shoulders.

'You're right, we all have to mind each other.' She had to be strongest of all. She couldn't expect Jack to be the breadwinner or her eldest daughter to fend for the little ones. They too needed stability.

Dar's voice echoed in Peggy's thoughts, his resilient words giving her the courage to face an uncertain future. Although, as her heart wavered between desperate hope and paralysing fear, she silently pleaded with a higher power for the strength to continue.

Gradually, Millie's words began to sink in, and a growing determination rose up inside Peggy. She had a duty to do what she must, to make sure her family were as well cared for as they had always been. She had to make sure Dar still had a proper, loving home to come back to. 'Dar would be so disappointed if I fell apart and let our family, and our house fall to ruin.'

'You'll never let that happen, Mam,' said Millie, 'you've got too much fight in you.'

Peggy looked with loving eyes towards her, and she nodded, but Millie could still see a hooded glimmer of defeat in her eyes, even though she was doing her best to hide it.

'There will have to be changes,' Peggy said, watching Millie undressing little Jane, who was to be washed in front of the lively fire, while Eddy was polishing off his toast and malt drink, sitting in front of the fire without the fireguard up – something Dar would never have allowed.

'We will all say an extra-special prayer for Dar tonight,' said Peggy. Dipping the flannel into a round white tin bowl of hot water she rubbed it vigorously with green soap and began washing little Jane's mucky hands and face.

'We'll get by somehow, Mam, we always have.' Millie moved her sister to the end of the table, while her mother prepared to wash Eddy, who needed a bit more of a scrub than his sister, being the rough-and-tumble kind of boy. Millie gently dried Jane's pretty face with a clean towel, thin through years of meticulous washing, but not yet ready for the rag bag, and still serviceable.

'Aye,' said Peggy, 'we must do what we've always done, love,' she told Millie, determined to try not to show the uncertainty that had threatened to overwhelm her. The insecurity that had once been as much a part of her life as the air she breathed. 'We are going to soldier on, and make sure everything is kept as comfortable as it has always been, for when Dar finally comes back to us.'

There were women in worse situations, money-wise, than she was. Peggy thought of the suitcase under the bed and the hoard of money inside that should be tucked up safely in the bank to buy the house. Then she realised she would need that money to pay Dar's medical bills, which would not come cheap, given the amount of specialist care he would need. At least they wouldn't starve, and the rent would be paid. Something would turn up, Peggy was sure. The least she could do was to keep the house and children as secure as possible. But for how long would she have to keep chasing shadows?

7

'Next!' Daisy, Molly's daughter, called, as the line of eager customers flowed up the back yard like a meandering River Mersey. In no time, news had got round that there was bread being baked and sold in Mary Jane's bakery in Beamer Street, and the line grew longer, stretching from the back gates of the bakery and weaving its way along the dock road, a testament to the desperation of women who needed bread to feed their family. Some had even enlisted their children to stand in line to make sure they got more than their fair share.

Mary Jane, Daisy and Percy found themselves swamped in the relentless tide of customers. Their hands moving in a blur as they fought against time to meet the insatiable demand.

'Something has got to be done.' The bleak realisation dawned on chief bread and pie maker, Percy, that the precious supplies of yeast and flour were rapidly dwindling. 'Demand is threatening to leave us short of ingredients,' he told Mary Jane, who nodded in agreement.

'Supplies are scarce, and we can't get any more for love nor money,' said Mary Jane. 'We don't know how long the strike is going to last, so we need to protect what ingredients we already have, otherwise we will all be out of work, and worse than that,' a shrewd smile lit up her emerald eyes, 'I'll be out of pocket.' Mary Jane was determined the strike was not going to cost her business, she had worked far too hard for that to happen.

'What are we going to do?' Daisy asked, her eyes widening. 'What about our regulars?'

'For a start, we are going to put a stop to the amount of people we serve, the ones who have been turning up out of the blue, I've never seen so many strangers in this shop.' Mary Jane was glad of the custom, but her loyalty lay with her regular customers who were having their noses pushed out when they could not get the bread they were accustomed to buying.

'I've heard tell there's a lot of stockpiling going on,' said Daisy. They were almost dead on their feet at the end of another busy working day.

'One man's meat is another man's poison,' Mary Jane said, picking up the sweeping brush when business had eventually ceased for the day, and they were cleaning the shop ready for tomorrow.

'This strike will make or break a lot of businesses, you mark my words,' Percy said, 'people have long memories, and our regulars won't stand for being put on the back burner in favour of new faces who will disappear as fast as they came when the strike is over.'

'We're going to have to ration the bread, Percy, like they did during the war,' Mary Jane told him as she brushed loose crumbs and flour from the bakery floor.

'I suppose you're right,' said Daisy. 'I can't see any other answer. The customers won't like it, but there's nothing else we can do under the circumstances.'

* * *

The following morning, Mary Jane put a notice in the bakery window, saying that the shop would close until further notice. Molly and the other Beamer Street wives passed on quiet whispers, to let the local regulars know they must be discreet if they wanted their supply of bread, and the usual array of pastries would be limited due to the shortage caused by the strike.

Usually busy at this hour of the morning, the bustling front shop now looked abandoned. Its doors shuttered and locked. The window blinds pulled down.

However, the back of the shop told a different story. The local housewives had slipped into the stable yard through the back gate and were served their regular bread from the back window.

'Is this all we're allowed?' said an indignant Ina King, inspecting the bread that was smaller than usual. 'Just one small loaf a day, is that it? That is not going to feed my family.'

'It's better than nothing,' Daisy told her. 'You'll have to slice your bread thinner.'

'I can read the *Echo* through me butties as it is,' said a disgruntled Ina. 'My lot think they've been put on workhouse rations.'

'Think of your trim waistline,' said Daisy, passing the loaf across the counter.

'I'm thinking of me washing line,' said Ina, obviously irritated, 'it can hardly take the strain of the family wash now, with the young'uns being off school. They think green soap grows on trees. If the teachers don't go back soon, we'll all be going around in last week's knickers.'

'You're not the only one, Ina,' said Daisy, 'but the strike can't last forever.' As Ina turned from the window, Daisy called her back. 'You will make sure you don't let slip that we are providing bread to our regulars.'

'What you tellin' me for?' said Ina. 'You know I can be trusted to keep a secret.'

Daisy gave her a perceptive smile, knowing the local newspaper was nowhere near as fast as Ina King for spreading news, good or bad. 'Just tipping you the wink, Ina. We don't want to be overrun by strangers again, otherwise there won't be enough bread to go around our regulars, you get me?'

'Loud and clear,' said Ina, not wanting to go without her regular supply for the sake of strangers. 'We can't let that happen.' Ina liked to think she had a vital role in the community. She would make sure everybody understood the message that the sombre façade of the bakery was doing a good job of concealing the activity at the back of the shop, and she'd make sure word got around that Mary Jane's bakery was closed to strangers from other districts, unless people wanted to go without their daily bread. And nobody wanted that. 'You won't hear me telling anybody that you're open.' Ina shrugged her thin shoulders and Daisy smiled, secure in the knowledge Ina would never risk her own supply and would diligently ensure only the familiar faces of the neighbourhood were looked after.

Nor were the regular working men ignored. The ones who usually called in every morning awaiting orders to be taken on for a morning or afternoon's work now manned the picket line in the pouring springtime rain and received a free cup of tea for their trouble, in the teashop, surrounded by the smell of the newly baked bread that lingered on their senses.

'I had to give short shrift to an out-of-town baker,' said Percy as he brought in a batch of dinner cobs hot from the oven. 'The bugger tried bribing me to sell him yeast and flour to make his own bread.' He placed the crusty cobs onto a wooden pallet, knowing they wouldn't be there for long.

'It's a good thing you're an honest man, Perce,' said Daisy as the queue dwindled to nothing and they gladly sat down, enjoying a much-needed cup of tea at the end of another working day.

'I told him – *on your bike, mister.*' Percy jerked his thumb over his shoulder. Daisy found comfort in Percy's reassuring presence when the women could get a bit fierce and could give a burly docker a run for his money. 'Mind you,' Percy, who was as honest as the day was long, laughed when he said, 'imagine if we'd sold him the flour and yeast, we'd have made a killing.'

'Why's that, Perce?' asked Mary Jane who knew he would never do such a thing.

'The news has just come out the strike will end at midnight tonight. By tomorrow, it will be back to work as normal.'

'Well, that didn't last long, thank goodness,' said Daisy.

'Nine days was more than enough for some folk,' said Mary Jane and rolled her eyes.

'It didn't do those poor miners a lot of good though, did it,' said Percy. 'I imagine a lot of them will get their marching orders after this.'

'Not just the miners either,' said Daisy, feeling the strike had dragged on for much longer than nine days.

'I passed our yeast to your mam,' said Percy, knowing staff were allowed either a part of yeast and flour or a freshly baked loaf in addition to their wages. 'We can't have our Molly wasting away now the strike's nearly over,' he told Daisy. His gentle wit had offered them a brief respite from the misery of the strike, and Daisy smiled, suspecting he had a bit of a soft spot for her mam.

'Poor Peggy,' said Molly, as she gripped a biscuit-coloured mixing bowl with one hand and expertly tipped the contents of bread dough onto a scrubbed and floured tabletop, 'if she didn't have bad luck, she'd have no luck at all – what with Dar in hospital, and her mother poorly, too.'

'None of us have had it easy, Molly.' Ina King had popped into Molly's kitchen, to get away from her brood and on the off chance she would get a fresh cup of hot tea and a bit of local gossip she might have missed elsewhere.

'Did I tell you Dar can't be moved just yet?' Molly began to knead the dough, nodding to the pot, knowing Ina usually called in around this time and was quite happy to help herself.

'No, I haven't heard anything.' Ina looked a little put out. 'How come you always get to know first?'

'They say he's too ill to be moved just yet,' said Molly, ignoring her neighbour's question. 'Peggy said he's had his leg put in something called traction.'

'What's traction?' Ina was scooping a third spoonful of sugar from the cut-glass bowl, before noticing Molly's watchful eyes offering a silent warning and giving her cause to put the sugar back into the basin.

'It's all ropes and pullies, from what I can make out,' said Molly, suspecting Ina would have emptied the sugar bowl had she not noticed. 'A Thomas splint, I think Ellie called it, invented during the war and used in the casualty clearing stations.'

'Never heard of it,' said Ina, not really interested. The talk of war and casualties and brave men was not something she could engage in. Molly knew Ina wouldn't have heard of the apparatus, seeing as her husband never served on the battlefield. But Molly continued to enlighten her.

'Ellie said, this splint revolutionised the way the injured men were treated and reduced the rate of mortality from fractures of the femur.'

'Fancy.' Ina didn't have a clue what most of Molly's words meant, thinking she sounded like some kind of medical book. She was bored with this conversation, and was more interested in drinking her tea, than listening about Dar's treatment. He wouldn't be in hospital, said her husband, if he'd been out on strike like other men.

'Mary Jane said her Cal had gone through the same treatment on the battlefield.' Molly noticed Ina's ears prick up. After she'd recently discovered Cal owned every house in Beamer Street – his inheritance from his father – Ina would not hear a word said against him or Mary Jane. A far cry from the days when Mary Jane had first moved into Beamer Street, when Ina would not give her the time of day, let alone a civil word.

'Well, if it's good enough for Cal Everdine, it must be good enough for Dar Tenant. But it seems I'm the last to find out anything these days.' Ina was most put out. 'Since Mary Jane was forced to close the bakery doors, to stop outsiders from other parishes muscling in, and buying up all the surplus bread, there has been a noticeable lack of local news.' Ina's pinched expression told Molly that she wasn't just put out, she was downright livid.

'Haven't you heard?' Molly could feel her delight rising. 'Our Daisy told me the strike is ending at midnight tonight.' There was a long silence in the kitchen, and she knew Ina was annoyed at not being the first to find out such important news. Opening her mouth as if to say something, she thought better of it.

After a couple of seconds, Ina could stand the silence no longer. 'Is that bread you're making there, Molly?' She knew full well her neighbour would have been supplied with yeast from her daughter Daisy, or even Percy.

'Aye,' Molly answered, not committing herself to telling Ina that Percy had brought yeast so she could bake bread for her family, nor the more essential information that she had invited him to tea. The strike had been going on for nine days and the mothers of Beamer Street had had enough. Tempers were not only frayed, they were bursting at the seams.

'I knew the strike would be over soon,' Ina conceded. 'It's not getting them anywhere.' By 'them', Molly took it she meant the workers.

'The government were well prepared by the look of it,' answered Molly, 'enlisting all those volunteers to keep the essential services going. But what a waste of time in the end. The miners still have not had their hours reduced, nor their pay increased.' The more she spoke, the firmer she kneaded the bread.

'Toffs who'll never know what it's like for dockers to suffer the humiliation of standing around in the pouring rain,' said Ina, 'just waiting for a hand on their shoulder, to show they've been hired for the morning. And then they must go through the whole thing again in the afternoon.'

'I suppose,' said Molly, a widow who had lost her husband in the Great War. She knew full well that Ina's husband would have been the first to throw his hand up for a strike.

'I suppose you'll be well supplied with bread, what with your Daisy working over the road,' said Ina and Molly knew she was edging for a handout.

'I'm just the same as everybody else, Ina,' said Molly. 'I only get the same as you.'

'Aye, but I don't have a cupboard full of flour and yeast to fall back on.' There was no mistaking Ina's accusing manner, and Molly felt a guilty heat rise to her cheeks that had nothing to do with the weather or the heat of the oven. 'Mind you, it's a good thing the strike's nearly over, Mary Jane wouldn't be able to keep it a secret much longer that she sells her bread out the back door.' There was a peevish edge to Ina's words. 'There was a definite whiff of freshly baked bread coming from her shop as I passed.'

'If she hadn't been so shrewd, none of us would have had bread.' Molly knew Mary Jane had provided a glimmer of comfort to her customers during the unrest.

'Those loaves she sells for the same price are smaller than they were before the strike.'

'She's making sure everybody gets a fair share, Ina,' said Molly. 'At least people are getting something, which is more than can be said for other parts of the town.' Having her ears to the ground, Mary Jane had seen the signs and had headed off trouble before it reached crisis point. Not that Ina would see it that way, she knew.

'Aye, she's got a real business head on her shoulders has Mary Jane,' said Ina, pouring tea into her saucer and blowing on it, before noisily slurping the contents.

'And wasn't that a good thing she did.' Molly admired Mary Jane's business nous and the way she had trained her eldest daughter, Daisy, who told her Mary Jane had ordered in more supplies, knowing bread would be one of the first commodities to be in short supply, if the whole country should down tools, which they had done. 'Mary Jane is bound to have heard the rumours,' said Molly, defending her best friend. 'She'd have overheard trouble brewing from the teashop tables.'

She knew Mary Jane had listened keenly to the whispers of growing discontent from the men who went into the teashop every day. And Molly could well imagine how soon those whispers grew to a harsh murmuring of unrest and mingled with the blue haze of curling smoke from matchstick thin hand-rolled cigarettes.

'If it hadn't been for their hard work and good judgement, we'd have all gone hungry,' said Molly, 'so I think they should be praised not pilloried.'

* * *

'How are you feeling, my love?' Peggy asked the following week when she was allowed into the long ward to see her husband, who was lying in one of the two rows of beds, overlooked by sister's table in the centre.

'I won't be dancing, that's for sure,' said Dar, who, dressed in striped pyjamas, was lying flat on his back without pillows. His right leg was in the air being supported by a splint that looked none too comfortable. 'When I'm able, I'll be moved to Lavender Green for rehabilitation, but that won't be for another month or so.'

'A month!' Peggy was glad he was near home for the foreseeable, grateful he had survived his accident, but she wanted Dar home as quickly as possible, and that would not happen until his leg was better and he learned to walk again.

'It's going to be a long job,' said Dar, taking hold of her hand, 'but at least I know we have our savings until my sick money comes through.'

'What sick money?' asked Peggy, her spirits lifting a little.

'I've been paying insurance since I started work at Hutton's in case something like this happens.' Dar's brow met and he looked concerned. 'Has nobody been to see you?'

Peggy shook her head.

'Leave it with me,' said Dar. 'Sister said Cal Everdine is coming in later, I'll have a word with him. He'll know what to do.' Cal was the man everybody went to if they needed good solid advice.

'Houseman is a liability, and you know it.' Cal Everdine glared across the desk at Hutton the following day. 'Either you kick him the hell out of here or you are going to pay the price. The men are ready to walk off the job, and that means only one thing – penal-

ties.' Penalties were the rising costs incurred when a job went over
its designated deadline, and Hutton knew penalties would be detri-
mental to his bank balance. 'You will have to pay the price one way
or the other.'

'I can't sack him, he's family,' Hutton answered, and the
commencing silence told him Cal Everdine was right. Miles was
never going to amount to much. No matter how much he tried to
appease his sister, Henry Hutton knew his nephew's drinking was
getting beyond the safety limit.

There was drinking on the dock, Hutton knew. Apart from
there being a public house on every corner, where some of the men
would spend their lunchtime break and forget to go back to work,
there was usually a wooden crate of something alcoholic that was
'accidentally' broken on the quayside, and Miles would always be
there with his tin mug ready to whet his whistle.

'Have you been to see Dar Tenant's family yet?' There was no
mistaking the accusing tone in Cal's voice. 'His wife and family
cannot be expected to live on fresh air.'

'I will see Mrs Tenant,' Hutton did not mention a day or time
but left the comment hanging, 'but there is something I have to do
first.' He was going to get his nephew's version of the accident, but
Miles had taken time off to visit his mother in Southport. Hutton
suspected his nephew was lying low until the dust settled; however,
knowing a bit of damage limitation was called for, he had tele-
phoned Miles to get his arse back here to explain himself. Hopefully, Miles might be able to shed a different light on the matter.
Although, Hutton wasn't holding out much hope on that score.

'Make sure you do see Mrs Tenant; her husband has been a
good worker for this firm.' Cal knew he had no need to verbally
threaten Hutton to do the right thing. At thirty-six years old, Cal
was not only the older man's equal in terms of money and authority, he had the advantage of being strong, muscular and in his

prime. Cal was a force to be reckoned with, although he preferred to use good old common sense and fair-mindedness.

When the office door slammed closed behind Cal, Henry Hutton knew this wasn't the end of the matter. Something would have to be done if he didn't want a riot on his hands.

8

Sitting behind his enormous mahogany desk, Hutton sighed.

Having heard the rumours surrounding Dar Tenant's 'accident', he now had to go and see Tenant's wife. He had put the matter off as long as possible, realising he would need to conjure up a story that would save his business from ruin.

Drinking on the job. That's what the men were saying about Miles. Drunk in charge of the winch. An instantly sackable offence. Not only that, but Miles had at once abandoned his station. Not hanging around to give a proper account of himself when his negligence caused a man to be almost killed and injured so badly, he may never work again.

If Hutton had done the right thing and insured his men, Dar Tenant would be entitled to full pay – and compensation. But he hadn't done that. He had penny-pinched to keep his wife in furs and his nephew in a fancy car, to keep his sister happy. A fool for a pretty face and an easy life, his chickens had now come home to roost.

Burying his face in his hands, Hutton knew he was going to have to find a way out of losing the shirt off his back in compensation payments. Tenant's condition was critical, and Hutton knew he should do something to help the family.

Aware of every dodge, cheat and light-fingered pilfering known to man, he had a reputation for keeping his eye to business. Making sure nobody would bleed him dry, knowing he had tried the underhanded tricks, at some time. Nevertheless, he knew it was going to be difficult worming his way out of the mess his nephew had created.

Tenant had the law on his side, and if this went to court, Hutton knew he didn't stand a hope in hell of winning. This catastrophe would cost him his business and, what was worse, his accumulated fortune. He couldn't let that happen.

A large, white-haired man in his mid-fifties, Hutton had owned this business since the beginning of the war. He made his money loading and unloading cargo, turning his dockside business into a growing, thriving concern. He and his partner, Harris, had conned a huge amount of money out of the government when he'd assured the powers-that-be he was a bigger fish than he actually was.

The import and export work had paid well during the Great War and made the two men richer than their wildest dreams, as well as giving local men regular work. He enjoyed the esteem his workers showed him almost as much as he loved the money. There was no shortage of cheap labour, and they took full advantage. In a time of high unemployment, the mere hint of being sacked was enough to keep the workers in line.

It was a pity about Harris though, thought Hutton, recalling the day his partner fell from a ship's derrick and broke his back. Never to work again. Stupid bugger, he thought, what fool of a man his age would even consider climbing a ship's rig? But that was Harris all over. Always devil-may-care and gung-ho. It may have served him better to keep his eyes on the financial situation though. If he had done so, he would not have been medically retired on a paltry pension when, by rights, he should have been living off the company shares.

However, as the weight of the business was on his shoulders, Hutton decided he alone had every right to be suitably remunerated.

Shame about Tenant. He'd been a good worker. But there was no sentiment in business. Nearing footsteps on the outside stairs stilled his thoughts before they began to turn benevolent. He had considered paying Tenant some kind of recompense. But the thought was quickly scotched when he realised that a show of generosity could be seen as an admission of guilt, and where would that lead him? Every man would expect to be compensated for the slightest injury. He could not allow that to happen. A small sum would be enough, as a mark of goodwill, to tide Tenant's wife over until her husband was discharged from hospital. *If he was discharged from hospital*, he thought, as the office door opened.

He raised his head. Nobody entered the office without knocking, and Hutton knew there was only one cocky young bugger who would dare doing so, safe in the knowledge he had his mother's backing. Or so he thought.

'Ahh, Miles, just the man,' Henry Hutton said in a cunningly light-hearted tone, which he knew his nephew would be wise not to ignore. However, Miles never had been the brightest spark in the box. The fool took everything at face value.

'Busy, Uncle Henry?' Miles asked, unconcerned. Or maybe plain ignorant of the fact he had caused a situation that had left one of Hutton's most qualified workers significantly injured, almost killed.

'Busy.' Henry Hutton's tone was a deep Lancastrian burr that put most people at their ease. Or, as he was doing to his nephew now, threw them completely off guard. 'When have you ever seen me *not* busy?' Hutton's words grew stiff, and he stretched his neck, looking directly at his sister's lad, all gangly six feet two inches of him.

A warning light went on in Miles' head when he saw the cold steel in his uncle's eyes and he realised he may not be given the unchallenging ride he had expected. Apprehension rose inside him as Uncle Henry gave him the latest update on Dar Tenant's situation. As presumed heir to all he surveyed, Miles could weather a scolding without too much difficulty.

'Shame. But I'm sure Tenant will be fine; his sort is made of tough stuff.' Miles' manner, conversationally indifferent, obviously irritated his uncle, but Hutton said nothing for the time being, until Miles said, 'I thought he was supposed to be competent to do the job.'

'He is!' snapped Hutton. What little patience he had left for this idiot had now dissolved completely. 'I've been hearing stories.' Hutton's voice was now low, even, and deceptively calm. 'You were supposed to be lifting slings of sugar, not knocking his head off. If he hadn't managed to push that young lad to safety, you could have killed him.'

'I didn't see the kid. The fool was on the wrong side of the crane.' Miles knew he could lie his way out of anything, usually. He had been doing it for years, so he'd had enough practice. The liquid lunch he had enjoyed earlier, in the Tram Tavern on the corner of Reckoner's Row, had given him a layer of self-assurance, which he did not usually have when dealing with his uncle. Thankfully, the sound of his own heartbeat was drowning out Uncle Henry's jaw-jawing. All he had to do was look suitably contrite and then sneak off for a pint.

'A little bird tells me you spent midday in the Tram Tavern before the accident.' Henry Hutton was in no mood for lies or liability. 'You didn't even hang around to see if the man was hurt!' What if Tenant did decide to sue? Hutton had heard Dar had more than a few shillings put to one side to buy his own house. What if he died? The recriminations would be disastrous, and this jumped-up fool of a nephew didn't give a rat's arse. 'A very dependable little bird, as it happened.'

Henry had questioned the men he knew would have seen the accident first-hand, and to a man, they all said Miles was oblivious when they were trying to warn him the sling, full of hessian sugar sacks, was unsafe.

'It was my lunch break. *My* dinner hour.' Miles felt he was entitled to that much at least. 'I thought—'

'You know what *thought* did?' Hutton's voice rising with every syllable was booming by the time he stood up. 'It followed a cart of shit, thinking it was a wedding!' Hutton's enormous bulk, brought on by too much sitting at a desk, a taste for fine wine, and a liking for rich food, seemed to fill the room as he leaned towards his nephew. The spoiled offspring of his younger sister, whom he should have ignored when she'd pleaded with him to employ her only son and show him how to run the business, which, being his only relative, she expected Miles to inherit.

Miles felt the office grow smaller and become a suffocating cage, trapping him in his uncle's wrath. The look of disgust on the older man's face told him he had to tread carefully.

'You weren't watching what you were doing, were you, lad? Did the work spoil your afternoon nap, is that it?' He could smell the beer and whisky on his nephew's breath even now and it had only turned one o'clock.

'I only had a couple of pints.' He waited for the inevitable wrist-slap he had been expecting.

'I'd say you had more than a couple of pints, lad. It looks to me like it's a daily habit.'

'I wasn't aware my intake was rationed.' Miles felt his stomach dip when he realised his uncle was as angry as a spitting cat, and grasped the fact there might be dire consequences to his actions.

'If you were anybody else, I'd haul you out in front of those men and flog you to within an inch of your life!' White balls of frothy saliva formed at the edge of Henry's angry mouth. 'And you can wipe that stupid smirk off your face, too, before I forget my promise to your mother to give you a second chance and put you on your arse.' Miles' cocky retort had enraged Henry Hutton beyond family loyalty, knowing his mealy-mouthed nephew would never backchat him if he were sober. 'You could have killed both Tenant and the kid!' He slammed his fist down hard onto the desk, wishing he did not have to consider his sister's feelings, wanting to wipe the smug look off his nephew's self-centred face.

Hutton was beginning to rue the day he paid for Miles to go to a select boarding school that had given him ideas above his station.

'Tenant will need more than surgery to fix the break in his thigh bone,' said Hutton. 'Did you know it is the longest and strongest bone in a man's body? A critical part of his ability to stand, let alone walk again.'

'Too bad, Uncle.' Miles' words sounded hollow even to his own ears. He did not even try to show concern, eager to get out of the office, away from his uncle's incessant nagging. 'If I'd known Tenant was incompetent, I would never have let him do the job.'

'Incompetent? How dare you? You arrogant bastard!' Henry walked around the desk and Miles took a step back towards the door. 'Don't you dare believe for one minute that Dar Tenant was incompetent,' Hutton growled. 'He is not the one to blame in all of this. He saved that young lad's life.'

Hutton stopped shouting momentarily, realising his words were carrying to the men below, and he didn't want to fill their mouths with facts that could finish off his business.

Lowering his voice, he leaned forward, inches from his nephew's face. 'Now it is up to me to clean up your mess.'

'So, you think it was my fault?' Miles, sounding incredulous, could not lose face.

'I don't *think* anything. I *know* this cock-up was your fault.'

'The man was useless. The kid was on the wrong side of the sling when it snapped. Tenant should have made sure the rope was in good order.' Miles struggled to keep eye contact with his uncle, obviously annoyed he was being interrogated in this manner. If it wasn't for the fact his mother had threatened to disinherit him if he didn't reduce his drinking and gambling ways, become a sober, upright member of society, he would walk out of this office right now. Spending the afternoon in the Tram Tavern was favourable to putting up with this schoolboy scolding. But he knew he had to put up with it for the sake of his future.

Uncle Henry, vindictive bastard that he was, would make sure he lost his inheritance. It was the only reason he acted so servile to this blubbery excuse of a man. And if the puce colour of his face was anything to go by, thought Miles, he would inherit sooner than even he expected.

The thought made him feel giddy, imagining the day, when *he* would be the one sitting behind that huge desk giving the orders. His herculean effort to keep a straight face failed, and a high-pitched laugh erupted from his lips, enraging his uncle even more.

'You think it's funny, *boy!*'

The emphasis on the word *boy* and the sound of Uncle Henry's fist slamming onto the desk once more brought Miles' intoxicated amusement to a sudden halt.

'No. Of course not, Uncle, I... I just thought—'

'I don't care what you thought! You have lost me one of my best workers. You spend more time in the alehouse than you do in work.' Henry was getting angrier with every word. 'Don't think I haven't heard the men talking about your afternoon naps.' Henry's words were suddenly quiet, more forceful. 'You are a waste of my time, and if your mother was not my sister, you would have been out of the door long ago.'

'I'm sorry, sir,' Miles grovelled, knowing his uncle's delicate ego was always in need of a good stroking. 'I thought I could trust Tenant to do a good job. After all, you were the one who told me what a decent worker he is.' He intended to share as much culpability as possible.

'Oh no you don't,' said Hutton, aware of his slick nephew's trick of always finding a scapegoat. 'This time the responsibility is all yours.' He dug his forefinger into Miles' chest. 'And if he dies, it will be you who will be held accountable – in a court of law – not me!'

'He won't die. Will he?' Miles felt the blood suddenly run ice cold through his veins. If there was an investigation, he was certain he would be found to be negligent. The men looked up to Dar Tenant. And there were plenty who would vouch for him. But he could not think of a single worker who would say a good word about him – or his uncle. 'I thought he knew what he was doing.' The obvious panic was coming out in short bursts. 'I would never have... If I thought—'

'Enough! I don't want to hear any more of your drivel,' roared Hutton, beyond exasperated. 'You'd better hope, for all our sakes, that Tenant does survive, and that he walks again, because if he doesn't, there will be nothing left to inherit.'

'Mother won't be happy.' Miles, regaining his earlier cockiness, knew his mother owned a share in Hutton's, which, he presumed, gave her a say in the whole company and its employees.

'Don't be under the illusion I worry what your mother may say.' Hutton's voice was cold.

'She is a shareholder in the firm.' Miles raised his chin and Hutton longed to ram his meaty fist into it.

'Celia has no authority in this firm, whatsoever. I am sure she will agree with me when I say you deserve a good flogging, for what you have done to that poor man and his family, not to mention the trauma you have put that young kid through!'

Miles Houseman should have been wise enough to say no more. But wisdom was not his strong point. 'Mother may not have authority in the firm,' he said, bored of his uncle's overbearing reprimands, 'but she will certainly have something to say about the way I have been spoken to and accused.'

'Really?' Hutton had been offered a challenge, which he could not resist. 'Let me tell you something, you poisonous upstart. You have been spoiled by that mother of yours since the day you were born, and she has done you no favours whatsoever.'

Henry looked over his nephew's shoulder to see the workforce below working diligently, yet he knew to a man, they would have an ear cocked, eagerly listening to the outcome of the meeting. Tenant was well liked. They would want to see justice done.

'You feel entitled because of who you are. Yet you do not have a qualification, nor a farthing, to your name!' Hutton roared, working himself into a frenzy, giving the workforce something to talk about, but he was past caring. Tenant's *accident* could cost him a fortune. The kind of money that would be taken from his own bank account to be used as compensation. Because Henry Hutton had never paid one penny to any insurance company, against possible injuries in the workplace, since the day he commenced trading. And this wasn't the first time he realised what a foolish, ridiculous, penny-pinching way of running such a risk-laden business. He knew that years ago. Yet he still took the gamble that was now in danger of ruining him.

When he had finished here, he would go and see Mrs Tenant. Square things off. She would be grateful he was a benevolent man.

'I will do better next time.' Miles conceded defeat, for now.

'So, you'll finish off the next poor sod, good and proper,' said Hutton, who did not believe anything that came out of this drunkard's lips, and his next words came from the back of his throat like a growl. 'You are a liability, a jumped-up nowt!' He moved forward, looked Miles in the eye and said, 'Pack your things. Get out of my sight. Out of my office. And out of my business. Do you understand me, boy? You're sacked! And don't expect another penny from me.'

* * *

Miles Houseman, outraged, ignored the sly glances of the working men as he stormed down the wooden steps and out of the double doors leading to the dock gate. He needed a drink.

Heading for the bridge that led to Reckoner's Row, he turned into Beamer Street and glared at the woman from No. 3, who was sitting on an upstairs windowsill cleaning her bedroom windows.

Not knowing she was the wife of the man he believed sabotaged his inheritance, he decided if Tenant was as skilled as the old man said he was, then, surely, he knew the dangers of the dockside and would be suitably insured. Uncle Henry must be forced to understand, the accident was not his fault. Nothing was ever his fault. Didn't these stupid people understand that?

Taking the concrete steps of the bridge two at a time, Miles headed towards the Tram Tavern to assuage his craving thirst and get his side of the story straight in his head. Mother was going to want every little detail and he had to be convincing if he was going to keep her onside.

As he walked along Reckoner's Row, Miles shook his head. He could not understand how Uncle had taken Tenant's side over his own flesh and blood. Who would do such a thing? His mother would have something to say when she heard about this. She wouldn't allow it.

As he ordered a pint of light and dark accompanied by a whisky chaser, Miles made a vow. When Uncle Henry changed his mind and took him back, he was going to make sure Tenant was never getting his job back. Not after this.

* * *

'Here, Molly.' Ina King looked both ways before she said any more, and when she knew the coast was clear she continued in hushed tones. 'You'll never guess who I've just seen going into Peggy Tenant's house.'

'Well? Go on then,' said Molly impatiently, she didn't have time for Ina today, she had washing to mangle.

'It was only himself... Henry Hutton.' Ina nodded, confirming her words, satisfied her revelation had the desired effect she was hoping for when Molly's jaw dropped.

'Henry Hutton? Well, I never did...'

9

Peggy was putting her last batch of washing through the mangle in the scullery when she heard the knock. The front door was open from morning till night since Dar went into the dockside hospital.

Molly, Ellie and Mary Jane, her strongest support, called in every day to see if there was any news, and to offer their help if she needed it, and Ina would call if she needed to borrow a cup of sugar or a penny for the gas meter.

Usually, they knocked on the vestibule door and waited for her to invite them in, so Peggy knew her visitor wouldn't be any of her friends with a heavy knock on the brass door knocker.

Turning the handle of the mangle faster, she was suddenly filled with an all-consuming trepidation. The loud hammering on the door knocker was what the women called the rent man's knock, and she prayed it did not mean unwelcome news.

If it was the rent man, she hoped he had not come to give her and her family their marching orders for missing last week's rent. She would explain she had been at the hospital, hoping he would accept double this week. The houses around Strand Road were very much sought after, so the agent had his pick of good tenants on behalf of the landlord, Peggy thought. Dar would not be pleased if she had lost the house, which they had come so close to owning.

As she put the folded towel into a white enamel basin ready to hang on the washing line in the back yard, she knew their safety net of savings would need to be used to pay for necessities. The money, which they had strived so hard to accumulate, shilling by shilling over the years, would be eaten up with no wages coming in.

When Dar was eventually well enough, he would need to go to Lavender Green, to learn how to walk again. The doctor had told her the treatment would not come cheap, but she had assured him she had the money to pay. But without his wages coming in, everything, including the housekeeping money, would come out of their savings from the cardboard suitcase under the bed.

Peggy shuddered at the thought of not being able to pay the rent and losing this house if Dar needed specialist care for any length of time. If that were to happen, it would mean having to throw themselves on the mercy of her mother, who would no doubt remind her that pride came before a fall. Not only that, but Peggy also had no doubt whatsoever her mother would never allow Dar to move into her house. With him not being a good Catholic man in her mother's eyes, even though Dar was one of the kindest men she had ever met. What if they had to move into a slum-dwelling in a lower end of the dock road?

Peggy knew Dar would never contemplate moving back to the cramped courts. The thought of leaving Beamer Street made her feel sick, but what choice would they have?

Her thoughts were doing somersaults as she hurried down the narrow hallway and opened the half-glazed vestibule door. Standing on her front step was Henry Hutton. The last person she expected to see. He tipped his grey fedora and introduced himself.

So, she thought, her husband's boss had finally deigned to honour her with his presence.

'To what do I owe the visit, Mr Hutton?' Peggy's voice sounded abrupt and a lot more confident than she felt, imagining any good employer would have sent a foreman to see the family of one of his best workers long before now. Instead, one of Dar's workmates had been around with an envelope of money after having a whip-round. Peggy had been embarrassed to take the money. They might be frugal, but they weren't dirt poor, and when she had tried to refuse, her rejection had been looked upon as an insult, so she had buried her pride and graciously accepted. There had been not a word from Hutton, until now.

'I've come to enquire about Dar, Mrs Tenant.' He gave her a pleasant smile, which immediately raised Peggy's suspicions.

'Come in,' Peggy said before leading the way up the narrow passage to the kitchen.

'Please, sit down,' she said, nodding towards the fireside chair, eager to hear what he had to say, 'I'll make a cup of tea.'

'Not for me,' said Hutton, trying not to admire the homely comfort of the Tenant household, with its polished floors and sparkling windows, every surface dust-free and spotlessly clean. The furniture was not lavish, but sturdy and well kept, there were no ornaments on the fireplace, apart from a domed wooden clock with filigree fingers pointing to Roman numerals.

Peggy imagined he was going to finally explain why Dar's wages had not been paid. Dar had told her he was entitled to sick pay, as he had been paying an insurance stamp since he'd joined Hutton's, and Peggy expected Mr Hutton had come to tell her how she should collect her husband's money every week.

'I've come to give you this as a small token of my appreciation of your husband's work over the years,' he said, holding out a crisp, white, five-pound note.

Peggy looked at the money for a moment, then she looked at Hutton. Five pounds? Was that all Dar was worth? After the back-breaking work he had put in over the years to line this man's pockets? She didn't trust herself to say anything as a feeling of indignant rage rose inside her. Peggy knew no matter how much she longed to voice her thoughts, Dar would not appreciate her speaking out to his boss and jeopardising his job. Jack had already lost his because he'd joined the strikers.

There was an awkward silence before Peggy thanked Mr Hutton and, clearing his throat to cover her obstinate pause, he put the money on the sideboard. She would wait and see what Dar had to say on the matter when she went to visit him, hoping he would be allowed a visitor today. A bone infection meant he had been put into isolation, and she had been prevented from seeing her husband.

* * *

'Five pounds, is that all?' Molly said when Peggy told her about Hutton's visit. 'The cheek of him. Did he say anything about Dar's sick money?' Peggy had confided in Molly.

'No,' said Peggy. 'To be honest, I was so shocked at him bringing the money, I forgot to ask for details.'

'Well, if I were you, I would be hotfooting it over to his office and finding out for certain.' Molly rolled her shoulders, a sure sign she was feeling vexed on Peggy's behalf. 'It's men like him who worm their way out of their responsibilities, and to blazes with the rest.'

Peggy wondered if Molly was speaking from personal experience, but she didn't ask. She had said enough already. Dar would not be best pleased to have his private, family dealings bandied around Beamer Street.

'Did I tell you my sister Violet mentioned she had a job for me cleaning the ships on the dock?' Peggy said, quickly changing the subject. 'I'm not work-shy, but I do think Dar would have something to say if I told him I would be working on the docks.'

'A lot of men think the dockside is no place for a woman,' said Molly, 'but that's not my way of thinking.'

'I'll talk to Dar when I go to visit next,' said Peggy, having second thoughts, knowing the work would boost her finances and was not to be sniffed at in a time like this.

'You've got to do what's right for your family,' said Molly, picking up the galvanised bucket of water she had just used to wash down her window ledge and front step. 'There's no shame in being poor, but in my opinion, it would be a terrible shame to see a good job go to waste when your need is great.'

'I knew I could depend on you for a bit of common sense, Molly,' Peggy said, relieved she had taken Molly into her confidence. However, when she saw Ina King heading across the road, she said a swift ta-ra to Molly. Peggy did not want to get in conversation with the woman who asked far too many questions for her liking.

10

The hospital ward was so calm, Peggy could hear herself breathing, and when she spoke to the nurse, it was in whispers. Dar had been moved back into the main ward and her excitement soared when she was told she could see him today.

The iron beds, set out in two long pristine rows, were filled with men of various ages. Looking along from the bed nearest the door, her eyes followed the line to the one near the arched window, next to Matron's office.

When Peggy saw her beloved husband, her heart skipped a beat. His hair was freshly washed and parted down the middle, his thick dark moustache neatly trimmed, and his tired eyes lit up when he caught sight of her.

Dar had been lying on his back staring at the ceiling; his leg in traction was suspended in mid-air by the Thomas splint. His hair had grown, she noticed, and his skin was all smooth and shiny, not rugged and sun-baked like it was when working out in the open on the river. The time that had passed, not being able to talk to him, had been agonisingly slow. His muscles seemed to have shrunk, and he looked pale, making him appear much older than his years.

The hospital-supply pyjamas seemed to be suspended, like his body was a coat hanger. That was because of the infection, she surmised.

'How are you, my love?' Peggy asked when she reached Dar's bed. 'We're all missing you so much.'

'I'll be right as ninepence in no time,' Dar said, a beaming smile going some way to oust the sombre expression from moments earlier when he thought nobody was looking. Always the optimist, he did not want to worry Peggy any more than was necessary. 'How are the kids?'

'They miss you, we all do,' Peggy answered, slipping her hand into Dar's gnarled work-worn hand, and he gently folded it around hers. He didn't have his usual strength, she could tell, but she didn't comment. Instead, she said, 'I've brought you some new pyjamas, and some slippers and a dressing gown.'

'I've missed you so much, Peg.' Dar's words held an intimacy she had forced herself to let slip from her memory. She could not allow herself to dwell on thoughts of her and Dar entwined in each other's arms, enjoying the deepest love only a married couple can share, when there was every chance she might have lost him.

'I've missed you too,' she answered. 'Our bed is much too big and lonely without you.' She could feel a nervous heat rise to her cheeks. She had never spoken to him in such a way before, but knowing how close Dar had come to losing his life had given her the courage to speak as she felt. And judging by the softness in his face, she could tell he was happy she had spoken so openly. 'Maybe you'll be allowed outside for a bit of fresh air soon,' Peggy said and Dar told her he hoped so.

The weeks were flying by and, the beginning of June saw the weather growing warmer. Even though she knew her husband's recovery would take time, she never imagined how much she and the family would miss him, and this wasn't the end of it.

Resting against a hill of pillows, Dar patted the bed, encouraging her to sit closer, and Peggy raised her eyebrows. For as much as she would love to be enfolded in his arms for even a little while, she would never do something so racy.

'The children send their love,' Peggy said, regaining her composure and pulling the chair closer to the bed, 'and they want you to know they say an extra-special prayer for a speedy recovery every night.'

She thought of Dar as he was before the accident – vigorous, robust and strikingly handsome – not this husk of a man whose skin and emaciated muscles hung on skeletal bones. The thought frightened her, but she did not love him any less, in fact, his fragility only went to make her love him more, and she knew that when he was back home, sitting by his own fireside surrounded by the people who loved him most, he would soon become as robust and energetic as he had always been.

'Did the doctors say when you will be moved to Lavender Green?' Peggy asked.

'If all goes well, it should be soon.' Dar was putting on a brave face. 'I'm looking forward to getting out of this bed and working on getting back on my feet.'

'You will be back home before you know it,' Peggy said, trying to sound upbeat, and Dar told he might not be home until Christmas. How was she going to cope being without him until then?

'The doctors said it is a long process, your thigh bone is the longest, strongest bone in your body and takes months to heal, if at all.'

'Just as long as you're on the mend.' Peggy smiled, aiming to reassure Dar she could cope. 'I'll keep the home fires burning.'

'That's my girl,' said Dar and she recognised the twinkle in his eyes that had not diminished.

Christmas was such a long way off. Six whole months without him. She could hardly bear it.

'How have you been managing? Did Hutton pay my sick money? After all, this is all his nephew's fault.'

'He sacked Miles Houseman,' Peggy told her husband. 'Mr Hutton called, and he gave me five pounds in case you needed anything.'

'He did what!' Dar's face paled with rising anger. 'Five lousy pounds. Is that all?' Five pounds was more than a week's wages to Dar, but he knew he was worth more than that. 'And the rest?'

'He didn't mention any sick money, and I didn't question it,' Peggy explained. 'I didn't want to do anything until I spoke to you first.' She could see Dar was turning the matter over in his head. He wasn't one for making rash decisions. Everything he did would have been carefully thought through. 'Do you think I should go and see him?' Peggy asked, and Dar said she should. 'I'll go first thing tomorrow.'

'Don't let him fob you off,' said Dar. 'Remind him I paid my dues every week. He has an obligation to pay my dependants.'

'He doesn't live by anybody else's rules, we both know that.'

Peggy knew their savings would not last forever. Once Dar was moved out of the local voluntary hospital and into the specialist hospital in the Lancashire countryside, the cost of his treatment would escalate. For a start, he would need to learn how to walk again. The recovery would be long and arduous. Nevertheless, Peggy knew if she had to pay every penny of their savings to get Dar back to the man he once was, she would do it, and gladly. Anything to have him back home with his family where he belonged.

She squeezed his hand, and they shared that private look only a happily married couple could share. 'Oh, I nearly forgot,' Peggy said, reaching into her bag. She took out an apple and an orange from her shopping bag, along with two sandwiches, neatly wrapped in greaseproof paper. 'Best ham on the bone,' she said, knowing they were Dar's favourite sandwiches, and seeing his face light up, she put them in the little wooden cupboard at the side of the bed. 'I brought you some of that aniseed twist you're so fond of, and Ellie sent a bag of liquorice she made.' Peggy looked around to make sure nobody could hear her when she said, 'They'll help to keep you regular. I don't think I'll have enough time to get all the news out before end of visiting...' She hoped this other news wouldn't diminish the light in his eyes. 'Violet is in charge of a group of ships' cleaners—'

'I hope she doesn't think you'll be joining them,' said Dar, and Peggy suddenly felt a surge of something she had never felt before. She knew he had never been cock-a-hoop about women going out to work, but nor did she reckon on him forbidding her outright to do so.

'I didn't say she'd asked me.' Peggy's indignant voice was strained. For the first time, she felt as if her choice didn't count. Like the women who had kept the country going during the war. Who then lost the jobs they had been so capable of doing in favour of the returning soldiers.

'I'm sorry, Peg, but I don't like the idea of you working on the docks!' Dar said. 'I've heard stories.'

Peggy looked at her husband. Really looked at him. Lying in his bed with his plumped-up pillows, being waited on hand and foot, while she scrimped along, trying not to make too big a dent in their savings, knowing every penny would be needed for his recovery. Peggy, trying not to be unreasonable, felt she was being taken for granted. Like most women of her generation. Always putting other people's needs above her own, without complaint. While struggling to stay positive. She cooked, and cleaned, and scrubbed the house from top to bottom. She made sure her family were as well cared for as she possibly could. With what little money she allowed for housekeeping. While dashing along to the courts, to help her ungrateful mother every day. Cooking and cleaning for her. All without a word of complaint. Not to mention the half-crown she had handed over for the last seventeen years.

Her mind was like a runaway horse. Peggy could not stop the thoughts racing. Recalling the days Dar would come home from work, his slippers warming by the fire, his tea on the table, the children playing happily on the mat, so as not to disturb him while he was reading the evening newspaper. Eking out the housekeeping to provide small treats for him and the children.

Nothing had been a trouble to her, because she knew Dar saw them both as a team, a force for good. So, she thought it unfair he should suddenly become a man who ordered her to become the little woman who did as she was told and stay at home, because his manly pride was dented.

'Come on, love.' Dar's coaxing tone was one she recognised. 'Don't look so fed up, you know I only have your best interest at heart.'

'But I didn't say I was going to go out to work, even though I can't see the problem – lots of women do it.'

'Maybe so,' Dar said gently, taking hold of her hand again, 'but I don't want you worn out before your time, too tired to enjoy your home and family.'

'Is that how you felt?' Peggy asked, realising the long hours her husband worked to keep them respectable.

'It's my job to bring home the bacon, not yours,' Dar said softly, 'and maybe I was a bit heavy-handed when I said I didn't want you working on the docks, but I didn't mean it the way it came out. Those women work so hard.'

'I'm not scared of work,' said Peggy. 'I think women's work is as relentless as their husbands' – cooking, cleaning, washing, ironing and scrubbing floors.'

Dar gave his gentle laugh and held up his hand. 'All right, I get the message,' he said. 'But how is all that going to get done if you are going out to work?'

'Our Millie is quite capable of helping out,' said Peggy, who was in no doubt her daughter would help look after the little ones. 'And our Jack is too.'

'You know I would do anything to make you happy,' said Dar and Peggy relaxed a little.

'I know you would,' Peggy answered, glad they were back in harmony again, 'and maybe I was a bit quick to take umbrage.'

'Let's just see what happens,' Dar said, kissing his wife's hand. 'We never know what tomorrow will bring.'

Peggy jumped a little when one of the nurses rang a huge brass hand bell to signal the end of visiting; her nerves were beginning to get the better of her, she knew.

'I'll be in tomorrow.' Peggy gave Dar a kiss and stood up to leave. 'I'll go and see Mr Hutton in the morning.'

11

'They let me in to see Dar,' Peggy told Molly when she arrived home from the borough hospital. 'He's out of the isolation ward, and the infection has subsided.'

'That is good news,' said Molly. 'Does that mean he's on the mend?'

'He's not out of the woods yet, but the infection is waning. So, it won't be long before he's on his way to Lavender Green and learning to walk again,' Peggy told Molly, who was out brushing her front step when her daughter, Daisy, and Mary Jane left the shop and crossed the road, the usual gathering place for the women of Beamer Street when they fancied a natter. 'Dar confirmed what the men have been saying,' she continued. 'Miles Houseman was drunk in charge of the crane.'

'I knew it,' said Molly. 'He's never out of the Tram Tavern. Anyone would think the bar would fall down if he shifted himself from it, the idle bugger.'

'I promised to take the little ones to see Dar on Sunday after-noon,' Peggy told Molly, Daisy and Mary Jane, who had finished work in the bakery and were on their way home for their tea, but not before they found out how Dar was getting along. 'Our Eddy and Jane are missing Dar so much.'

'I'm sure you all are,' said Molly and Peggy gave a tight smile, she didn't want any of her family to worry, but nor did she want to hide the truth and give them false hope.

'We have to be prepared for what's facing us.' She knew Dar had a long way to go before he was back home, and *if* he would be back to his normal walking self again. She also knew that even though the future looked bleak, they were not in the impoverished situation that people around and about were forced to endure.

'Does this mean you won't be buying the house?' Molly asked, then looked apologetic when Peggy's mouth set in a straight line. 'Sorry, Peg, you know me, my nose won't rust through lack of use.'

'We will have to wait and see.' Peggy laughed, knowing Molly was never slow off the mark when she wanted to know anything. But her friend was not underhanded like some. If she asked a question, the enquiry usually held good intentions.

Mary Jane, excited, showed Peggy a picture of Lavender Green, which had been featured in one of her magazines.

'It looks like a five-star hotel,' said Daisy, who had drooled over the article earlier.

Peggy's eyes widened in surprise. She knew Dar's rehabilitation was going to be expensive, and now she understood why.

'The place has an excellent reputation,' said Mary Jane.

But even so, thought Peggy, it could still take months to get him walking properly again. It went without saying, the treatment would not come cheap, and she knew she would need the extra funds that working on the docks would bring. If it meant Dar was going to walk again, sacrifices must be made.

'I'll light a candle for Dar when I go to mass,' said Molly, while Daisy and Mary Jane nodded in agreement, and Peggy thanked them. Dar needed all the help he could get. She also knew she would have to be more frugal to cover all the household expenses. The loss of Dar's wages meant she was now dependent on their life savings more than ever.

'Dar received a letter off one of the men who told him Henry Hutton had sacked his nephew.'

'Why would he do that if Miles did nothing wrong, I wonder?' Molly sounded suspicious.

'That's what I thought,' said Peggy.

'Houseman doesn't know the job,' said Ina King, who had also joined them and didn't like to be left out. 'He's only waiting for the old man to pop his clogs, then he'll get the lot.'

'Aye,' Molly answered, 'Hutton hasn't got any children of his own, so Miles will automatically step into his shoes.'

'Well, I can't see that firm lasting if Miles Houseman inherits,' Mary Jane said. 'Cal told me he knocked Dar twenty feet into the ship's hold.'

'Dar's lucky to be alive,' said Peggy, appalled the man who expected to inherit the firm could be so reckless.

'Houseman was in no fit state to heed the warning. It's a disgrace.' Mary Jane was so angry she could hardly speak.

'Dar deserves a medal for saving that young lad,' said Molly, 'and I don't care if Hutton has sacked him, Miles Houseman needs locking up.'

'Anyway, I'll have to be off, our Millie will have the tea on, and I haven't had a bite to eat all day,' Peggy said, weary now; it had been a long day.

Peggy, who missed her husband more than words could say, prayed he would soon be in the best place at Lavender Green as she made her way up Beamer Street. She knew the place had been used as a military hospital during the war. Returning soldiers, whose bones were shattered on the battlefield, were taken there for expert treatment. She prayed it would do the same thing for her man. All Dar had to do was avoid another infection. Then he could be moved to the countryside and his recovery could begin properly. That way, he would be home before Christmas.

The cost of travelling would only allow her to visit once a week, but she and Dar had already decided they would keep up to date by writing every day.

'I'm home,' Peggy called to her eldest daughter Millie, who was out in the back kitchen preparing the evening meal.

'Tea's nearly ready,' called Millie. She was relieved Mam had been able to see Dar. Her parents had not spent a single night apart, since he came back unscathed from the trenches. Millie thought the house felt strangely empty without her father. She longed for the day he walked through the front door, to make them one happy family again. Also, to reignite that familiar look of tenderness in her mam's eyes.

'Mary Jane showed me this picture of the hospital.' Peggy opened the magazine Mary Jane had given her to the page that showed a large red-brick mansion nestled in acres of countryside, standing proud against the backdrop of healing tranquillity, which held the promise of hope. 'It wouldn't look out of place in a painting.'

'It's quite a long way from the train station,' Millie said, and her heart fluttered with excitement as she traced her finger along the map, imagining Dar's face when they turned up to see him, imagining a warm breeze enveloping them as they made their way across the huge lawn and the scent of wildflowers and freshly cut grass filling her senses.

'Just a good stretch of the legs,' said Peggy. Her voice quivered with a mixture of awe and longing as she whispered, 'Imagine being surrounded by such beauty and peace after being so ill. Lavender Green could make all the difference to Dar's recovery.'

As Jack stared at the grandeur of the fine building, a pang of indignation, fuelled by the injustice of a society where wealth determined access to quality, ignited a fire of determination within him. 'I suppose they can have fine buildings like that when we're paying through the nose,' said Jack, who believed good medical care should not be consigned only to the rich.

* * *

'He still doesn't look as strong as he was,' she told Millie later. 'He's been through a lot, since we last saw him.' There was a catch in Peggy's voice as Millie listened quietly. 'And I could tell by a little involuntary wince every now and again, Dar was in a lot of pain.'

'Oh Mam,' Millie said the only words she could manage to get past the lump in her throat.

'I gave him all your best wishes,' Peggy said, rallying, when she noticed how close to tears poor Millie had come, 'and the pictures the little ones had drawn. He has put them on his bedside table, to cheer himself up. Knowing we are all thinking of him and praying that he will be home soon is a comfort to him.'

Fighting back her own tears, Peggy didn't tell her children that the hospital regulators would not allow the drawings to be kept beside Dar's bed, stating that paper carried infection.

'The fruit I took in, to cheer him up, was swiftly taken away by a diligent nurse.' Peggy looked a bit put out. 'She explained later that not all patients were lucky enough to receive gifts from their own visitors, and the fruit would be shared out equally among all patients, as was hospital policy.'

'I suppose it's the right thing to do, if some don't have visitors.'

'You're right, love,' said Peggy, giving the matter thought. 'Some patients don't have the means to buy fresh fruit.' She told Millie and Jack everything Dar had told her, and by the time she had finished, it was time for the little ones to get ready for bed. She was thankful Millie was so mature she was able to help her.

'I've made a shepherd's pie and bought some new potatoes and vegetables from the money you left on the mantlepiece.'

'It's a good thing I've got such a capable daughter.' Peggy gave Millie a hug, grateful they had such a good relationship. Although she did wonder if she should tell Millie everything. Even though she did not want to put the burden of worry onto her daughter's young shoulders, Peggy realised she had no choice. 'Dar's recovery is going to be a long one.' She told her daughter. 'Months, maybe even longer.'

'I know, Mam,' said Millie, 'but we have to stay positive for the young ones—' Eddy and Jane were missing Dar so much '—we have to remind them every day brings him a little closer to coming home.'

'You're right, Millie,' said Peggy, wishing she could be as certain as her daughter.

12

'Wotcha, Dais, me auld cock sparrer!'

Daisy Haywood's heart gave a full-on twist when she heard Max Hunter's simulated attempt to torture the English language, and she battled without success to appear indifferent as a smile lit up her pretty face, even though she tried her best to ignore his sudden arrival, after weeks of going AWOL.

Max, a reporter on the *Liverpool Evening Echo*, was as dashing as he was charismatic. At twenty-one, he was three years older than Daisy and was always on the lookout for the next big story. But his habit of chasing a 'scoop' meant he could be gone in the blink of an eye. Any poor girl who tried to pin him down was going to be sorely disappointed. So, even though he made her heart soar, she had to appear detached. Not let him know how much she cared.

Max came into the bakery or the teashop most days to glean snippets of local news that appeared interesting, seeing that such information seemed to arrive here first. He was following in his father's esteemed journalistic footsteps and knew he had the perfect name for an inquisitive journalist.

'Here he is,' whispered one of the customers, 'the happy wanderer. I bet you're made up.'

Daisy appeared not to take any notice as she served Mrs Lamb from number thirty-two, although stealing a glimpse towards the bakery door. She hoped that, even though her heart gave its usual bolt-of-lightning surge at seeing him again, the pleasure did not show too much on her face. If confidence was an Olympic sport, Max would win gold. Although, she did admit, but only to herself, that he did have something to be self-assured about. Max was the most handsome man she had ever seen. He dressed like an American film star, in his black and white brogues and 22-inch bottom Oxford bag trousers, a striped shirt and a fashionable cricket pullover. He was the height of style, standing out from the usual rough-and-ready men around here. His straw boater was worn at a jaunty angle and Max always stood out from the crowd.

And his eyes, Daisy felt a swoon coming on, those dreamy blue eyes which could drown her in their penetrating gaze. Max could show Harry Houdini a thing or two.

One of his most successful disappearing acts saw him not turning up, yet again, for an arranged date, like he had done before. Only this time, she knew, mumps did not last for nearly a month, which was the length of time he had been gone without a word.

'I'm sorry, do I know you?' Daisy's face remained passive, a mask hiding a whirlwind of hurt feelings, her heart hammering against her ribs like a caged bird desperate to break free. Max had promised to take her to the pictures last month but had not turned up. Not only that, but he had not called into the tearoom for his usual bacon on toast either. Daisy surmised he was likely too ashamed to show his face. But she had missed him. Much more than she thought she would. 'What did you say your name was?'

'Ahh, don't be like that, Dais,' Max pleaded, pushing back his straw hat, to show the light in his gorgeous eyes, and she almost yielded to his persuasive manner. But hurt feelings overcame her natural show of sociability. Max had let her down once too often. 'I never meant to hurt you, Dais.' His voice softened as he leaned across the counter, his words meant for her alone, but he hadn't reckoned on the interested women of Beamer Street who were waiting to be served and enjoyed a bit of local information themselves, especially when it came to matters of Daisy's tender heart. 'I am truly sorry.'

'Tell it to the sparrows, Max, they might be more interested.' Her voice quivered slightly as she fought to keep her composure and the women nodded under their headscarves, taking in every word.

Daisy knew it wouldn't do to show the customers she had been a love-struck girl who had been taken for a fool – twice! Even though she longed to forgive him for standing her up, she couldn't lose face in front of her neighbours. Why did he have to make such a big show of turning up unexpectedly again?

Daisy passed a customer her change, and in return she was offered a sympathetic smile. She didn't know which was worse: the customer's pity or her public show of humiliation. Everybody knew she had a soft spot for Max, and he might as well have put it on the front page of his newspaper. But it hadn't been enough to keep him here for the past month.

'I'll serve Mrs Tenant,' said Mary Jane, who had just returned to the bakery from the back of the shop and knew Max and Daisy would make a handsome couple, if only he would stay in one place for long enough.

'I'm sorry I haven't been in to see you, Dais.' His eyes suddenly lost their ever-present sparkle and Max looked quite sombre, which was unusual, she thought, knowing he was one of life's perpetual optimists, always looking on the bright side. He enjoyed having a laugh and a joke. Usually at her expense, but she took it in good sport. 'I had a bit of business I had to deal with,' he said simply.

'You always have an excuse, I know that much,' she said primly, making a big job of tidying the tissue paper on the other counter, away from waggling ears. 'I told Mary Jane you'd have a good excuse. *Full of them,* I said. *Nobody can come up with an excuse quicker than Max,* I said. *He's got one for every occasion,* I said.'

She stopped shuffling the tissue paper when he did not answer with one of his usual quick-fire quips, and she raised her head to find herself looking into his tender pale blue eyes.

'Well? Go on then,' she said, determined not to weaken. 'Spit it out before it chokes you.'

'I'm sorry to have to tell you, Dais.' Max lowered his eyes, seeming to examine his polished brogues, the height of fashion worn on the feet of every stylish man-about-town. 'My old man died and...'

The words stopped Daisy in her tracks, her mouth falling open, her jaw dropped, but no sound came. The customers did not even try to hide their curiosity, watching Daisy's interaction with Max, their eyes filled with interest and a hint of envy, remembering the days when a young man looked at them that way.

'Oh Max, I am so sorry to hear that.' Daisy's anguished whisper was apparent to all as she lifted the counter flap, hurried to the other side and threw her arms around his neck, hugging him to her. 'I take it all back.' There were tears in her eyes and Max looked concerned. 'I knew you wouldn't stop coming into the shop for no good reason.' She could have bitten her tongue off for being so off-hand with him.

'Dais, there's something I have to tell you.' However, Max soon realised she wasn't listening to a word he said. 'I didn't mean—'

'Was it sudden?' Daisy asked, feeling like a shrew for the way she had behaved towards him. 'Did he suffer?' Her heart was breaking for his loss.

'I don't know, Dais, I wasn't there.' Max was contrite, even though he enjoyed the hug immensely. He had waited a long time to have her in his arms, but not like this. Not by a misunderstanding. He had to make her listen. 'He didn't die recently,' Max blurted out the words and Daisy's brow wrinkled in confusion. 'Remember. I told you he died at Ypres in the Great War.'

'But you said...' Daisy stepped back, unravelling herself from his arms. Confusion flooded through her. She had been tricked. Not only that, but half the women in the street had been witness to her humiliation. She had fallen for one of Max's towering tales, again. 'That was very cruel of you, Max.' Daisy could not believe she had been so gullible. The heat of mortification rose to her neck and face as more customers came into the shop.

She turned on her heel and went over to help Mary Jane. Thankful that in no time at all she was rushed off her feet. A blessing in disguise, she thought. Having always been a peace-loving person, she now felt she could willingly box Max Hunter's ears good and proper. Serving the customers, she tried to keep her usual composure. But it was a struggle.

Max watched her from the other side of the counter, admiring the way she always took the time to have a little chat, making the customers feel she had only turned into work to serve them, proving her ability to manage pressure even when she was rushed off her feet. She was one of a kind, was Daisy, and he thought the world of her. He would go as far as to say, Daisy was the love of his life. But was she enough to keep his feet on the ground? He was ambitious. He still hadn't decided to take the promotion he had been offered. The move meant leaving Liverpool for London. He was certain Daisy wouldn't leave her hometown to live among strangers. What girl would?

Thankfully, the promotion was not available until next year, so he had six months to decide. He wanted to prove himself as an established journalist. He wanted to uncover important stories full of impact. Exciting news that had influence on the world like his father had done.

Yet, he could not do that if he had a girl waiting in the wings, hoping for more from their relationship. Like marriage! He could not take off at a moment's notice to cover a story and leave a wife and possibly children while he travelled far and wide to discover the next big story.

He and Daisy would remain close friends, he told himself, knowing she had ambitions of her own. She wanted to run her own catering business, organising functions and events. Making a name for herself. She felt the same as he did, Max was sure. She had dreams of her own to pursue. She had told him, she would be her own boss, like Mary Jane.

'Are you still here?' Daisy tried to ignore Max, who she now considered some kind of vagabond who stole women's hearts and turned up unexpectedly whenever the mood struck him, acting like he had done nothing wrong.

'Did you know your nostrils flare in the most delightful way, when you are angry?'

'Mary Jane, will you please serve this gentleman, I think he wants a strychnine sandwich and has far too much to say for himself.' Daisy promised not to look at Max as she served another customer. His cheeky smile did her runaway heartbeat no good at all.

'A slice of your delicious toast, cut in half and filled with a crispy rasher of mouth-watering bacon, please, Mary Jane,' Max called over his shoulder, heading to the three wooden steps that led up to the tearoom, 'and a refreshing cup of your excellent tea.'

'I don't know where he gets his cheek from, I really don't!' Daisy sighed, rolling her big brown eyes.

* * *

'This note was left for you,' said Mary Jane, later, coming into the tearoom from the baker's shop. She handed Daisy a neatly folded sheet of lined paper ripped from the notebook Max always carried with him.

I know tomorrow is your day off, so I've arranged for us to go into town and see a show tonight, not the music hall, a real swanky show. Spend the whole evening together. How's about it, Dais? Pick you up at seven? I won't be late.

Your fondest friend,

Max xx

'The cheeky blighter!' Daisy spluttered. Every time she thought she had won the battle, he went and started a commotion in her heart. Well, she had no intention of going into town with him tonight. Not a hope. Not a chance.

The rest of the day went by at a crawl. Every time she looked at the clock, the fingers never seemed to move, which was in stark contrast to Daisy, who could not keep still. At times, she had the urge to run out into the street, open her arms wide and spin around until she was dizzy, to calm her racing heart.

'Are you feeling all right, Daisy?' asked a customer. 'You're looking a bit flushed.'

'If that beaming smile and those sparkling eyes are anything to go by,' said Mary Jane who was serving, 'I'd say she was feeling just fine.'

'I don't know what you mean, I'm sure.' Daisy tried to sound baffled, but her rosy glow told a different tale. *I wonder if Mam has ironed my new pink blouse.* Not that she had any intentions of changing her mind. No intentions whatsoever.

* * *

'Oh Mam,' cried Daisy, looking in the ovel mirror over the fireplace, 'my hair looks like an exploded mattress.'

'No, it doesn't,' exclaimed Molly, who was sitting at the fireside knitting a man's pullover ready for winter, 'it looks lovely.' She knew her Daisy had been in a complete tizzy since she came in from working at the bakery, and it hadn't taken much probing to find out why. 'So, what time is Max picking you up?' asked Molly, breathing a sigh of motherly pride. She knew Daisy had her sights set on Max, since the first day he'd walked into the bakery, and his cheeky banter had set her daughter's pulse racing.

'He said seven o'clock, but I'll never tame this hair by then,' Daisy answered, licking her index finger and thumb to shape a curl above her eyebrow.

'Mam's finished with the potato sack,' teased Freddy, her younger brother. 'You could always put that on your head.' He was obviously amused at his sister's nervous excitement, but when Daisy turned from the mirror to glare at him, Freddy could see she was in no mood for funny comments. 'Sorry, Dais,' Freddy said, 'I was only joking. Your hair looks lovely and if he doesn't like it, then he's not the man for you.'

'Don't say that.' Daisy sounded disappointed. 'Anyway, I'm not looking for a lifelong commitment. Max is taking me to the theatre, that's all. Just two friends having an enjoyable time. Under no obligations. Like Mam and Percy.' Mam, at forty-six, was much too old to know what it was like to be in love.

'Well, that's all right then, Dais,' said Freddy. 'Can you hear the band playing Gershwin's, "The Man I Love"?' Freddy threw his head back and roared with laughter, and Daisy sent a silent plea to her mother to tell him to stop teasing her.

Molly, enjoying the entertainment of her offspring's wit, fondly instructed her second son to stop teasing his sister.

'Is that clock right, Mam?' Daisy asked, checking the time again.

'Yes, lovey, only another hour to go.' Molly smiled, knowing exactly how Daisy was feeling, remembering the first time her beloved Bert had taken her out to the music hall. But those days had long gone, even though Bert would always be her first love, the father of her beloved children. Time had a habit of moving on and changing things around a bit.

'Did you launder my pink blouse, Mam?' Daisy asked.

'All washed and ironed, and hanging in your wardrobe, lovey,' Molly answered, hoping her daughter wasn't going to be stood up by Max again, knowing such a thing would break their Daisy's heart and no mistake.

'I won't be late home, Mam,' said Daisy, winding her curly hair around her hand into a bob. 'I wish I had smooth straight hair like Louise Brooks.'

'You look beautiful just the way you are, my lovely,' said Molly, proud of every one of her children, who had been an absolute godsend to her.

'But if I had straight hair, I could wear it in a glossy short bob like a movie star.'

'A movie star, no less,' said Freddy, careful not to rumple his sister's ego.

'That reminds me,' Molly said, looking the picture of innocence and not taking her eyes off her knitting, 'did I tell you Percy asked me to go and see the new Buster Keaton film?' She could feel all eyes on her.

'That'll be twice in one week, Mam!' Daisy and Freddy said in unison, then giving her brother a silent warning, Daisy said, 'It'll do Mam good to get out.'

13

Peggy, determined to sort out the family finances, tried desperately not to let her nerves get the better of her when she got up after a fitful night's sleep. The fear of what could happen if Dar couldn't walk again brought back her insecurities of the past. Gauzy memories of a cold, hungry child huddled in the shadow of the court's stone steps, leading up to a paint-cracked door, from behind which loud, viciously angry voices rang out and played in her head.

The nightmare was always the same. But what, or who, was the child hiding from? Her mam? No, not Mam. Her mother was inside the crowded two-storey house. The keening sound of an injured animal was coming from her mother's lips.

Yelling and pounding of fists. Furniture smashed to smithereens. Father home from sea. Violet running. Out of the door. Down the steps. Sobbing, she disappeared through the darkness of the alleyway. Then she was gone.

Neighbours huddled together. The child, watching from the cold, wet ground beside the forbidding stone steps. Her small hands clasping her bony knees close to a scrawny chest, her wet face buried in her arms as the wind and rain battered down upon her head.

The memory dissolved, as it always did, into a fog as thick as the one rolling in off the River Mersey. Memories lost in the murky depths of her thoughts. But the suffocating grip of dread was still there. Sharp. Tightening around her heart.

Peggy found it hard to breathe and sat upright in her bed, stretching out her hand to the empty space Dar had occupied. There was something in her past that had burrowed into her soul and came terrifyingly close in her sleep. Try as she might, Peggy could never get to the end of the nightmare. Nor did she know why it only came when she was at her lowest ebb, knowing Dar was the only one who could ease the night terrors, console her, make it all go away.

* * *

'Morning, Mam,' said Millie.

'I've made a pan of porridge.' Peggy, a little distracted, was relieved when Millie came down the stairs and interrupted her jumbled feelings of confusion. Living in her own thoughts did no good for herself or her family. She had overcome challenging times in the past, and she would do it again. A small flame of hope flickered inside her when Peggy realised that it was performance, not thoughts, which got things done and there was no time like the present to put those thoughts into action. 'I'm going to see that Mister Hutton and find out what he intends to do about the money owed to Dar.' Peggy was determined not to let Hutton get away with doing Dar out of his sick pay. She had heard nothing from Hutton since he came that day and left five pounds. 'If he thinks five pounds is all your father is worth, he will have another think coming.'

'I was surprised the high and mighty Mister Hutton came at all.' Millie's look of disgust distorted her pretty face. 'I thought he would have sent someone.'

'He was trying to show what a benevolent man he was, but I reckon that was a ploy; he hoped I wouldn't stir up trouble about the accident,' Peggy answered with a look of determination. 'But he didn't reckon on the grit of a woman who has a family to support.' The resolute edge in her voice, belied Peggy's stomach-churning anxiety. Going cap in hand to Hutton was not something she was comfortable about. Nevertheless, she must push the feeling deep down inside herself. Be strong, if only for her children. 'We'll soon see who comes off best.'

'You tell him straight, Mam,' said Millie, her resolve matching her mother's words. 'The old skinflint should have coughed up long before now.'

The rain lashing against the corrugated roof of Hutton's office drowned out the sound of Peggy's footsteps as she marched past the machine operators, who stopped what they were doing to gawp at her, climbing the wooden steps to Hutton's office – a place nobody entered without an invitation or a summons. But Peggy was in no mood to wait. If she lingered, waiting for the invitation to enter, she might well lose her nerve. And that would not do. Her children's well-being depended on her being strong and forthright. She had come for what they were legally entitled to. From what Mary Jane had told her, Peggy had the law on her side. The thought gave her the assurance she did not know she had. Her husband had been a hard-working man. He had never missed a day's work since being set on, at Hutton's, after the war. He had paid his dues every week without fail. Surely that should count for something.

With every determined step she took, her resolve grew. Hutton was a demanding man to work for, she knew. He wanted two bobs' worth of work for a shilling's pay. But no matter, Peggy thought, she was not leaving here without the reassurance her husband would get what he was owed.

Hutton looked up from his paperwork at the sound of the tarnished brass knob turning and inhaled a gasp of cigar-flavoured saliva. He had not expected to see Peggy Tenant again. Yet the woman standing in the doorway was like a ghost from his past. Tall, her back was ramrod straight. And there was no mistaking that insolent tilt of her chin. That steely glint in her eyes, so like her mother's, caused the blood to pump through his veins.

'Mister Hutton?' Peggy's voice broke his train of thought, and he looked at her. Proud. Unsmiling. 'I have come to talk to you about my husband, Mister Tenant.' The sounds of the dockside seemed to grow louder. The smell of oil, and dust, and wood permeating his senses.

'Ahh, yes. Unfortunate business.' Hutton's body grew tense. His hooded eyes darting about as if trying to find an escape route. He would have demanded Peggy leave his office at once had she been anybody else. If she had come here to seek more money, she had enough witnesses to back her up.

'Unfortunate is not the word I would use, Mister Hutton,' Peggy said stiffly, noticing the distinct musty smell, reminiscent of damp wood and black mould, skirting the ceilings and leaching around the walls, causing her nose to wrinkle in disgust. How could anybody work in this filth, she wondered, distracted by the gloomy, dimly lit room that created an atmosphere not only of grime but decay. Nor did she sit in the chair opposite his desk, to which he gestured. 'I won't, if you don't mind.' Peggy tried to be civil, but it wasn't easy. 'I have a family to support. As you may know, my husband is still in hospital. And will be, for a long time, under-going expensive rehabilitation.'

'What is it you want, Mrs Tenant?' There was a sharp edge to Hutton's voice that had not been there when he'd visited the house, to offer a paltry five pounds, for all the months Dar would be out of work. 'I suppose you have come looking for more money?'

'You suppose right, Mister Hutton.' Peggy's shameless response showed an equal determination to the man glaring at her from the other side of the desk. 'However, I have not come grovelling for handouts. I have come for my husband's sick pay, that is all.'

'What sick pay?' Hutton's bushy white eyebrows pleated, and although the feeling did not register on her stern features, Peggy's heart sank. She waited for him to explain himself. 'Who said he is entitled to be paid when he is not working? I've never heard anything so ridiculous in all my born days!'

'What about the insurance money you took from his wages every week?' Peggy argued. In the ensuing silence, she could hear the lashing rain intensify, creating a sense of foreboding.

'What insurance?' Hutton, shrugging his shoulders, looked puzzled as if such a thing had never occurred to him. His direct gaze, which usually put grown men in their place, challenged her to defy him.

A sudden gust of wind rattled the rotting window frames, the damp smell reminding her of the dreaded courts, and she shivered. But this was not the time to cower. She refused to be intimidated by this charlatan.

'The insurance money the law says you must take from his pay packet each week, so he is covered for sick pay and medical treat-ment, if he is unable to work through illness.' Peggy's answer was equally challenging.

'Your husband did not pay any such insurance.' Hutton leaned back in his chair. His thumbs hooked into the shallow pockets of his waistcoat, he made a steeple with his fingers, his hands resting on his over-fed belly. 'He worked on a week-by-week basis. If he wanted the protection of sick pay, then he should have taken the necessary steps to secure such finances.'

Peggy's infuriated mouth dropped open, and she stared at this mountain of a man with growing rage. He, obviously, had never seen a hungry day. She knew without any doubt, if Dar was working for himself, he would have put all the necessary insurance protection in place to secure their well-being. 'Dar is far too astute to do something as stupid as leaving the security of his family to chance. So, I think you might be mistaken, Mister Hutton.' Peggy's voice was deceptively low, but there was no mistaking the force behind her words. 'You took the money out of his wages every single week, and you have done so since he came out of the army in 1918. That's eight years of contributions.'

'That money was for the tools he hired to do his job.' Hutton had a crick in his neck looking up at her, waving his words away as if swatting a fly.

Peggy realised her coming here may be as effective as carrying water on a knife, knowing he expected her to take his words at face value. However, that was not her way, she knew that now. 'Those are some very expensive tools, if it takes eight years to pay for them, Mister Hutton?'

Her voice held the same determination he recalled from another woman in years gone by. The same tone, coming from Mrs Tenant's mouth, gave her words a wasp-sting quality. The last woman who spoke to him in such a forthright way was little more than a girl. A beautiful, feisty girl with fire in her belly and passion in her soul. His one lasting regret, among many of life's disappointments, was the day he told her he could not marry her, because he was engaged to be married to Helena, the daughter of a wealthy merchant who was going to set him up on the first rung of the ladder to riches and power.

What good had the choice done him? None. That's what. Something stirred within him. A feeling of regret he had forgotten existed.

He had told the girl he could not be connected in any way to the child she was carrying. And when she had told him he would rue the day he turned his back on her, she was right.

Helena, unable to have children, had blamed him. He had accepted her belief as a self-punishment for not being honest with her. Helena had spent her barren life attending fund-raising charities, hobnobbing with the rich and influential, and offering their marriage nothing but spiteful recriminations.

'Well, let me tell you something for nothing, Mister Hutton!' Her words broke through his thoughts and Peggy Tenant leaned forward, spreading the palms of her reddened, work-worn hands flat on the green leather inlay of his huge oak desk. His pride and joy. The inanimate, unfeeling symbol of success. The cost of which would have bought Tenant's house, he was sure. 'You will never have a worker as good as my husband,' Peggy almost spat the words, 'and if you had designs on making Miles Houseman your successor, I don't rate the chance of this business surviving, because he will drink this business dry and will almost certainly attempt to kill your workforce.'

'Will that be all, Mrs Tenant?' Hutton showed no emotion one way or another, silently enraging Peggy.

'I'll see my day of you, Mister Hutton. Just you see if I don't.' Contempt gleamed in her eyes across the desk, and Henry Hutton felt truly deserving of her unmitigated scorn. If only she knew he felt the very same way about himself, he thought. 'Your kind think you rule the roost, but you're wrong,' said Peggy, her cold, forbid-

ding eyes meeting his with no hint of recognition before she
slammed out of the office.

His kind? He rubbed his chin as the opaque glass in the top half
of the door quivered in its frame. If only she knew. She was *his kind*.

He forced his spine upright, his vision clouding. If ever he
needed proof of who she was, he had just seen it with his own eyes.

* * *

Peggy no longer worried about what anybody on the quayside
thought of her. Hardly caring that all eyes were on her. She was too
focused on trying to get away from there and calm the thundering
beat of her heart. Her hands, trembling uncontrollably, fumbled to
lift the rusting latch of the dock gate and get out of here as quick as
she could.

Once outside, the west wind from the river blasted in her face.
She couldn't think straight. Her breathing, which came in short,
painful gasps, told Peggy she needed to stay calm, let the feeling
pass, as it usually did. This wasn't the first time she had experienced the heart-racing palpitations. The terrifying tremors and
tight compressions stopped her ribs expanding. She felt like she
was drowning. Fighting to get just a little air into her lungs. The
attacks had come on her since she was a child. But never as
strongly as they were coming now.

Exiting, into the smoky street, her silent tears of anger and frustration mingled with the torrential rain. Peggy knew she had no
choice. She must go to the local priest and beg relief from the
parish fund. Something she promised she would never do.

Placing her hands flat against the rough, red-brick wall, Peggy
bent her head, trying to catch her breath. She had never asked
another living soul for anything. Everything they had, she and Dar
had earned and worked hard for.

'Mrs Tenant, is everything all right, can I help you?' The male voice came from behind her and Peggy's head shot up to see Ellie's husband, Aiden, standing close by.

'Just a little dizzy spell, Mister Newman,' said Peggy as he offered to help her back home, which, thankfully, was only a short walk away. 'I'm much better now,' she said as she reached her front gate. 'Thank you for your help.'

'It might help if you let Ellie have a look at you,' Aiden said, and Peggy nodded.

'Maybe I need a little tonic.' She thanked him once again before he carried on down the street towards the apothecary.

Peggy told Millie, in detail, what had happened in Hutton's office. 'Can you believe that Dar has paid all those contributions, yet he has nothing to show for them?'

'I heard there were jobs going in "the baggy", I could try there.' Millie's words were tentative, she knew how much her mother wanted her to get a trade, better herself, be someone, not work in a factory sewing an assortment of utility bags.

'You will do no such thing!' Peggy would not hear of it. 'I've got better things in mind for you than factory work, sewing canvas bags for horse feed. Never in my lifetime.' Peggy's lips, white with indignation, tightened at the injustice she had been dealt. 'I will have no daughter of mine throwing her life away in a sweatshop.' Peggy could feel the squeezing in her chest, and she dreaded another attack. Millie mustn't see the panic. She had to be strong in front of her daughter.

'Mam?' Millie's voice was full of concern. 'You're not well.' Her mother's face drained of all colour, and Millie rushed out to the scullery to fetch a cup of water. Unbeknown to her mother, she had seen this happen before. And these sudden bouts terrified her. 'You're having one of those attacks again, aren't you?'

'What attacks?' asked Peggy when Millie returned and offered her the cup to take a sip of freezing water, her mother's hands trembling as she placed the cup back on the saucer, straightening her slumped shoulders.

'Mam, I'm not blind, I can see what you're going through.' Millie's voice was soft, like she was talking to a child. 'You don't have to keep everything bottled up inside you. You've got me and our Jack. We'll always be here.'

Peggy took a deep breath, and her eyes softened as the attack released its grip, allowing her to breathe easier. Reaching out for Millie's hand, she looked to her daughter. 'Don't you worry, queen,' Peggy said, using an affectionate, local term of endearment, 'it won't always be like this. We'll get by, somehow.'

14

'Is this the shop where our Peggy gets me ma's chest medicine?'

Ellie smiled, as she did to every customer who came into the apothecary. She had never seen this one before, but there was something familiar about her. Maybe it was the colour of her eyes, so pale they were almost silver-grey. The same colour as Peggy's, if she wasn't mistaken, but this woman's hair was a wiry rust-red, whereas Peggy's was as black as a raven's wing.

'Can I help you?' Ellie asked the woman.

'I need some of that liniment for me mam's cough,' Violet answered. 'Me sister, Peggy, who lives in number three, told me she gets Ma's medicine here.'

'You must be Violet, I'm Ellie.' She took in Peggy's sister with a single sweep of her eyes and could see the resemblance.

'Yes, I'm Violet.' She did not say anything else while Ellie went to fetch a bottle from the back of the shop. Looking around the shop, Violet was interested in the lotions and potions on display and noted that they could do with a place like this near the courts, where there was always somebody ailing.

'Hello,' said Aiden, who had come to put some more concoctions on the shelf behind the counter as the shop door opened and a scruffy-looking man in a gabardine mac tied with string sidled up to the counter, 'is Ellie attending to you?'

'Aye,' said Violet, 'she has just gone out the back.'

'I'm sure she won't be long,' said Aiden as he stroked the white cat lying on the counter before attending to the other customer, whom he recognised as Miles Houseman, and realised that the nephew of one of the town's biggest employers had really let himself go since he'd got sacked. 'Ah, here she is. I hope you're feeling better soon.'

'It's not for me,' said Violet, but Aiden was already serving a bedraggled customer at the counter near the door.

'Here we are,' said Ellie, 'that'll be three ha'pence, please.'

'Thank you very much,' Violet said politely, handing over a penny and a halfpenny, 'you'll find that's just right.' She gave Ellie the impression she was putting her best foot forward. 'Peggy's gone to visit her husband at the hospital.' Violet looked around the shop and taking all in. 'It's unusual to see a shop open on a Sunday, unless it's a newsagent.'

Ellie nodded, took the copper coins and handed over the linctus. 'People still get sick on Sunday,' she said with a smile, knowing Sunday was usually her best day for trading.

'I should say,' answered Violet, 'my Fred had a terrible cough when he got up this morning, too. I told him he must have been drinking out of a dirty glass in that public bar last night.' She raised her hand in a cheery wave and let out a cackling laugh that was loud enough to wake the sleeping cat.

All signs of laughter had gone when the scruffy man barged past Violet and dragged open the shop door. She let him pass through it before making her way up the street.

'I think working with Violet would do Peggy the power of good,'

Ellie told Aiden, 'but she told me her husband would not hear of it.'

'What did she say to that?' Aiden asked, believing that women should have just as much right as men to choose how they lived their lives.

'You know Peggy, she keeps her cards very close to her chest. Although, I think the independence would bring a glow to her cheeks.' Ellie smiled.

'Not to mention the money it brings in.' The twinkle in his eyes told Ellie how much he absolutely loved her. 'You thrive on being independent, and I wouldn't want it any other way.'

'You are the strength I need to continue my ma's good work, my love.' Ellie accepted the kiss on her cheek with the utmost pleasure, knowing Aiden was so much more than her husband, he was her best friend and her soulmate. She genuinely believed they had been together in a past life and would be together for all eternity.

'I've just remembered where I saw that man,' she told Aiden.

'Yes?' Aiden said and Ellie shook her head.

'The bloke who shuffled in after Violet. He bought methylated spirits. You must remember him – scruffy beard, rough-looking, yellow-tinged skin, very dishevelled.'

'Miles Houseman.' Aiden raised an eyebrow. 'He's on a slippery slope,' he told Ellie, who was tidying paper bags into the drawer of the counter.

'Peggy's taking the children to visit Lavender Green.'

'Will you ever go back?' asked Aiden and Ellie shook her head, leaning against the counter and thinking how lucky she was to have a husband like Aiden. 'It was kind of you to let Dar have his treatment for free,' said Aiden, who had once tended the acres of land that surrounded Lavender Green, the huge mansion house that had once held Ellie prisoner to a loveless marriage but was

now the dedicated establishment for both specialist healing and
the well-being of deprived children.

15

Peggy made sure her youngest children were scrubbed clean in the tin bath, which usually hung on a six-inch nail outside the back door. Their faces were smooth and shiny, their clean clothes freshly ironed, and their hair was glossy after being washed in Derbac soap.

Giving her excited children one last look to make sure everything was perfect, Peggy made sure the back door was locked, and the four of them made their way to the tram stop to take them into town to catch the train, while Jack chopped wood for the chandler to earn a few shillings.

Travelling was not usual practice for Peggy or her children, and all were busy looking out of the tram window on the journey to Lime Street station.

'Hold Millie's hand,' Peggy told her youngest child. 'When we get on the train, we will open the sandwiches and have something to eat.' She smiled when she saw the enthusiastic glance pass between her children, who had never been on a train before, glad she had brought a couple of sandwich parcels: one for the journey to Lavender Green and one for the journey back. When she went to visit Dar last week, she hadn't thought to take food with her, not realising how long the trip would take, and she was starving by the time she got back home.

'There's a cow!' Eddy shouted excitedly, nudging Jane. 'And there's a rabbit!'

The summer's day was gloriously hot and sunny, and the blue sky was high and cloudless, but by the time they got near to the hospital, the younger children were wilting a little.

'Is it much further?' asked Millie, carrying Jane on her shoulders as the novelty of the countryside walk had lost its appeal for her little sister.

'Not long now,' answered Peggy. 'Just think how surprised Dar is going to be when he sees you all.'

'I can't wait to see him.' Millie's voice was high with excitement. 'I just want to give him a great big hug.'

'It's such a glorious day they might let him come down to the garden,' Peggy told them as they neared the red-brick archway through which a long path bordered by colourful flowers led up to the hospital. Dar was still unable to walk, Peggy told her children, but he would be allowed to come into the garden to be with them, as the sun was shining and the day was so warm, even if he was in a wheelchair. There was much more freedom here at Lavender Green than there had been at the borough hospital and the children were so excited to see their father.

As their mother disappeared into the building, the children sat on a wooden bench that was on the edge of a large, neatly trimmed lawn, and waited impatiently for the signal from their mother to go to the garden at the back to see their father.

However, they were surprised when Peggy came out of the hospital less than ten minutes later. Millie was concerned when she saw her mother's eyes were red, as if she had been crying, and Millie felt her heart sink. She stood up, quickly telling the children to stay on the bench, while she hurried over to their mother.

'Mam, what's wrong?' Millie asked, fearing the worst kind of news.

Her mother was quiet for a moment, as if gathering her thoughts.

'Dar's not allowed off the ward, he's got another chest infection.' Peggy's voice was dull, she so wanted Dar to see the children. 'They've given him a sleeping draught. He was spark out when I got up to the ward.'

'He's going to be so disappointed when he wakes up,' Millie said.

'Come on, let's make our way back to the station. Maybe he'll be well enough to see us next week.' The journey back was going to be a long one, she knew, and not nearly as exciting as the one they'd had coming.

* * *

'How's it going, lad?' asked Cal in that friendly way he had about him.

'Not so good, Mr Everdine,' said Jack. 'I got the sack as you might have heard.'

'That's bad luck,' Cal said, his voice keeping the North American drawl he'd developed from years spent in Canada. He paused, a look of confusion on his open face. 'I was coming to see you anyway.'

'Oh aye,' said Jack, a tall, gangly youth of sixteen, 'what can I do for you?'

'I was hoping to speak to your mum, too,' said Cal.

Jack told him she was visiting Dar. 'The house is empty, except for me,' Jack answered.

'That's why you didn't hear me calling,' Cal answered, 'but I could have sworn I saw someone going into your house.'

Without another word, the two of them looked at each other and hurried along the street.

Something troubled Jack Tenant as he approached the front door, which had not been open when he left it to go and borrow a chopper from Molly Haywood. Then, he noticed the parlour curtains were closed and was distracted momentarily when Mr Everdine, hands in pockets, started whistling a jaunty tune. Jack wished he would stop whistling; he needed to listen.

The front door was wide open, and the skies had darkened, as the first spots of rain began to fall, promising a storm to come. Why would the parlour curtains be closed? Mam never closed them during the day. She liked to show off her brass ornaments on the windowsill.

He knew for certain he had closed that front door after promising his mother, he would chop wood for later. And even though the people of Beamer Street rarely closed their front door before bedtime, there should be nothing unusual in seeing their door open. But this time there was. Knowing the family would be out for best part of the day, and knowing there was a suitcase full of money under his mother's bed, he had taken no chances, making sure the front door was closed tight shut.

When he entered the house, everything was quiet. As he expected. Then he heard it. A creak in the bedroom above. Mice perhaps? The thought was fleeting. Jack knew they'd have to be wearing ruddy great hobnail boots to make a sound like that.

Jack very quietly opened the vestibule door and shivered. In the darkening skies of the summer evening, he felt a chill now that the sun had disappeared behind low black clouds. Tiptoeing across the polished linoleum, he noticed the tea caddy in which his mother kept her rent money, upended against the wall of the narrow hallway. He knew the caddy would be empty today, because Ma paid the rent only yesterday. Something was very wrong.

When he heard Cal's hushed voice behind him, Jack's head turned on a swivel and he put his forefinger to his lips. Passing the parlour, he ventured into the kitchen, and as he entered the room where his family spent their time, his eyes grew wide in horror and astonishment. Gripping the handle of the chopper, he could not believe the state of the place. Every drawer had been turned upside down. The cupboard at the side of the fireplace, where Mam kept her letters from Dar, and any other household items, had been ransacked, the door hanging off its hinges.

Jack had never seen their house looking like this. Then they heard a creak above, both looked up to the ceiling.

'That's Mam's room,' Jack whispered, and Cal motioned for him to lock the back door, silently creeping out to the hallway to close the front door. Then they both waited. There were definite sounds of someone moving around up there and as Jack made to rush up the stairs, Cal stopped him and mouthed the words *not yet*.

Jack knew the living room had never looked as chaotic as this. He imagined it couldn't look any worse if a herd of elephants had charged through the place. The sideboard drawers had been dragged out and the contents spilled over the floor. Cushions were ripped open, and the duck feather filling covered the furniture in a frenzy of disarray. He could not even begin to imagine his mother's reaction if she came back to see the place looking as bad as this.

'Whoever did this, they have not left yet, Mr Everdine.' Blood rushed through his veins and his heart pounded in his chest as his eyes scanned the room. 'Did you hear that?' His voice deepened, giving way to the feeling his insides were vibrating. He should feel scared, but he wasn't. As Jack felt the rush of adrenaline oozing through his body, it made him feel invincible and he made for the stairs.

'No!' Cal whispered and pointed to himself. 'You go and call a cop from the police box down the street.'

Jack's mouth was dry, his senses heightened, he could hear every breath, every hair bristling on his head before hurrying towards the door.

'Whoever did this know what they're looking for,' he hissed, 'but they don't know where to find it.'

'Well, whoever, ain't leaving with anything from this house,' Cal whispered back.

'I'll be back before you know it,' Jack said and, in a moment, he was gone, racing down the passageway out of the front door. Dragging open the wooden gate, he bumped into Molly Haywood.

'What's the rush?' asked Molly as Jack nearly knocked her over in his haste to get to the police box on the corner of the street.

'We've been burgled,' said Jack, still running, throwing the words over his shoulder. 'Me mam's at the hospital and the house has been ransacked.'

'Oh, my goodness!' Molly's hand flew to her face, and, indignantly outraged, she hurried towards No. 3, quickly followed by Ina, who was determined not to miss anything. Looking past the open vestibule door, Molly could see Cal, moving with panther-like grace and calm to stand at the foot of the stairs. Ina gripped Molly's shoulders tightly until Molly shrugged her off.

'This intruder might have no qualms about killing a woman,' Ina said, standing behind Molly, but not so far back she could not see inside Peggy's usually pristine house.

'Stay back,' Cal warned.

They listened. Not a peep.

Cal nodded to Jack, who had just returned and was about to head up the stairs when the shrill signal of a police whistle rent the thundery air, quickly followed by a horse-drawn ambulance, when the only word in the garbled message which Jack had relayed to the police was 'chopper'.

The police vied with the ambulance men for entry to No. 3 just as Peggy rounded the corner with her children to see a large crowd gathered outside her house.

'Something's happened!' Molly told her needlessly, elbowing her way to the front of the burgeoning crowd of neighbours who were not in the least concerned when the sky let out a deep rumble and the heavens split, allowing a deluge of rain to soak the gathered crowd.

'What's going on?' Peggy's voice was sharp as she moved closer.

'Well, police and ambulance men don't turn up for nothing,' Ina said, 'what do you think it could be?'

Everybody in Beamer Street milled around the Tenants' front door. Kids stopped their games and pulled cardigans and coats over their heads to watch uniformed men race into the house.

'I'm going to ask what's going on!' Ina said, never behind the door where news was concerned. Molly followed at a lick now, too. However, they did not have long to wait to see who the intruder was.

Miles Houseman, busy concentrating on stuffing money into every pocket, didn't spot Cal Everdine waiting for him at the bottom of the stairs. A swift right hook from Cal's iron-strong fist put Houseman on his backside, too dazed to do anything except lie there and take what was coming to him.

'Here,' said a toothless voice under a flat cap, coming from the back of the crowd, 'he's the bloke what's been mouthing off in the Tram Tavern, moaning about it being Dar's fault he was sacked and threatening to get even.'

16

'Millie!' Peggy's voice was trembling, and at the sound of her name, Millie raced up the stairs two at a time, quickly followed by Jack. They stopped dead in their tracks, almost knocking each other over when they got to their mother's bedroom. 'Is it all here?' Peggy gasped, kneeling on the linoleum-covered floor. Her heart had sunk like a stone and tears had streamed down her face at the terrifying thought their savings had all gone.

'We got most of it back,' said Jack as he pulled pound notes out of his pocket. 'There's more downstairs. Don't worry, I've locked the front and back doors, so nobody can get in.'

Millie watched her mother slump onto the bed, her breathing coming in short gasps, her face grey with worry.

'I don't know what we would have done if he had got away with our savings,' Peggy stammered. 'What would I have told Dar?'

'But he didn't get away with the money, Mam,' said Millie, who had never seen their mother so upset. 'Come on, let's go downstairs and have some supper. Jane and Eddy are both starving.'

Downstairs, Millie pulled the children towards her, holding them close, knowing her mother needed to keep busy.

'You do the food while I clean up the mess,' Millie whispered, her voice filled with determination, while Jack put his reassuring arms around their mother.

* * *

Miles Houseman's fall from grace was the talk of the street for weeks.

'Even his mother has disowned him,' Molly told Percy, who had missed the whole thing because he lived in Seaforth, but not for much longer.

Percy decided he would leave his news for another time. There had been a lot going on lately. The surrounding streets might be a bit rough, and ready for anything, but stealing from local houses was rare. Usually, there was nothing to pinch.

'Fancy Peggy having all that money,' said Molly, 'who'd have thought it.'

'They've been saving since they got married, apparently,' said Daisy. 'Poor Peggy.'

* * *

Peggy felt as if someone had fired a cannon and put a big hole in the middle of her body and resurrected those almost forgotten feelings of insecurity she once knew. The money they had saved so carefully for the last seventeen years had almost been stolen. And with it, their dreams of Dar getting back on his feet. Because if that money had been stolen, they could never afford the rehabilitation Dar would need to help him regain the ability to walk again. Owning their own house was not nearly as important as keeping her family safe and healthy.

'Has anybody from Hutton's been along to see you?' Mary Jane asked when Peggy went into the bakery the following day. Having her own business, Mary Jane knew how it worked if any of her staff were off sick. 'If anyone's off because they've taken bad, they get sick pay, because that's what they pay their national insurance for. So, surely someone should have been to see you with money.'

'Mr Hutton came a few weeks ago.' She recalled the five pound note he left on the sideboard. 'Although, Dar did mention something about national insurance,' said Peggy.

'Well,' said Mary Jane, 'I think you need to go back again to see that man Hutton, tell him what you know and get what's owed to Dar.'

'I will,' said Peggy, feeling a little better after receiving their support, which reminded her that, even in her darkest moments, she was not alone.

'Things will look better soon,' said Molly, who had followed her into the bakery, knowing her words were as hollow as they sounded. Peggy's husband had a long job to get back on his feet and walk again, not to mention building up his strength if he wanted to get back to work. 'I don't know anybody who could stoop so low as to steal from the very people they have injured.'

'If I had my way, I'd chop his bloody hands off!' Ina joined in.

Peggy didn't tell Dar about the break-in when she went to visit the following Sunday. Dar was still not well enough to take such news. She did, however, put the money in the local bank for safe-keeping, drawing out a set amount for housekeeping and rent. Although she knew she could not keep the details secret from him forever.

* * *

The burglary was the talk of the neighbourhood and would have made headline news, had it been for Max, who interviewed many workers from Hutton's Logistics and knew Hutton had not paid national insurance for any of his workers. It was a scandal that would be of interest not only to the local people, but also to the authorities.

He paid Henry Hutton a visit to let him know he was aware of the repercussions of his workforce losing their own jobs if they spoke out about Dar's accident, and anything else to do with the Tenant family. However, Max would never reveal his sources as Hutton demanded, especially when work was so difficult to come by.

Hutton told Max the results of the accident would not be left at his door and he sang like a canary when Max revealed he was going to do an exposé of Hutton's Logistics working practices, blaming his nephew for everything that was wrong with the business. Daisy had already told Max how unfairly the owner treated his workers. Max told Hutton that a local break-in was in the public interest, and if the perpetrator happened to be related to a successful businessman who was doing wrong by his employees, there was no telling what would happen after such a disgrace was uncovered.

Nevertheless, Henry Hutton refused to accept liability for anything his nephew had done, stating that if Miles had been released on bail pending further investigation, the police could not have much in the way of evidence to prosecute.

'All that after her husband saved that young lad's life and almost getting himself killed into the bargain,' said Daisy, 'it's just not fair.'

'I agree, Daisy Duck,' said Max, using the affectionate name he called her by, 'and I intend to do something about it.'

'What do you intend to do?' Daisy asked, believing what Max always said about the pen being mightier than the sword. 'Are you going to challenge him?'

'I really think I ought to, don't you?' Max was so adorable when he had a question that needed answers, thought Daisy. He was like a terrier, always digging for information. Standing up for the common man, he would say, and Daisy told him she hoped he didn't think of her as 'common'. 'Never, Daisy Duck,' he assured her. 'I'm still working on the exposé to uncover the working practices of Henry Hutton, a sort of David and Goliath kind of story,' said Max, who enjoyed thumbing his nose at those who took advantage of the ordinary working man.

17

The money was dwindling faster than even Peggy had expected. It had been months since Dar's accident, and the medical bills had eaten into the savings. As well as keeping the house going and hardly any money coming in, Peggy could see Christmas was not going to be a time of good cheer in this house. If she didn't do something to subsidise their savings, Dar would not be coming back to Beamer Street when he was finally allowed out of hospital; they would be doing a moonlight flit to dodge the rent collector. Not only that, but she'd have to pawn some of her furniture to hire a horse and cart to move them, which wasn't going to be cheap in the dead of night.

Peggy collected her housekeeping money from the bank. Not a penny more, or less. After paying the hospital bill for Dar's treatment, the rent, coal, food, gas, and anything else that unexpectedly cropped up with four offspring to support, she spent frugally in the local shops. She knew if things continued like this, the money they had so desperately saved for years would be gone by New Year, along with their security for a long time to come. But she wasn't going to allow her pride to raise its ugly head again and ruin her chances of keeping her family safe and secure. They would be worse off than they had ever been.

'I know we always said, no matter how stricken our money situation,' said Peggy to her daughter after the young ones had been put to bed, 'we would not resort to having a lodger in the house. But—'

'Mam, you can't. Dar would never allow another man to move in.' Millie knew her father would not be pleased to hear another man was moving in under his roof. 'He doesn't like having strangers in the house.'

'We haven't got a choice in the matter,' Peggy said, keeping her eyes lowered, deliberately concentrating on the sock she was darning. 'I've got to pay for everything now, and with Jack not bringing in a wage, and finding it almost impossible to find a job after being sacked for going on strike, I'm worried we soon won't have enough to pay the hospital bills, as well as keeping the roof over our heads.'

Peggy's words left her feeling traitorous for even voicing such thoughts. Jack was doing his best, going out every morning tramping the streets looking for work, but so far his efforts had been in vain. She had to convince Millie that they must carry on the best way they could.

'I don't know how long Dar's going to be in the hospital.' Peggy sighed. She felt the need to confide in her daughter, so that Millie understood the enormity of their ever-precarious position and did not think she was moving another man into her beloved father's position as head of the family. 'Even when he does come home, it's going to be a long while before Dar's able to work again, if he can get a job. There's not many about.' Peggy doubted Dar would be fit enough to go back to the docks. 'And I'm certainly not going to the parish to ask for charity. We've always paid our way – never relied on anybody else – and always lived within our means.'

'I know, Mam,' said Millie, they might not have the best that money could buy, but the family had never gone without the things they needed. Not even now.

'We've been beholden to no man, and we won't start now,' said Peggy.

* * *

'Here,' Percy said to Mary Jane and Daisy, who was closing the bakery door after another busy day, 'did I tell you I'm moving into the street?'

The two women stopped their cleaning and stared at him, agog.

'You most certainly did not!' said Mary Jane. 'Come on, tell us everything.'

'Well, I saw an advert in a shop window,' Percy informed the two surprised women, '*room to let*, it said, so I thought to meself, Percy, lad...' He stopped talking when Daisy let out a most unlady-like snort of laughter.

'It's been a while since you were a lad, Perce,' she said, knowing he would take her announcement in good sport.

'There might be snow on the roof, young Daisy,' he answered, 'but there's still a fire in the grate.'

Percy's playful retort brought a hot flush of pink to Daisy's cheeks. She hadn't expected him to say something so racy.

'That'll teach you.' Percy laughed loudly, and Daisy threw a tea towel at him, barely missing Mary Jane, whose laughter also filled the shop with infectious mirth, enjoying the camaraderie and good humour that came at the end of every working day, no matter how tired they were.

'So, come on, where are you lodging?' asked Mary Jane, eager to hear the news.

'Number three,' said Percy, 'and very nice it is too.' He was scraping the last of the dough off the table before giving it a good scrub ready for the morning.

'That's Peggy's house,' said Daisy, and Mary Jane nodded.

'She'll need a man about the house while Dar's in hospital.'

'Aye, that's what I thought,' said Percy. 'She's got a lovely front room, big enough to take my sofa, and my piano.'

'I didn't know you played, Percy,' said Mary Jane, 'won't you be popular when there's jars out at Christmas.' They hadn't had an excuse for a good old knees-up in a long time.

'It seems so long since there's been a hooley in the street,' said Daisy, lifting her skirt a little and doing a soft-shoe shuffle across the bakery floor, wishing the time would soon come to enjoy some sort of social gathering. Laughter and lively music was what the community needed.

'I doubt there'll be any parties in Peggy Tenant's house for a long while,' Mary Jane answered and Percy surprised the two younger women by telling them he had already been to see the room Peggy was renting out.

'She keeps the place spotless, does Peggy. There's not a speck of dust in that house,' he said. 'Spick and span it is. A real credit to her.'

Daisy knew what he said was true, recalling how her eyes danced in admiration when they fell upon Peggy's meticulously polished, hammered-brass pot holding a huge, polished aspidistra, which Peggy had proudly placed in the front parlour window. The white lace nets that adorned the windows were immaculate, the whitest in the street apart from her mam's, ornamented by shining brass bells of assorted sizes, reminding Daisy of a posh Victorian parlour she had once seen pictured in a magazine.

'What will Peggy do with her furniture when you move yours in, Perce?' asked Mary Jane.

'Well, there's the thing,' he said, pushing back his peaked cap and scratching his head. Never usually one to divulge the living arrangements of other people, he trusted Daisy and Mary Jane not to spread the information everywhere. 'I was a bit surprised to see the parlour was completely empty. No wallpaper on the walls, no lino on the floor, no furniture, nothing.' He suddenly noticed the two women exchanging glances and he said quickly, 'But that suits me down to the ground – a blank canvas, you might say.'

Daisy's dark eyebrows almost met in the middle of her forehead, and Mary Jane's vibrant green eyes were hooded, giving nothing away. The long silence made it plain they hadn't expected to hear there was a completely unfurnished room in Peggy Tenant's house.

Percy cleared his throat. He had said something out of turn, he could tell. 'Well, if the room isn't getting used,' he said, breaking the long silence, 'there's no point in filling it with furniture you will never sit on.'

'You are so right, Percy,' said Mary Jane and Daisy nodded in agreement. 'It's nobody else's business but Peggy's.' Mary Jane vividly recalled her own shock when she saw Cal's room over the bakery that first time she'd visited. There was hardly a stick of furniture in sight. A chair, a bed and a rickety table, he had lived like a pauper before she took him in hand and married him. Although, unbeknown to most people, herself included until after their marriage, he was one of the richest men in the north-west. The only luxury he had afforded himself was a plumbed-in bath, which he had installed to ease his aching leg, which had invalided him out of the army during the war but had never stopped him from working hard for his family. 'Who are we to talk anyway,' Mary Jane said. 'Peggy can do what she likes with her own front room.'

'Aye,' chuckled Percy, 'less dust to wipe.'

'Mam always says Peggy is the most houseproud woman she's ever met,' Daisy remarked.

'These last months can't have been easy,' said Mary Jane, 'but we'll all help out where we can.'

'Not that Peggy would ever ask for help from anybody, she's too proud,' Daisy said, wiping down the countertops with a clean dishcloth.

'Aye, and from what I saw, she had plenty to be proud of, those nippers are a credit to her. I was hardly inside the door when I was offered a cup of tea,' said Percy as he cleared away the bowl of water and swept the floor.

'Well, that's me done for another day,' said Daisy, rinsing out the dishcloth before putting on her coat. *Fancy Percy moving into Peggy's parlour.* Daisy couldn't wait to get home and tell her mam.

* * *

She wouldn't swear to it, but Daisy was sure her mam looked more than a little put out when she told her about Percy moving into Peggy's house.

'What does he want to go and do that for, when he's got a perfectly good house of his own?' Molly said, her colour rising as she lobbed mashed potato onto the plates like a navvy cementing a wall.

Daisy could see her mam had not taken the news well and felt the unspoken need to explain on Percy's behalf. 'Percy said he will be closer to the bakery, that'll mean another half an hour in bed on a cold winter's morning.'

'Are you sure that's all it means?' asked Molly, her expression pinched, her jerky actions impatient as she pushed her sleeve up her arm like she was ready to have a set-to with someone.

This is most unlike Mam, thought Daisy.

'Is anything the matter, Mam?' she asked a little cautiously.

'Why would anything be the matter?' her mam answered, her back towards her as she slammed the sideboard drawer shut after noisily removing the cutlery.

'You don't sound very pleased that Peggy's getting a lodger.'

'She can do as she pleases in her own house,' Molly answered. 'She can have the king himself in her spare room if she's a mind. It's got nothing to do with me.'

There was a moment's silence and Molly's lips pressed in a straight white line, avoiding Daisy's questioning gaze. As the air hung heavy with questions, Molly lifted her hands as if she was going to speak, and then she hesitated as if she thought better of voicing her thoughts.

'Where you going to say something, Mam?' Daisy had a suspicion her mother was jealous, not because of the extra money he would bring to the table, especially not now three of her offspring were working, but she suspected her mother had as much of a soft spot for Percy as he had for her mam.

'Oh, would you listen to me. I'm sorry, Dais,' Molly said, her whole demeanour hesitant, as if she was struggling to find the right words. 'I was just a bit surprised, that's all. What with Peggy being so private, like. She's had enough to put up with lately and doesn't need tongues wagging when her husband has been so ill. She doesn't need me putting two and two together and coming up with four, either.'

'Two and two does make four, Mam.' Daisy smiled, knowing her mother could always be counted on to get her words mixed up when she got herself into a bit of a tizz. Nevertheless, with a heart bigger than herself, Molly's reaction was a surprise to Daisy. 'What have you got against Peggy having a lodger?' she asked, and Molly shook her head, obviously ashamed of her outburst.

'I've got nothing against her having a lodger,' said Molly,

surprised the news had brought out feelings she never knew she had, 'we all take someone in when times are hard.'

'Is it because the lodger is Percy?'

'Don't be daft, our Daisy,' Molly gasped as a bloom of pink coloured her cheeks, and she quickly turned away as unruly thoughts jabbed at her like a sharp stick. Percy had never been anything except a good friend who took her to the pictures every Saturday night and treated her to a box of Mackintosh's Celebrated Toffee, which they both enjoyed as they watched the film. 'Percy never mentioned wanting to move closer to the bakery, that's all.' Not even when he came for Sunday dinner each week. 'But then, he doesn't have to tell me anything.' She was quiet again for a moment and then she said with an apologetic laugh, 'If I'd known he was looking for a room, I'd have offered.' Molly sighed.

'Hmm,' said Daisy, refraining from asking if that was the only reason her mother was so put out.

18

Dusk began to close the day down and the children were collecting their night things from the sideboard when there was a knock at Peggy's front door. She went to answer it, surprised to see Percy standing on her doorstep at this time of night.

'Hello, Percy,' she said, suspecting he might want to move his personal stuff into the parlour before moving in proper, which was fine by her. She was glad of his financial contribution to the coffers; it meant she wouldn't have to work on the dock, as her sister, Violet, had hinted last time Peggy saw her when she visited her mother. And her daughter would not have to look after the young ones for so long. Percy had already paid a week's rent in advance. 'Come in, our Millie's just put the kettle on.'

'I won't if that's all right with you, Mrs Tenant.' Percy's tone was formal. Having taken off his flat cap, he circled it through his fingers and thumbs, looking anywhere but in her direction. 'Well, the thing is...' His words were hesitant, as if he didn't know what to say. 'It's like this, you see.'

'Like what, Percy?' Peggy said in her straight-talking way. 'Is something the matter?' She thought he looked a bit embarrassed, if truth be told.

'Well. You see...' He paused momentarily, and then, like he had no control over them, his words sped up like they were in a rush to be out of his mouth. 'Well, what it is, my sister's husband, Horace, died last year, and she's friends with Mrs Blake who lives next door to you at number five...'

'Yes, I know Mrs Blake lives next door,' said Peggy, wondering where the conversation was going, and wishing it would get there soon, because her cup of tea would be cold by the time she got to it.

'Well, Mrs Blake is going to live with her daughter. Because her eyesight is not what it was. And she's asked our Phyllis – that's my sister – if she wanted to take over the tenancy and move into number five. She'd already spoken to the landlord's agent,' Percy's circling cap turned a little faster with each word, 'and he said it would be fine for our Phyllis to take over the rent book, what with me working in the bakery, and all that, – better the divil you know, I s'pose...' When he finished speaking, he let out a long sigh, looking relieved to get the information off his chest and out in the open.

'Oh,' said Peggy, her shoulders slumping. She lowered her head, trying hard not to show her disappointment. 'I see.' There wasn't much more she could say.

'I thought I should let you know as soon as I knew, so you could re-advertise.' Percy scoured his brain trying to think of something positive that might make the situation less awkward but could think of nothing. 'I'm ever so grateful for the offer.' He paused. 'You keep a lovely home, Mrs Tenant. I'm sure anybody would be glad to move in.'

'Well, thanks for letting me know, I'll just get your rent money.' Peggy's clipped reply told him she was not happy about the situation.

'No, that doesn't matter,' Percy said as she put her hand in her apron pocket for her purse, 'please, take it, for messing you about, like.'

'I will do no such thing.' Peggy raised her chin and pushed back her shoulders, taking the ten-shilling note from her purse and pushing it into Percy's hand. 'I don't expect to take money for nothing.'

'But you could have had somebody else lined up,' he offered, but Peggy was adamant.

'Don't you worry yourself on my account,' Peggy answered.

'I'm ever so sorry to let you down.' Percy could not feel more guilty than he did at that moment.

'You haven't let me down, Percy,' Peggy rallied, forcing a smile. 'I was in two minds about renting out the room in the first place. My husband isn't keen on having strangers in the house, you see, and when I told him, he wasn't at all happy about the situation.' She could not bear the look of pity in his eyes. 'So, now you've made my mind up for me. So, thank you for letting me know.'

As she closed the front door, Peggy wondered what she was going to do about the dwindling money. Although they weren't destitute, there was always the need for a little extra, and her mother still expected her half-crown every week.

Thinking about it now, Peggy wished she had never told her mother they had been saving to buy this house. Ma thought they were better off than they were and felt no compunction in accepting the weekly money without a thought for Dar recovering all the way out in the countryside and the expense that went with it. The demands on her money situation were getting more troubling with each passing week.

Pushing her aching back against the closed front door, Peggy's muscles were tense, rigid with the burden of it all. Her jaw clenched tightly, and Peggy had to console herself with the thought that once Dar came out of the hospital, everything would start to be all right again. He would be itching to get back to work. Good stevedores were not easy to find. Hopefully, Dar would soon be on the mend, and then all their troubles would be over.

Swallowing the tears that threatened, she held in a heavy sigh and made her way back to the kitchen, forcing a smile when she saw the fire was now burning brightly in the hearth, a fresh cup of tea was on the table, and her children were playing contentedly on the mat, not a care in the world.

'That was Percy.' She tried not to sound defeated, but her words were flat with disappointment, knowing she would have to dig deeper into their savings until Dar was well enough to come home. 'He's not taking the parlour now. He's moving in next door when Mrs Blake moves to her daughter's house.'

All those years of scrimping and scraping just to put a few shillings by each week. For what? There was no hope of doing any more saving for the foreseeable. The fees for the hospital were eating into their savings, not to mention Dar's reconstruction aid – a revolutionary intensive treatment in manipulation, massage, stretching and exercises on his leg that promised to improve the strength and flexibility. The therapy was used during the war in the treatment of soldiers, and doctors were still working to get Dar's legs working now the bone had knitted.

Peggy's dream of not having to work such long hours was sliding rapidly from her grasp. But Dar was growing stronger, that was the main thing. Also, she had to be strong for her children's sake.

'Another cup of tea, Mam?' Millie felt treacherously relieved to hear the news that Percy would not be lodging in the parlour. 'Maybe it's for the best. You know Dar doesn't like strangers in the house.'

Peggy gave a tight smile. 'Maybe you're right, it did worry me. I lost sleep, knowing Dar likes to let his braces dangle after a working day. He could never do that if we had a lodger.' Sitting at the table with her four children, Peggy began counting her blessings. They weren't as hard-up as some, but they soon would be if Peggy didn't come up with a way of finding funds to protect their savings.

'We'll get by,' Millie assured her mother, 'like we always have.'

'Aye, we will,' said Peggy. *But at what price?*

19

Millie entered the cosy confines of the apothecary. The air, heavy with the scent of herbs and spices, was a pleasant change from the sooty rain pelting against the windows, casting a gloomy shadow over what Millie believed was her mother's sanctuary.

'Hiya, Mrs Newman.' Millie's heart was racing, knowing she had to help her mother, but not knowing what to do. She was torn between wanting to protect her mother's privacy and her need to find advice outside the family. Millie did not know who else to ask, except Mrs Newman. Being so private about their life behind the front door of No. 3, Mam wouldn't be one bit pleased to learn she was telling outsiders about the attacks she was having, but Millie knew her mother trusted Ellie. She saw the healer as a valued friend.

'Hello, Millie love,' said Ellie, standing behind her polished wooden counter, her ever-present smile lighting up her pretty face even on a miserable afternoon like this one. 'What can I do for you?'

'I'm a bit lost as to how I should go about this, Mrs Newman.'

Millie's voice trembled. 'But I don't know what's happening to me mam...'

'Don't fret, lovey,' said Ellie. 'Anything you tell me will remain strictly confidential.'

'Mam doesn't even know I'm here.' Millie looked behind her, expecting the door to open any minute. 'And I don't want her to know either.'

'I understand.' Ellie's soothing tone encouraged Millie. 'I'm sure you will not be speaking out of turn if you want to help your mam. Take your time.'

Millie hesitated, as a mixture of fear and hope battled within her, unsure of what Ellie or the apothecary could offer. 'As you know, Mam just gets on with things as best she can,' Millie's shoulders slumped, like an invisible weight was pressing down on her, 'but I can't bear to see her suffer like this, she's so lost without Dar...' Her voice cracked with emotion. Absent-mindedly, she stroked the soft fur of the white cat curled up in its usual place on the counter and felt a peaceful warmth through the gentle vibrations of its purr against her fingertips.

'She likes you.' Ellie's voice softened, noticing Millie's hesitation, wanting to put the young girl at ease. 'She only allows a select few to stroke her.'

'Have you had her since she was a kitten?' Millie asked, gently running her fingers over the cat's silky fur, her thoughts racing as she tried to decide how she was going to tell Ellie about her mam's situation, without sounding like her mam was going mad. Because she wasn't. She'd heard of women who went to see the doctor and said they were going mad, and they were put in the workhouse. If that happened, they'd all have to go there. And what would become of them after that? Before Mrs Newman could answer her question, Millie asked another. 'How old is she?'

'I don't have a clue,' Ellie answered, gauging Millie's questions were a delaying tactic for the real reason she had come here. 'She strolled in behind me that first morning when we opened the shop, then she leaped up onto the counter, made herself comfortable, and she has been here ever since.'

Millie liked Ellie's cat, considering it the most amazing creature she had ever come across.

'She's a free spirit,' said Ellie, who, although she would never make her belief known, had a fancy this peaceful feline was the reincarnation of her beloved mother. She believed, like her ancestors before her, that white cats were protectors. Guides from the spirit world. A reassuring sign she and her little family were being watched over by her cherished mother, whom she still missed so dearly.

The apothecary walls were adorned with ancient tapestries once owned by her mother, depicting scenes from folklore and legends, visually transporting visitors – *never customers* – to a bygone era.

Millie's eyes travelled the shelves, holding traditional remedies and potions, which had been passed down through generations of healers, carrying the wisdom of centuries, while Ellie, who would not push her beliefs onto the shoulders of the young girl at the other side of the counter, waited patiently for her to speak.

'Some say white cats are a symbol of good luck and prosperity, but I feel Serena is my protector.'

'Serena?' said Millie. 'That's a good name for a cat.'

'It's a suitable name for such a peaceful feline, don't you think?' Ellie smiled. 'I believe she adopted us, not the other way around.' Ellie looked towards the latest addition to the Newman household with unrestrained fondness. 'She came and lived here, and we love her dearly. I feel reassured by her presence.'

Millie continued stroking the cat and noticed she did not feel as nervous as she did when she first came into the apothecary. And even after such a brief time, she felt she could tell Ellie anything.

Taking down a large, clear-glass jar from the shelf behind her, Ellie gave Millie a stick of barley sugar, which Ellie had made only yesterday, and it did her heart good to see the girl's eyes light up.

'I'll save it for later,' said Millie. 'I will share it when I get home.' It had been such a long time since they had tasted sweets.

Intuition told Ellie the girl must be particularly worried to seek her advice. Because in these rough-and-ready streets surrounding the dockyards, women kept their troubles to themselves.

'You see, it's like this...' Millie began, as the barley sugar gift relaxed her enough to say what was on her mind. 'Mam has been having these... *feelings*.'

'Feelings?' asked Ellie, her forehead pleating, not wanting to rush the girl.

'Yes, like she's gasping for breath, then she says her heart beats dead fast,' Millie pulsated her chest with her fist, 'and all the colour drains from her face like dumplings.'

'Dumplings?' Ellie looked concerned, knowing the doughy balls that thickened stews had no colour whatsoever, and Millie nodded.

'I was sure if anybody would know what was wrong with me mam, you would, Mrs Newman.' Millie suspected this woman who had only been in Beamer Street for the past two years knew everything about everything.

'How long has your mam been having these feelings?' asked Ellie, remembering Aiden had seen Peggy leaning against the wall, and she did not look too good then.

'I think they've been happening for a while,' answered Millie. Before she realised, Millie had told Ellie the whole sorry tale. Her mother's sickness was too big for her to carry alone. 'She went to see Mister Hutton about Dar's sick pay... but Mister Hutton said he had no sick money for Dar, and so Mam had to go to work on the docks. Then, when she was telling me, she had this sort of a quickening, she called it.'

'Ahh,' said Ellie, 'I see what you mean.' From the sound of it, poor Peggy was having attacks of panic, the body's natural response to extreme worry, which soon escalated to intense fear and dread, making the sufferer feel they were having a seizure or, even worse, a heart attack. Ellie knew people who did not believe in the body's 'fight-or-flight' response to severe anxiety, but she knew Peggy had cause to feel anxious, given what she had been through lately. The feelings could cause such terrifying sensations the sufferer felt they were going to die. Those disturbing sensations added to the fear and made the matter worse. 'Do these feelings come on without warning?'

Millie nodded. Her big brown eyes looking troubled. 'Since Dar's accident, they come on even when she isn't worrying about anything,' said Millie, 'and Mam is getting to the point she doesn't like to leave the house, in case she has an attack in the street and makes a show of herself.' Leaning her elbow on the polished counter, Millie was glad she could tell Mrs Newman about poor Mam. 'They started out as flutters in her chest,' she said, 'but they've got much worse now, and they happen when she's doing her washing, or cooking the tea.'

'Do you think it might help if I went and had a word with your mam?' asked Ellie.

'Well, she won't come here and ask for help,' Millie said in that straightforward way she had about her. 'She's never asked nobody for nothing. But don't tell her I told you.'

'I won't.' Ellie smiled. 'I'll just pop in, by the way I've called to see how Dar is.'

'Thanks, Mrs Newman,' Millie sighed with relief. 'I'm sure she'll be ever so grateful.'

I doubt that, thought Ellie, watching Millie leave, knowing how independent Peggy Tenant was.

20

Ellie arrived with the herbal tonic after the apothecary closed, giving Peggy the impression her visit resulted from seeing Aiden, after she had been to Hutton's office, and Ellie did nothing to dissuade her otherwise.

She noticed Peggy, looking haggard and careworn, was not a bit like the proud woman she had been before Dar's accident. Her hair, which had once been glossy and neatly waved, was now wiry and bedraggled. Her sleep-deprived eyes sank into the sockets. She seemed to endure an air of hopelessness.

'I think you may need a tonic,' said Ellie, knowing Peggy would volunteer no information, guarding the privacy of her family like a lioness protecting her cubs. 'I've brought you some calming tea.' Ellie handed over the packet of chamomile and lemon balm tea. 'All you do is steep the leaves in hot water as you would with ordinary tea. If you want it sweeter, add a little honey.'

'Honey?' Peggy did not mean to be rude when she let out an incredulous laugh, but she could not help herself. 'Where on earth am I expected to get the coppers to buy honey?'

There was a moment of silence before Millie watched her

mother's face crumple as Peggy lowered her head so as not to show her anguish.

Staring at the brown paper package, the tears, which welled painfully behind Peggy's eyes, refused to flow. She had to keep a semblance of dignity and not frighten her children.

'I'm sorry, Ellie,' said Peggy, quickly regaining her composure. 'I didn't mean to be rude. This is a lovely gesture, but I feel it's going to take more than a cup of tea to help me out.' Peggy, exhausted, felt every day brought another worry. The security of her husband was gone in the blink of an eye, and it felt like a bereavement.

She reached into her apron pocket for her purse, hoping she had enough money to pay for the tea.

'There's no charge.' Knowing how proud Peggy was, Ellie added: 'I was wondering if you would do me the kindness of trying it out for a couple of weeks, and let me know if it helps you sleep better?' Ellie was having to think fast, suspecting Peggy was about to refuse the tea. 'You told Aiden you felt light-headed because you hadn't slept very well.'

'Yes, that's right,' said Peggy as her eyes registered her conversation with Ellie's husband, but that was ages ago. 'It was very thoughtful of him to let you know.'

'The ingredients in the tea will help you relax.'

'I could make you one now, Mam,' said Millie and dashed off to the kitchen with the bag of herbal tea. A short while later, she brought Ellie and her mother a freshly brewed cup, and she gave Ellie a knowing smile. Her secret was safe.

'Also, if you still have trouble sleeping,' said Ellie, handing Peggy a muslin bag, 'slip this inside your pillowcase.'

'It smells lovely, Mam,' said Millie, urging her mother to have a good sniff.

'Oh, I do like that,' said Peggy, inhaling the sweet scent of lavender. 'But I can't just take...'

'Think nothing of it,' said Ellie kindly. 'If the tea does the trick, then I can sell it in the apothecary.'

'You've got a good head for business,' said Peggy, and for the first time that day, she smiled. It seemed such a long time since she had anything to smile about, but Ellie's kindness had lifted her spirits, restoring her good humour. 'I can smell the lemons.' Peggy inhaled the fresh, fruity zing while sipping the hot brew. 'I like it.'

'Let me know how you feel in a week or two,' said Ellie. 'You should feel much better after a few nights of good sleep.'

'I don't know about that, but thank you,' said Peggy, as she walked Ellie to the door, while Millie beckoned her brothers and sister, to sit up to the table, giving each a bowl of thin stew, consisting of potatoes and vegetables commonly known as 'blind scouse' because it contained no meat.

'I'll leave you to enjoy your evening meal,' said Ellie as she reached the front door. 'But there is just one more thing, if I may?' Ellie knew Peggy needed less worries if she was to grow stronger, and there was one positive way in which she felt she could help. 'As you know, I am actively involved with The Deborah Kirrin Retreat, a place for children to enjoy the wonders of the countryside.' Ellie knew she had to choose her words carefully. If Peggy thought she was being offered charity, she would turn Ellie's idea down flat. A proud woman, Peggy was not the kind of person who took donations from anybody, not even the church. 'The thing is, I have two places that need to be filled by under-tens and I was wondering if you would do me the kindness of allowing Jane and Eddy to fill those places. There is a huge bonfire and a firework party,' Ellie was about to play the ace she had been saving, 'and the children even go over to Lavender Green to sing for the patients.'

Ellie watched Peggy's face for any sign of rejection, but there was none.

'Everything is organised by local Scout and Cub leaders, you don't have to worry about clothes or money, everything is organised...'

'They sing for the patients of Lavender Green, so does that mean...?'

'Yes, they will get the chance to see their father, but you must promise me you won't tell them, it's a surprise.'

Peggy hesitated. She needed her children to have a bit of respite from the hardship they had suffered over the last few months. And what better way than a visit to their father, something she could not afford to offer them? Peggy was so delighted that Ellie could provide her children with a few days' respite from her worries, she did not have the heart to refuse. She could no more deny them the right to three good meals a day, fresh air, green grass, trees to climb, and a visit to their father whom they missed so much. Eddy and Jane needed a place where they could run about and play in complete freedom under the loving supervision of their father.

'I'll think about it,' she said simply, and Ellie could only smile, knowing Peggy hadn't refused outright. So that was a good sign.

* * *

'Cooee,' called a voice from the front door and Peggy went to answer.

'Ellie, come in,' Peggy said, wondering if she had enough tea to offer her friend a cup.

'I can't stay long,' Ellie answered. 'I just came to drop these off and give you the timetable for the trip. The coach leaves at nine thirty.'

'Today?' asked Peggy astonished.

'Yes,' Ellie answered, 'didn't I tell you? Silly me. I know that doesn't give you much time to get the children's clothes ready, so I've brought these.' She didn't give Peggy time to refuse or to object, but she was sure her friend would never deny her children the possibility of seeing their father after he had been gone for so long. 'You are doing me a great favour, otherwise there would be two empty seats on the charabanc,' Ellie said, not looking at Peggy as she took out some clothes. 'These are some new under-things, galoshes, gum boots, that kind of thing, which I'm sure you already have, but they're going to go to waste otherwise, and I know I've left it a bit late for you to pack, so there we go.'

Peggy wondered if Ellie was going to take a breath, but she just kept on going, like a speedy locomotive, churning out timetables and activities her children would be involved in. In the end, Peggy felt she had been worn down by words and explanations. How could she say no to the children going for a week's respite?

'I don't know what to say.' Her voice was low, humble.

'You won't say anything,' Ellie refrained from putting a friendly hand on Peggy's arm, knowing that might be a step too far. 'Although, you might want to tell the children to get a move on, don't forget, the charabanc will be here at nine thirty.'

'I won't forget. Thank you,' Peggy said, noting that the earth didn't swallow her whole for accepting charity. Ellie had given with a good heart, and asked for nothing in return, which was just as well, as Peggy had nothing left to give.

21

'Don't make tea on my behalf, I'm not stopping,' said Violet in that clipped tone, which usually made Peggy feel as if she was a young child being scolded, which happened often in the past. Rarely told off by her mother, always by Violet. But those days were long gone and now she could match her sister in pitch and tone.

'So,' said Peggy, 'this is an unexpected honour. I've only lived here for sixteen years, what's the rush?'

There was a moment's silence.

Violet knew how difficult Peggy could be since she married that Dar Tenant, and she was trying to choose her words carefully. Peggy was proud as can be. She always had been. Even as a child. She thought she was different.

And she was, thought Violet.

'I haven't come for an argument, if that's what you're thinking,' said Violet, who would never have come to this house if Dar Tenant was not in hospital, fearing he would not let her over the door. Her pale blue eyes, once so beautifully striking, were now hooded, taking in the immaculately clean and tidy room in one swift glance. The room was bare of any knick-knacks, but Violet could see the house was spotless, nevertheless.

The brown leather suite was polished to a high shine, as was the chiffonier on the wall between the door from the long passageway to the back kitchen. The smell of furniture polish mingled with the clean washing airing on a wooden clotheshorse by the fireside, which Dar had made. There wasn't so much as a fingerprint on the oval mirror above the fireplace and the cloth on the dinner table by the sash window was pure white cotton, unheard of in most households around the dockside. White table-cloths were kept for best, like weddings, funerals or christenings. Trying to keep anything so white would be a day's work, thought Violet.

'I came to ask if you want a bit of work?' Violet didn't sit down, instead she hovered near the open door, ready to be off at a moment's notice if Peggy took offence as usual.

'What kind of work?' Peggy asked, her tone holding more than a hint of suspicion.

'I need cleaners for a luxury liner that's in dock for repairs.'

'Cleaning ships!' Peggy knew for certain Dar would never hear of her working on the docks.

'You think it's beneath you?' Violet's question seemed more like a challenge to Peggy, who had never been frightened of demanding work, far from it. 'You've got no idea, have you?' Violet's words were low now, almost tender. How she longed to tell Peggy the truth. *But Ma would have a fit of conniptions if I ever tried.*

Peggy was the reason her father never came home. If she was ever encouraged, Violet would willingly tell Peggy the truth. But Mam wouldn't hear of it. She said the shame would break the family apart, and her father would never return home again. By not airing the truth, Ma expected there was every chance he would come back.

'Remember last time?' Mam had said to Violet when she threatened to tell Peggy. Her father had not been back home since. Peggy had been three years old when her father came home from sea. The first time he saw the dark-haired child he fell in love with her. He'd visited every alehouse on the dock road with his seafaring pals when his ship docked. Throwing his duffel bag precariously over his shoulder, he whistled a sea shanty as he wended his way back to Rose Cottages, where Maggie said she had a surprise.

And what a surprise, thought Violet who was preparing to marry Fred. Her mam had made her promise she would not tell her father or Fred the truth. Violet could see the scene as clearly as if it were yesterday, but she must put it out of her mind.

'You expect me to go working down the docks?!' Peggy said. 'Dar would have me guts for garters. He'd never allow it.' Hands on hips, Peggy knew she was capable, but Dar was a proud man, and she suspected he had been emasculated enough without her adding to his inability to keep their household in good order.

'You don't even know what the job entails,' said Violet, who had expected this reaction, but she couldn't let their Peggy go without money when she had the means to make her life a bit better.

'More scrubbing? Or maybe I'd be having my meals at the captain's table?'

'Some hope,' Violet answered, her patience wearing thin. 'There's a liner been in dock for six weeks, having repairs done, it needs a thorough cleaning before it sets sail again.'

'Aye, that sounds about right,' Peggy's lip curled, 'we do all the skivvying while those with money are waited on hand and foot.' She thought how wonderful it would be to be able to afford such luxury.

'That's the hand we've been dealt, and we have to put up with it,' said Violet. 'We have no choice.'

'Really?' Peggy's tone was caustic. 'Well, I do have a choice, and

I'll tell you what it is, shall I?' She didn't wait for Violet's reply. 'I choose to say thanks but no thanks, I'll not be skivvying. Dar will be out of hospital soon enough, and he'll be back at work in no time.'

'Suit yourself,' said Violet, 'but don't say I didn't offer.'

Peggy's mouth was pinched, her arms folded across a frame that had once been shapely, but now seemed lost in the clothes that hung on her body. She wouldn't lower herself to belittle her sister, but she was damned if she would sink to cleaning ships.

'You certainly know how to clean,' said Violet, unable to take the sting out of her words.

'I had a good teacher.' Peggy's scathing comment hit the spot.

'Look, I'm a bit short on staff,' Violet said, shifting from one foot to another, trying to make Peggy see sense. 'It's good money.'

'Oh, *you've* got staff? Lady Muck isn't in it.' Peggy, knowing beggars could not be choosy, did not like the idea that Violet would be entitled to bark orders at her like she used to do. Not after she had come so close to owning her own property. That was a far way to fall and no mistake.

'Do you want the job or don't you?' Violet's patience was wearing thin. 'I haven't got time to gasbag with you all day.'

'Is that right?' Peggy knew there was no change there.

'I get the point,' Violet answered as she stomped down the lobby and made her way to the front door. 'I'll see you when I see you, Peggy,' Violet called, opening the vestibule door.

How dare she come in here, to my home, and look down her nose at me? Peggy thought irrationally.

When she heard the slamming of the front door, it enraged her. Marching after Violet, and dragging open the door, she turned her head to the right to see her sister storming down the street in the direction of the dock road.

'Ta-ra well, Violet. Do call again if you're in the area,' Peggy called, then going inside, she closed the front door, leaned against the back of it and allowed scalding tears to roll down her cheeks. She knew Dar wouldn't allow her to take a cleaning job outside the house, especially not on the docks. Mind you, she thought, turning the idea over in her head, he didn't have to worry about where the next meal was coming from. And how else were they expected to be able to buy their house? She could hardly wait until Dar came out of hospital.

* * *

As the nights grew longer, stretching like an endless worry, Peggy struggled to piece together the decreasing funds that hacked away any trace of hope. After the two youngest came back from their holiday in the countryside, the struggle to keep her head above water felt even more futile.

'And we saw Dar!' said young Jane, who was so excited she couldn't get the words out fast enough. 'He was in the garden in a wheelchair. He spoke to us and told us he would be home for Christmas, and we sang songs for him, and he came to our bonfire party, and we had toffee apples.'

'We saw him every day,' Eddy joined in, 'so we didn't miss being at home so much.'

'I didn't know the countryside retreat was so close to Lavender Green,' said Peggy when she went into the apothecary and Ellie, serene as ever, smiled.

'Such a wonderful experience for the children.'

Peggy felt a frisson of something she could not put into words.

Over the next few days, Peggy pondered on Violet's offer of a job, tempted to reconsider. Nevertheless, she was reluctant to do so, knowing their Violet had a rigid, stubborn streak that would need no coaxing to refuse her the job. Some of her childhood memories were sketchy and a little disjointed, but she recalled Violet's stubborn streak and – Peggy's heart melted a little – her kindness when Ma wasn't looking.

One memory struck her. Mam had been cooking at the fireside, a large cast-iron pot of broth or soup taking centre stage on the kitchen table. Violet would ladle Peggy's food first onto her plate, letting it cool before cutting a thick slice of home-made bread for her to dip into the soup, even before she served their older brothers, home from working on the docks.

Then her father came home from sea. And everything changed...

A heavy knock on the front door curtailed her recollections and a shard of fear shot through her. Keeping the heat in the house was not Peggy's only excuse for closing the front door. The almost forgotten memory of another demanding knock had heralded the bailiff with an eviction notice. A sound that froze her heart with fear. She had nightmares about being forced to leave her beloved house and do a moonlight flit. Back to Rose Court Cottages. Back to the mercy of her mother, whose disapproving gaze always seemed to whisper, *You're not welcome here.*

When the knocking stopped, Peggy huddled as close to the dying fire as she could, the coldness of the room seeping into her bones making it difficult for her to move, knowing she had to save the coal for when the little ones came home from school.

Gone were the days when she could take her mother treats of potato cakes or pigs trotters, a nice cream cake from Mary Jane's bakery, or a home-made rice pudding. Last week, she had sent word to her mother she was ill, ashamed she did not have any money to give to her. The situation had got so bad, Peggy had taken to pretending to be out when the coalman called, knowing he had already emptied the sacks of coal down the coalhole in the front path, but she did not have the means to pay him. He left without being paid and put a note through the letter box telling her how much she owed. She was keenly aware she would have to find double the amount of money next week, otherwise they would have no heat to cook, or stay warm, and winter was coming in vigorously.

If nothing happened soon, she would have no choice but to give up the tenancy of this house and return to the courts. And what would Dar have to say about that? Her stomach twisted into a tight knot, a painful reminder of the choices she no longer had. The courts were only nominally better than the workhouse, she thought.

As the weeks wore on, Peggy was forced to pawn anything worth a few coppers, just to put food on the table. Meat was an unheard-of luxury. Bread was an inadequate sustenance that barely kept their hunger at bay, and even that was becoming scarcer, reminding Peggy of the life they had lost.

The family had only one meal a day if they were lucky, instead of the usual three good meals they had once been accustomed to eating. Peggy was getting deeper in debt with the rent. Days when she did not have the coppers to feed the gas meter, they took to going to bed earlier, and their once cosy kitchen was now transformed into a stark, barren room, devoid of warmth or cheer. Peggy had long since refrained from saying things would get better because they rarely did.

22

It was dark when Peggy got off the train at Lime Street from Lavender Green. Money she earned chopping wood for kindling had been spent on the fare, and if Mary Jane had not sent a fruity Sally Lunn Bath bun, Peggy knew she could not afford to take any sort of treat for Dar. But she was determined not to let him know how much she was struggling.

A cold autumnal wind blew in from the river as she crossed the city. Hurrying along the dock road towards the courts, her churning stomach left her feeling queasy and angry.

The train journey home had given Peggy time to think and turn the events of the last few months over in her head. And it was only when she was near the courts, she realised a few things.

One of them – the most important – was how much she had grown since Dar had been injured. Before his accident, she had freely accepted what Dar told her she must do, and as his dutiful wife, she had no doubt about that. After all, that was what she had vowed, when he had placed the gold band on the third finger of her left hand, and she had lived by those vows. But the time had come, she knew, when she would have to challenge the vows. She no longer felt able to *obey* the word of her husband. Peggy had no trouble whatsoever with the love and honour bit, they were fine, but the obey part was going to have to be kicked into the long grass, as Dar always said when he didn't agree with something.

Peggy felt relieved when she let herself into her mother's house and saw the fireside chair was empty. Nowhere to be seen, her mam was not in the kitchen, and there were no sounds of movement in the back kitchen either.

A glut of firewood had brought a few shillings extra as the weather had turned colder. But Peggy knew she could only afford to leave sixpence on the mantlepiece. The other two shillings would keep her children fed for a couple of nights.

'I thought I heard someone,' said Violet and Peggy spun around from the fireplace.

'Jesus, Mary, and Joseph! You frightened the life out of me,' Peggy hissed. 'I thought you were me mam.'

'Why? Don't you want her to see you?' asked Violet, who had brought up a shovel of coal from the cellar.

'Is she down the yard?' Peggy asked, nodding to the privy at the bottom of the back yard, and Violet shook her head.

'No, she's in bed.'

'What's she doing in bed?' Peggy asked, knowing her mother never went to bed at this time.

'She caught a chill.'

Violet looked concerned, thought Peggy. Everybody knew Maggie O'Day was a tough old girl.

'A couple of days in bed will be all she needs to get back to her usual self.'

'So, to what do we owe the pleasure?'

Peggy had not been to her mother's house for a couple of days, knowing she didn't have spare money to share. But Peggy had reached rock bottom, and Violet was the only person she could think of who could help her.

'I came to ask a favour,' Peggy said, wondering if she had made a mistake coming here to ask her sister for a job. Violet would crow about it till the cows came home. But what choice did she have?

Peggy knew money was tight. The coalman had threatened to cut off coal supplies until she paid off what she owed. And apart from the couple of shillings she had in her purse, there was no sign of any more money coming in until Jack got a job, which did not seem any time soon. She knew it was not his fault; Jack was not as skilled as Dar and so could not earn the kind of money his father had brought home. Jack picked up casual work here and there when he could, but nothing permanent. Even if she had to grovel to their Violet, Peggy would rather do that than see her kids out on the street without a roof over their head, which is what might happen.

She had not told Dar about Miles Houseman breaking into the house. He had enough to worry about, trying to walk again. If he knew their home had been threatened, he would sign himself out of Lavender Green – a decision which could see him lame for the rest of his life. The good Lord alone, knew what would happen after that. He might not like the idea of his wife working on the docks, cleaning ships, but he was not the one who was trying to keep body and soul together. Nor could she stay at home worrying about where the next penny was coming from when she had a good pair of strong working hands on her. No. She was going to swallow her pride and ask Violet for a job. Autumn days grew shorter, and soon, Peggy knew, Christmas would be galloping towards them. Her pride would not let her see her kids go without. They too had been through enough heartache, and missed their father so much. Every day they asked if he would be home soon, and every day, she had to answer that she didn't know.

Peggy had always wanted better for herself and her family. But beggars could not be choosers, and the only person she felt was able to help her now was her sister. Blood was thicker than water.

'You should have told me,' Peggy said.

'You've got enough on your plate, with Dar being in hospital,' said Violet. 'I brought her some beef broth.'

'Look, I can't stop. I have to get back to the little ones.' Peggy felt ashamed she had only brought sixpence, but she could not do any more. 'I'll get Ellie to make some linctus for her chest.'

'Don't mind me, Peg,' her mother croaked from her bed in the next room. 'I won't be troubling you for much longer.'

'Now, Ma, don't talk like that. You know it upsets me.'

'It hasn't upset you enough to leave that fancy house in Beamer Street for the last three days, has it?'

'It's not a fancy house, Ma. It's just a well-kept terraced house in a...' Peggy was going to say *a better-class area,* but she stopped herself. There was no point rubbing salt into this wound.

'Will he be home for Christmas?' Violet asked, not using Dar's name, but Peggy knew who she meant.

'We live in hope,' Peggy answered.

'Cleaning ships is not as bad as you think,' Violet said, putting a reassuring hand on Peggy's arm, and Peggy pushed a breath of air through her lips like she was blowing out a candle.

'Well,' said Peggy, 'you'll have no complaints about my work, if you want to offer me the job.'

'I know,' said Violet, who had seen how spotless Peggy kept her home, 'you could eat your dinner off your floor.'

Peggy tried to smile and accept the compliment with good grace. Instead, she shrugged a little lower into the coat. She had lost so much weight with the worry of the last months. Peggy shivered, not having the same ample covering as her well-proportioned sister.

She knew if she didn't take the job, she would have nothing to scrub or polish come Christmas. Because she would have had to pawn anything she could, to keep up Dar's medical care. Forcing a smile Peggy swallowed down the rising bile in her throat. She only needed the work until Dar was able to work again, she told Violet.

'This firm pays good money,' said Violet, 'these jobs get snapped up fast.' She headed towards the door and Peggy had no more time to think.

Pulling the woollen cardigan around her thin shoulders, she followed Violet to the door. 'What time do you want me?'

'Eight o'clock. Brown's, the ship cleaners,' Violet said. She was more than a little surprised when Peggy nodded her head.

'I'll take it.' She had heard of the women who cleaned the ships and never imagined herself being one, but anxious times called for speedy actions.

'Right, tomorrow morning. Eight till five, with an hour's dinner, and overtime when the ship's in need of a quick turnaround.' Violet's no-nonsense tone warned Peggy not to complain about the hours. The job would bring in money she sorely needed.

'And what do I have to do?' Peggy asked, knowing Millie would look after the little ones, but that was no hardship, she was sure.

'Clean the decks and the bulkheads – they're the walls. Then if there's a cruise ship in dock, we polish up the brasses and portholes, too. Everything must be done to an extremely high standard, but I can't see you having much trouble with that.'

'I'm sure I won't,' Peggy said. She had never feared demanding work, but she wasn't sure she could work with her sister. Peggy didn't know what it was about their Violet which made her hackles stand on end, but she always seemed to rub her up the wrong way, even on the rare occasion when she was being nice to her.

However, the thought of going to The Parish in Marsh Lane for bowls of soup or scouse was anathema to Peggy; she would rather starve to death. But she couldn't say the same for her children, making her decision to clean ships much easier to digest. 'And what are the wages?'

Peggy's jaw dropped when Violet told her how much she would be earning. The weekly pay was much higher than Dar had been earning at Hutton's, and that was without overtime or weekends.

'You get double time for working Sunday, with it being the Sabbath,' explained Violet, 'but it means you will have to miss mass.'

'As long as Brown's are providing the pennies, I'm sure the Lord will not be offended where I say my prayers.' Peggy's retort brought a peal of laughter from her sister that she had not heard in years. If it came between her children eating, and keeping a roof over their head, or starving and praying for any old roof on the streets, Peggy would put her elasticated principles to one side and have it out with the Lord when the time came for them to meet face to face. Anything was better than having to go to the dockside tenements in Ealing Street.

'Bring your own bucket,' said Violet, 'the firm supply the scrubbing brushes, green soap and wire wool. Paint your name on your bucket in case it gets mixed up.' Peggy assumed she meant 'pinched'. 'Will it suit?'

'It'll suit,' replied Peggy. It would have to suit. She had no choice.

'I'll walk along with you,' said Violet. 'Mam's asleep now, so I'll pick up the medicine for in the morning, save you coming all the way here to go all the way back again.'

'You can come in and have a cup of tea if you fancy it, the kids would love to see you.' Peggy was feeling unusually generous towards her sister, and knew it was about time the carping stopped.

* * *

Millie was just coming through the front door as Violet was leaving.

'Hello, Millie,' said Violet, 'your mam tells me you'll be leaving school at Christmas.'

'Hello, Aunty Vi,' said Millie politely, unaware there had ever been any animosity between her mother and her aunt.

'She could do a lot worse than—' Violet began to say, but Peggy cut off her words.

'She is not cleaning any ships,' Peggy said with a definite nod of her head, 'so don't even consider asking.'

'See you tomorrow,' Violet called over her shoulder. 'Canada dock gate, don't be late.'

'I won't,' said Peggy, watching her sister disappear into the gloom before closing the front door on the foggy street.

When Peggy pushed the 'raggy-snake' draught excluder up to the door to keep out the fog, she hurried up the passageway to the kitchen where, on the sideboard, she noticed the bundle of pound notes.

'Millie, where did these come from?' Peggy asked, holding the precious notes in her hand.

'Aunty Violet left them there; she didn't want me to tell you but said they might come in handy.'

Peggy felt her throat tighten. She had never known their Violet to be open-handed, nor to give money away, especially to her.

'She said you've done a good turn for her many a time and now she's able to return the favour. But she knows how proud you are; if you'd known she was leaving it there, you would have given it back to her.'

'You're right,' said Peggy who did not like taking anything she had not earned. 'But the money is a godsend right now. I'll send our Jack to the chip shop, and we'll have a slap-up supper.'

'That's the spirit, Mam,' said Millie, her mouth already watering at the thought of golden chips and crispy cod.

Peggy hugged her daughter, glad there was a bit of light at the end of this very dark tunnel. Surprised at how quickly their misfortune had turned.

23

A thick early-morning fog hung in the air as gas lamps flickered weakly, casting an eerie glow over the well-trodden cobbled streets as Peggy made her way towards the dockyard to meet Violet. Cutting through the jiggers, she knew she did not have much further to go when the smell of brine from the nearby docks mingled with the damp, musty smell of old Victorian houses lining the streets, and she shivered as another chilly gust of wind sliced through the only thin coat Peggy had left after her clothes had been exiled to Uncle's pawnshop.

The sound of flapping pigeons' wings echoed through the empty alleyways in their search for breakfast and the scent of salt water grew stronger as she approached the imposing gates leading to the dockyard, where a dark group huddled close to the dock wall.

'Come on, slowcoach, get a move on!' Violet's voice was unmistakeable, and Peggy swallowed a hasty retort. Today was her first day. She must not let Violet's rapier tongue get the better of her.

'I thought I was early,' said Peggy, slightly out of breath.

'You are, girl,' said another woman, her head covered by the ever-present woollen headscarf of the rest of the workers. 'She's having you on. We're just waiting for Winnie and then we'll go and find our ship.'

A short while later, another woman, whom Peggy assumed was Winnie, arrived breathless and blowing for tugs as they entered the dockyard and something huge loomed before them, accompanied by a symphony of creaking metal. Peggy, having never been behind the thick dock walls, was amazed at the labyrinth of towering masts. Heavy, tangled ropes and the clatter of porters' wheels on cobbles filled the air, as they manoeuvred their laden carts across the quay towards the warehouses, and Peggy knew she had to be careful where she walked as a trip could catapult her into the dock.

She saw groups of men huddled waiting, like cattle, to enter a shed, which was iron barred from end to end, then the doors were opened, and the rush for a good spot began.

'There he goes,' said Winnie, eyeing a bowler-hatted man in a three-piece-suit, 'cock of the walk.' She stood still, along with the other women, watching the foreman who would walk up and down the rows of men with the air of a dealer at a cattle market. 'Picking and choosing,' Winnie's words were scathing, 'from a crowd of hungry men who, in their eagerness to gain a morning's work, would trample each other underfoot and fight like beasts in the field for the chance of work.'

'It's not much different for us, Winnie,' said a thin, hungry-looking woman carrying her bucket over her arm like a handbag. 'We only get work when the ships are in dock.'

'Aye,' said another woman, 'if there's no ships, there's no work, and no money either.'

The women grew silent as they watched the looming figure of a man approaching, obviously heading their way.

'Do you have a full complement of women today, Violet?' asked the agency foreman and Violet nodded, saying she did. 'In that case, you will have to get your skates on, this ship is on a quick turnaround and will be leaving on the late tide, Wednesday.'

Peggy wondered how they were supposed to clean the whole ship in such a short amount of time but quickly realised the agency man's words were an order, not a request.

'We'd better get to work then,' said Violet, who was the forewoman of this team of ship's cleaners.

'By the sound of it, we can't stretch this job out until Friday,' said Winnie as the women moved off, all chattering at once as they collected their green soap and scrubbing brushes.

'Seeing as this is a quick turnaround, there may be some night shifts too for those that want it.'

Peggy felt her heart hammer in her chest. Work through the night. What about her kids? However, Peggy knew she had no choice. No work, no pay. And the good Lord above was the only one who knew when the next payday would arrive.

'I'll do it,' said Peggy and Violet smiled, making her feel included for the first time she could ever recall.

Violet handed her a scrubbing brush, wire wool, a block of green soap. 'If there's one thing, I can always say about you, Peg, it's this,' she looked Peggy in the eye, 'you never shirk. You're a worker through and through.'

The day's work started with cups of tea, which the women had sneaked from the galley, to keep them warm while they were working.

'As long as the work gets done,' said Violet, 'you won't hear me complain. Oh, and Peggy, don't forget to put your name on your bucket or it might end up who-knows-where,' she pointed to the murky waters of the Mersey, 'and nobody will be jumping in to get it back.'

'I'll go and see if one of the men has got a bit of spare paint,' said Peggy and went off to the ship's stores.

'Hello, beautiful,' said a softly spoken Italian sailor, 'what can I do for you?'

Peggy was surprised at the compliment. Nevertheless, she was not so gullible as to think he meant it. She had heard about sailors having a woman in every port and she was a happily married woman.

'I was wondering if you had a bit of spare paint?'

For the first time since Dar's accident, Peggy felt inexplicably exposed when he smiled at her. She had no cause to speak to men usually, unless it was the coal or the rent man and only then to make sure they gave her the right change. But they never looked at her the way this man was looking at her now.

'For you, my pretty?' said the Italian sailor. 'I'm sure I can find something.'

Peggy felt her pulse quicken and her mouth dried. It had been so long since she had heard a kind manly word, she didn't know how to react, so she just stood there clinging on to her bucket.

'Here,' said the sailor, reaching out his strong, work-worn hand, 'give it to me, I'll do a good job for you. What is your name?'

'Peggy,' she answered, then a sudden thought struck her. 'Peggy Tenant... Mrs.'

'Right, Peggy Tenant... Mrs.' He was teasing her. 'When the job is done, I will come to find you.'

'Are you sure you don't mind?' Peggy asked.

'Of course not. Peggy Tenant, Mrs...'

She felt the heat creep up her neck and her face.

'Thank you,' she called over her shoulder, making her way back to the deck.

'Are you all right, our Peg?' asked Winnie. 'You look a bit flushed.'

'I'm fine.' Peggy felt flustered, wishing her heartbeat would slow down just a little. She was a married woman. She had a sick husband. And four children. She was not a silly schoolgirl who was easily swayed by an unexpected compliment. There was no place in her life for such fancies. No place at all.

'You can leave at four, seeing as you are working through the night,' said Violet, ticking off her name on a sheet of paper, 'sort the kids out and be back here at seven. When you get your bucket back, I want you to wash the heads.'

'Heads?' asked Peggy, who was not familiar with the nautical names.

'The ceilings,' Violet explained, and Peggy hoped Violet was not going to put her down, in front of a group of women she had never met before.

'Don't worry,' Violet's words were a little softer, 'you'll soon get used to the new sayings. We all had to learn at one time.' Her unexpected kindness whipped the quick retort from Peggy's lips, knowing Violet meant well and she probably did not want her to show herself up.

A line of women, on their knees, were scrubbing the decks, as they would do many times until they were spotless, and Peggy wondered if she would rather do that than stand on the passenger rail of a ship that suddenly looked as high as Blackpool Tower, with her mop, washing the heads.

'Your bucket, my lovely,' said the storeman who had painted Peggy's name in beautifully copperplate handwriting, which brought a multitude of praise from the other women who talked as they worked.

'Here, he's done a lovely job on your bucket,' said Winnie, causing a riot of uproarious laughter from the other women.

'Whatever could you mean, our Winnie?' another woman asked, laughing on every word.

'I think 'e's got 'is eye on our Peg.'

'Behave yourself, Winnie, you'll scare her out of a job.' Violet knew Peggy was not used to the dry wit of the ship's cleaners, who, although they could be as earthy and funny as any man, did not usually engage in smutty talk.

'I never said a word!' Winnie looked innocently wounded by the insinuation, but she never could keep a straight face, and her toothless mouth opened to let out a loud cackle. 'You'll soon get used to us, our Peg,' Winnie said when the laughter died down, and Peggy felt a rare companionship she hadn't experienced before.

Waiting for her bucket to be filled with hot water from the galley, she noticed the Italian sailor collecting his food and realised she hadn't thanked him.

'Thank you so much for putting my name on the bucket. The other women are green with envy,' she told him, bringing another smile to his face.

'Green?' He looked comically alarmed.

'Jealous, envious,' explained Peggy, then realised he was teasing her again.

'I am glad you like it. I put in special effort.'

'Well, thank you.'

'Carlo,' he said, 'and you are Peggy Tenant, Mrs.'

'I'd better get back. I still have work to do.' Standing around here was not getting it done. She repeated her thanks, and her appreciation of his work, and turned to head back to her work, when he took the heavy bucket and gestured for her to climb the steep steps aloft.

When she was back on deck, Peggy heard a faint wolf whistle from one of the women and did her best to ignore it, as Carlo tipped the peak of his cap and made his way below, making her feel she missed Dar even more.

'I didn't say a word,' Winnie laughed, holding up her hands from her kneeling position on the deck, scrubbing brush in hand.

'You didn't have to,' Peggy laughed, encouraging a round of applause. 'What's that for?' she asked Violet.

'Now they know where they stand with you,' answered Violet. 'You've showed them you can take a joke with the best of them, and Winnie likes a good laugh.'

'I noticed,' Peggy said, although not unkindly. She didn't know why she had ever thought this job would be beneath her. The women were kind, down-to-earth and had enough of their own problems without wanting to delve into hers. 'I think I'm going to like this job.'

'Glad to hear it, because I've heard you are a natural scrubber.' Violet joined Peggy in a blast of uproarious laughter and both women set to work.

Peggy swished the mop vigorously, washing the ceilings until they shone. Only the younger women did this job, she realised, although surprised there were no safety precautions. 'Just don't look down' was the only safety advice she had been given.

The women were such a good crowd who did not judge, like some did. As *she* once did. Everyone was doing the same kind of work, and everybody got on with it.

'The company always want women in a hurry, because they're so busy,' said Violet, unusually chatty. 'We all need the money, so there's no shame in cleaning.' The job was a five-day week, she explained to Peggy as they scrubbed and polished.

'Sounds good to me,' said Peggy. Whether it was the briny air or the knowledge that every hour she worked she had earned another three shillings and sixpence, a fortune Dar could only dream of, she didn't know, but she felt more positive now than she had done in a long while.

The work was hard, but she enjoyed it. Her own spotlessly clean house was proof she was a worker who was not afraid to graft. But Peggy soon came to realise she could not have picked a worse time to work on the windswept docks as the dark nights were bitter.

'Bloody hell it's cold,' moaned Winnie. 'Winter's hell-bent on freezing the offal out of us this year.'

'I find the harder I work, the warmer I get.' Peggy gave a wry smile, even though her cracked hands were raw, and the work was hard. She was determined to earn as much as she could, knowing she would be a fool to turn her nose up at the money she would pick up on Friday. When Dar did come home, she wanted him to be proud of what she had achieved, not dwell on what they had been through.

Peggy was surprised when they finished the work they'd been assigned at the end of the week that there was no disharmony with the seafarers on board the ship, knowing if they did encounter them, the sailors were always courteous and did not swear in front of the women. If they did inadvertently curse in front of one of the women, they immediately apologised. Violet warned Peggy that if there were any grievances she must come straight to her, and she would sort it out. But Peggy never found any need.

The workers were well organised, each woman knowing what they had to do. Peggy wasn't sure whether there was a union, remembering that Dar thought they would receive sick pay when he was off, and she found out way too late that was not the case.

'Yes, the Transport and General is our union,' said young May, Winnie's daughter, 'but we've never needed to use them.'

Nevertheless, when the union woman approached her and asked if she was willing to pay fivepence a week out of her wages for the full backing of the union, Peggy did not hesitate. The other women assured her she would be well looked after if anything should go wrong.

The ship was extremely dirty, and her clothes were filthy in no time. The women wore a coarse apron made from a sack line cloth. Peggy worked below deck on a merchant ship and was not out in the harsh weather, and she found the whole experience, the work, the camaraderie, the whole thing, more exciting than she'd ever thought possible.

When she got home late at night, Peggy was too excited to go straight to bed, even though she was bone weary. Millie had done an excellent job of looking after the other three and she knew if there were any problems she only had to go and knock at Molly's door, and she would get any help she needed. And for the first time in a long while, Peggy felt the tide was turning in her favour.

'I've been asked to work through the night,' Peggy told Millie, 'will you cope?'

'I don't know, Mam,' answered Millie with the ghost of a smile, 'I'll be asleep for most of it.'

'That's my girl,' said Peggy, already feeling the weight, lifting from her shoulders. 'Right, off to bed, you've got school in the morning.'

Having brought home potatoes, vegetables and meat, there was plenty to eat and she had even gone to the expense of a pound of mixed biscuits from Costigan's as a treat for her children.

'I'll just make a couple of sandwiches for my carry-out, to eat during the night,' Peggy said, as she spooned loose tea and condensed milk into a little bundle of greaseproof paper, knowing she could get hot water from the galley.

* * *

Peggy didn't expect her life to be sunshine and flowers, a bit of peace from worry would do. She loathed the dark mornings when she had to leave her youngest children in the care of fourteen-year-old Millie, who gave Jane and Eddy their breakfast and they all went to school together as usual. Peggy knew that from dawn until dusk descended, she would toil in all weathers, each day growing a little colder than the last. But she also knew the sacrifice was worth it to make up the money they had lost in hospital fees.

The work was heavy and dirty, and she wasn't always working on the same ship and had to get back from whatever dock she had been working on. Lucky if the ship was docked in the north end of Liverpool close to home, and not over the water at Birkenhead, where she would often stand on the crowded tram carrying her bucket over her arm, tired after washing filthy cabin walls, ceilings and floors. Scrubbing the decks and bulkheads, panning-out the toilets – a disgusting job that called for a strong stomach.

When the weather was bad, the snow and ice settled on the ships, and the cloths would stick to the surface she was cleaning, her hands painfully red-raw. Peggy, thankfully, was robust. There was a first-aid nurse on the dock if you happened to fall overboard while cleaning the deck heads, Winnie told her. The women she travelled to work with on the tram for a penny a trip would laugh about it, because if they didn't laugh, they'd cry, and that would never do. Although, she loved the companionship of the other women who had taken to her from the very first day. The feeling of togetherness and of being in the same boat made the unenviable task of the work they had to do more acceptable. Peggy would even join the women in a song as they worked, helping the time go faster.

24

The winter months were the coldest she could remember, especially when working outside cleaning the rails of the ships. Peggy, considered one of the younger women, carried buckets of water up from the galley for the older women.

The best part of every week was payday, when her sister, being the charge hand, brought her wages around. Peggy could hardly contain her excitement, knowing it held a fortune. Not only did the packet have her wages, but also a payslip attached to show how many hours she had worked and what deductions had been made. Something Dar never had. She knew he was only glad to be bringing home a regular wage.

She also noted that she was paying her union dues, safe in the knowledge that if she had any kind of grievance, someone would sort it out for her, and for that she was incredibly grateful, knowing her husband would never know such security while he was working for Henry Hutton.

'Don't you ever go for your dinner in the dock canteen?' asked Peggy, who had quickly made friends with Winnie and was sitting in the hold of a ship to eat their sandwiches.

'Oh no,' answered Winnie, 'we only get hot water from the dock canteen, but we don't eat there 'cos it's full of men.'

Peggy threw her head back and roared with laughter. For all her bluff and bluster, Winnie was a bit of a prude on the sly.

'I've got the funnels to clean tomorrow,' said Peggy, knowing they were about thirty feet above the deck but earned her extra money. Danger money the other women called it.

'You're welcome to that job,' said Winnie with a shudder.

'I don't mind,' said Peggy, she was not afraid of heights and the extra five pounds for the job was well worth the risk.

The following day, to wash the superstructure and the funnels, she erected a trestle across two large ladders roughly twelve feet high and balanced a long plank of wood between them. Then she climbed up the ladder, carrying her bucket of water and brushes and stood on the plank to clean the paint. Everything was filthy with oil and grease.

Before long, Peggy wondered if volunteering for this job had been one of her most stupid ideas, as her raw hands started to crack and bleed, having to change the water every two feet because of the oil and grease.

'I want to see my face in that funnel,' called Violet, who seemed to be back to her usual catty self, 'it has to be sparkling.'

After Peggy had finished washing one part, she would drag the trestle along with to the next place.

If they weren't lucky enough to get hot water down in the crew's quarters, most of the time, Peggy and the other women had to haul buckets of cold water up the steep gangplank, knowing they either had to do that or go traipsing around a huge ship trying to find water, praying they would not get lost.

'Some of these ships are as long as London Road,' laughed Winnie, 'and there's doors all over the place.'

'You might have to bring a ball of string,' Violet laughed. 'Even I don't know my way around this one,' she said, 'and I've been on every ship in the fleet.'

'The only thing we don't touch is the kitchens,' said Winnie, 'that's where the cooks are, and they are very particular about their kitchens. Nor do we ever go up into the passengers' cabins. The stewards clean them; we're not allowed to go near them.'

'That's good, I don't fancy mooching around in other people's private things,' said Peggy, knowing Violet had already given instructions as to what part of the ship they cleaned, beforehand. Peggy gasped after putting her foot in her bucket of water, as the thick fog, rolling in off the Irish Sea, prevented her from seeing where she was putting her feet. 'How are we supposed to see what we're doing?'

'Let's concentrate on cleaning the insides of the ship,' said Violet as the weather grew worse.

'Thank goodness for that,' said Peggy, 'my washcloth was sticking to the side of the ship, it's that cold. I suppose we can always do the rails tomorrow.'

The shipping companies were strict about the rails being pristine, Violet told her. 'They're the showpiece. The company want them gleaming when the ship sails up the Mersey.'

'We all have to have a go cleaning the rails,' Winnie joined the conversation to have a little breather, 'but you won't have any nails left by the time you finish.'

The women chatted as they worked, and Violet left them to get on with the job.

'The ship's leaving a day early, girls,' Violet called later, 'so if you can help me out and do a bit of overtime that would be great.' Not surprising after a week of late finishes, none of the women were enthusiastic. 'Oh, and by the way,' called Violet, 'those who do stay are going to be offered a twenty-five-pound bonus.'

'Twenty-five pounds!' A gasp of disbelief went around the

throng of women, none of whom were accustomed to earning that kind of money. Every hand shot up, none of them were going to pass up the chance to earn that much. Peggy knew that kind of money could buy her wallpaper and paint, she could make the place nice for when Dar came home.

When the rain and wind subsided, Peggy knew she would have to resume her duties, working from her lofty height high above the deck, and the first thing she did was the one thing she was told not to do on her first day – she looked down at the infinite stretch of water below and the bobbing cargo boats looming on the oily water. Her vision blurred a little, but not enough to eliminate the numerous cranes criss-crossing the dark skyline. She could see the glow of the nightwatchman's fire on the quay and the west wind caused the water below to splash against the side of the dock wall and the rigging to judder, making a ghostly moaning sound that chilled her to the bone even more than the freezing wind.

To keep her mind occupied as she worked, she imagined what she could do to cheer up the family home.

Sunday, being her day off, Peggy promised to take the children on the train to see their father. She couldn't wait to tell him about her job and how much the work had given her the independence she never had before. Her only worry was that he might tell her to give it up.

'You need to be careful. I've heard the stories about women who work on the docks,' Dar said when she told him about the job. Although, having been nervous about revealing her news, and expecting him to tell her in no uncertain terms that she must give up the work, Peggy was surprised Dar seemed to be much calmer than she had anticipated.

'I haven't heard any stories.' Peggy felt annoyed at her husband's lukewarm response to the effort she had made to keep her home and family together in his absence. 'Everybody in the borough has someone in the family who work on the docks.'

'You could have gone to the parish,' said Dar, and Peggy raised an eyebrow.

'When have we ever asked for charity?' she said. 'I'll tell you when. Never! I refuse to go cap in hand for poor relief, when I've got a good pair of hands and a strong back to work with.' She knew poor relief came in the shape of food or food vouchers, but she was determined her children were not going to suffer the indignity she had to endure as a child. 'I couldn't bear the shame, and I don't care what you say about most people going to the parish at some time or other. I'm not most people.'

'Everybody's poor at some time, Peg,' Dar knew he had touched a nerve, 'and deep down we're all the same.'

'You've changed your tune,' she said, rolling her shoulders indignantly.

'I'd be happy to think you were at home looking after the kids,' said Dar.

'Aye,' Peggy told him in a straightforward manner that brooked no argument, and any sensible person would do well to heed, 'and our kids are happy when they're being fed regularly.' This was an attitude she would never have taken against her husband in the past, but things were different now. 'Ours don't have to get up early to go to school for their breakfast, like some poor kiddies. Ours have the comfort of eating their breakfast in front of a roaring fire. They have good shoes on their feet and a warm coat on their back – that's what my work provides.'

'You'll not have to go out cleaning ships in all weathers for much longer,' Dar said, reaching for Peggy's hand, while Jack and

Millie took the younger ones out for a winter stroll in the grounds to give their parents a little time to talk.

'We're a team, Dar, when one of us is poorly or infirm, we rally round, that's always been our way. You've no need to worry.' She wanted to put his mind at rest, ease his burden. Dar had been through enough, she thought. She knew he had been worrying, struggling so hard to find the strength to walk again so he could leave this place.

'I'll put in more effort to get walking and come home,' said Dar, 'I need to be with my family.'

'I know, and we feel the same,' Peggy told him, knowing Dar's accident had proved one thing at least: she too was capable of being a competent provider. Nevertheless, she could work until the cows came home, but she could never earn enough to buy him that manly pride Dar had taken for granted. 'You're a fighter, Dar, you'll be on your feet in no time.'

'Now listen, love,' Dar's words were softer when she bent to kiss him goodbye, 'don't forget to tell your Violet you'll be leaving when I get out of here.' He smiled, and that old twinkle returned, reminding Peggy why she had married him in the first place. He had been the only person she ever wanted to be with. She wouldn't have called it love at first. Not then. That came later, when they got used to one another. They were a team, working for the good of the family. 'I'll soon get back to work, you'll see, and everything will be just the same as it always was.'

As Peggy walked out into the frosty gardens that looked like they had been dusted with icing sugar, she wondered if Dar realised how scarce jobs were becoming these days.

25

The following week, Peggy heard the clatter of the letter box and went out into the long, cold hallway to see an official-looking envelope on the linoleum-covered floor. When she opened it, she saw it was from the hospital almoner, who wanted to come and see Peggy on Saturday for a chat.

'I wonder what she wants?' Peggy said aloud to the empty room. She knew Dar's payments were up to date; since she'd started work, she had paid every penny on the nail. No questions asked.

When the lady almoner called, Peggy realised she was not the ogre she had been dreading; in fact, she reminded Peggy of Ellie. Tall, softly spoken, she immediately put Peggy at her ease.

'I do hope my visit is not a nuisance to you, Mrs Tenant,' said the lady almoner. 'I'm Miss Hathaway, Florence Hathaway,' she said, holding out her hand, surprised at how cold Mrs Tenant's hands were. Florence Hathaway took in the chilly, sparsely furnished kitchen with the sweep of her eyes, but the clean smell of pine disinfectant was strong – a welcome change to other houses she visited.

'No trouble at all,' said Peggy. 'Please, take a seat, I've just put the kettle on.'

'None for me, thank you,' said Miss Hathaway, 'I've just had lunch.' She did not wish to deprive these poor people of their meagre provisions, but nor did she want to embarrass Mrs Tenant by saying so.

'If you've come about the money to pay for Dar's, my husband's, care,' Peggy began, and Miss Hathaway raised her hand like a policeman on point duty to stop Peggy going any further.

'No, I have not come to enquire about money,' she said, and Peggy let out a little sigh of relief, 'the fees have been taken care of. You need trouble yourself no further on that account.'

'The fees have been paid?' Peggy gasped. 'But who paid them?'

'I'm sorry, the benefactor made it quite clear that the donation must remain anonymous, so for as much as I would like to tell you, I cannot.'

'But I don't know anybody who would have the means to pay that kind of money.'

'Let's just say, you have no more to worry about, from now on you need pay no more for your husband's care and rehabilitation for as long as he is a patient at Lavender Green.' Miss Hathaway would not be drawn into further discussion on the matter. 'What I can tell you is good news. We hope to discharge Mr Tenant before Christmas, and I am here to learn if there will be adequate provision for his rehabilitation.'

'What kind of provision?' asked Peggy, her mind doing a quick calculation of what Dar could possibly need and how she would find the means to provide the equipment.

'Mainly good food, fresh air and plenty of rest,' said Miss Hathaway. 'We will provide crutches and any handrails he might need. Also, we will make sure he is able to climb stairs before he is discharged.'

'I can guarantee there will be no shortage of good food and rest, but as for fresh air, it's not the same as the air at Lavender Green,' said Peggy. She knew that as she didn't have Dar's fees to worry about, Christmas would look a lot cheerier, especially as he was coming home.

She was so excited she could hardly breathe. He had been gone six long months. If it hadn't been for the goodwill of the women of Beamer Street, and the camaraderie of her workmates, who had become such good friends and so supportive, she would never have got through the last months.

But Peggy also knew she had to get the house back to the way it used to be, restore it to the home Dar had left on that warm sunny morning. Peggy knew what she had to do. The time had come, when she had to find a way to make their house a home once more.

Over the course of the next half an hour, she did something she had fought against all her life. She opened her heart and told Miss Hathaway the truth about how much she had struggled and worked to provide for her family.

'That must have been so awful for you,' said Miss Hathaway, 'not just the money, but the love you and your husband so obviously share with your family.'

'Our Millie is leaving school when it breaks up for Christmas.'

'And what does she want to do?' Miss Hathaway asked, persuaded to accept that cup of tea, glad to see Mrs Tenant add more coal to the fire. Now she suspected the burden of paying for Mr Tenant's rehabilitation had been eased, Mrs Tenant might be able to enjoy the warmth of a good fire more often.

'She's not sure, but one thing I do know, she's not going into a factory. She's going to learn a trade, make something of herself.'

'Good for her,' said Miss Hathaway, enjoying the warmth of the hot tea she was cradling, to thaw her hands. 'It must be hard work, cleaning ships.'

'It's something you must do when you've got people depending upon you. We've never been ones for taking charity before now.'

'Like I said, Mrs Tenant,' Miss Hathaway answered, 'I have not come here today to batter your door down for any payment. My job is to make sure you have adequate means for your husband's return home. That is all.'

'I can assure you I have the means,' said Peggy, 'and when he comes home, I will make sure he is properly looked after.'

'I do believe you will, and with the help of your family, things will soon get back to normal.'

'I hope not,' Peggy laughed, feeling the weight of worry drop from her shoulders. 'I hope things will be much better than that. But please,' Peggy urged, 'please don't let him know our circumstances. Now that I don't have to worry about his rehabilitation fees at Lavender Green, Dar will come back to the cosy home he left behind. I might even decorate in here.' She felt she could speak openly to Miss Hathaway. 'He has been through enough, I don't want to set him back by worrying him.'

'I understand,' said Miss Hathaway, admiring Peggy's pluck. Her ability to shoulder the burden proved her to be a much stronger woman than she gave herself credit for. She also admired the way Peggy's friends had pulled together in times of need, especially Mrs Elodie Newman, whom the locals called Ellie, who owned the huge Oakland Hall, which she had turned into the rehabilitation retreat of Lavender Green.

Nevertheless, Mrs Tenant would never know about Ellie Newman's generosity unless her benefactor chose to tell her, and knowing Elodie as she did, Miss Hathaway doubted that very much.

* * *

When she finished work the following Friday morning, Peggy knew her first stop was going to be the decorator's shop on Stanley Road. She and Jack were going to make the house nice for when Dar came home.

Why shouldn't she have a nice kitchen, like Molly or Mary Jane, she thought. She was earning good money.

'Here's a job for the weekend, Jack!' Peggy sounded joyful when she came home with rolls of wallpaper and paint. 'We need to get this place ready for Dar coming home, and it will give you something to do while you are looking for work.'

'I'll start stripping the old wallpaper straight away,' said Jack, eager to get started.

'Not before we've had our breakfast, you won't.' Peggy smiled. Tired though she was, she was thrilled to see the look of happiness on the faces of her children.

'Come and have something to eat, Mam,' said Millie, placing two boiled eggs and a plate of hot toast before her. 'We'll eat like kings today.'

'No, we won't,' Peggy said, 'we'll eat like Tenants.' They all laughed.

'I didn't mean the King family,' Millie realised what she had said, and they all laughed. The atmosphere in the house seemed much lighter since Peggy had the security of her own money coming in and the knowledge that someone had taken away the worry of Dar's hospital bills.

* * *

When Peggy got home after a fourteen-hour shift the following week, she doubted she would be able to climb the stairs to her much longed-for bed.

'Oh, Mam, you're working too hard,' said Millie as she put down the warmed plate of dried-up mashed potato, desiccated carrots, bullet peas and brittle minced beef. The minced meat had to be chipped away from the edge of her plate, but Peggy was glad of it.

'We won't be saying that when I get paid,' said Peggy. 'They're a nice bunch of women, salt of the earth,' Peggy told Millie, reassuring her daughter the work was nothing she couldn't handle.

'But, Mam, look at the state of your hands, they're bleeding.'

'Only between my fingers, they'll soon toughen up.' Peggy winced as she folded her fingers around her knife and fork. 'The women I work with have been cleaning the ships for years and work as hard as any man.' She doubted any of them would give it up in favour of a cushier job with less pay. 'We have such a laugh.' Peggy paused, debating whether she should tell her daughter of the stories she had heard, then decided she could not keep Millie wrapped in cotton wool forever. 'You should hear some of the things they say.'

Millie listened, fascinated and amused in equal measure, as she ate her tea, thrilled to see her mam smiling again.

'Some of the things they say are quite outrageous, but it's all in good fun, and no offence is ever taken.'

Millie felt the experience was like a breath of fresh air to her mam, realising she had been coddled and protected by Dar all her married life. 'Well, it's certainly brought back the colour in your cheeks, Mam.'

'That'll be the west wind blasting in off the river,' her mam laughed, and Millie realised she hadn't seen her doing that for a long time.

'I know I've been getting in late, but I couldn't pass up the chance of making a bit more money,' Peggy told her daughter, who had been doing a sterling job looking after the two youngest with Jack's help.

'I forgot to tell you—' Millie's voice was barely a squeak as she brought a fresh pot of tea over to the table '—our Jack's been offered a job.'

'A job! Where? Who with?'

'Mister Everdine came to see him at tea-time,' explained Millie, 'said he's looking for an apprentice.'

'What about his indentures?' Peg thought aloud, knowing they didn't come cheap. Although, this was such a wonderful opportunity Cal Everdine was offering and would enable her eldest son to have a solid future.

'What are his indentures?' asked Millie, pouring tea as she sat opposite her mother.

'It's a legal document that binds an apprentice to his master for the length of the training, and they don't come cheap.'

Nevertheless, Peggy knew the training her son received would be first class. She also knew Jack wouldn't make good money for years as apprentices earned next to nothing in return for the training they would be given. However, the training would set her son up for life. He would never be short of work, unlike the men who worked on the docks, who had to go down to the stand each morning and afternoon in the hope of getting a few hours if they were lucky. She didn't want that for her children, and nor did Dar. They wanted their brood to have something better than they ever had, something that would set them up for life, so they didn't have to go cleaning ships in the freezing winter weather.

'I'll go and see Mister Everdine later.' Peggy knew she might have to stay on at the dock, but if that was what it took to make her son a better future, then so be it. 'Where is Jack?'

'He's gone to have a talk with Mister Everdine to see what the job entails.'

'He sounds eager,' Peggy said, knowing Jack would have set his heart on an opportunity such as this. Like Dar, her eldest son was ambitious. He wanted a better tomorrow. She knew Dar would be thrilled Cal Everdine was giving their son this opportunity. And she wanted that for him too.

26

_____

Percy knocked on Molly's vestibule door and stood back on the step, waiting. A moment later, he saw her bustle out to the door and his heart gave a little flutter. He liked Molly. He liked her a lot. She was a good woman, homely and honourable. She had raised a good family by herself. They all loved her, and would do anything to please her, which was what made it so difficult for him to do what he was about to do.

'Ahh, hello, Molly love,' Percy said, taking off his flat cap to reveal a thatch of thick steel-coloured hair. 'Are you decent?' He asked her the same amusing question every time he called.

'Am I decent?' Molly rolled her eyes and led the way into her cosy kitchen. 'Of course I'm decent.' She liked Percy and felt comfortable in his presence, never lost for words or something to talk about. They'd had a very comfortable friendship since he started working in Mary Jane's bakery.

'I've something I want to ask you,' said Percy, sliding the cup of tea, which Molly had just poured, across the table. He looked out of the sash window and down the yard.

'Oh aye,' said Molly, curious. 'And what's that then?'

'Well,' Percy spoke in a hesitant voice, 'you know my sister?'

'Aye,' said Molly, waiting. At the rate Percy was speaking, it would be Christmas before he got around to saying what he wanted to say. But she wouldn't rush him, knowing this must be something important if he was being so hesitant.

'Well, she's thinking of moving after Christmas, and I was wondering...' He paused, not sure how to word his request. 'I was just wondering if...'

'Come on, Percy, you'll have it dark by the time to get this off your chest. Stop airy-fairying around and spit it out before it chokes you.'

'Can I move into your parlour?' Percy blurted out the question before he had time to think on it any longer and Molly raised her chin, her mouth turned down at the edges as she considered his request. It might be nice to have a bit of company at the end of the day now that her offspring were all growing up and off her hands.

'I'll pay the going rate,' said Percy, not sure if he had over-stepped the mark. 'I know you've taken in a lodger in the past, so I thought I'd ask, but if it doesn't suit, I'll—'

'Of course it suits,' said Molly, 'the money will come in handy, what with Christmas coming up.' Molly surprised herself by the excitement she felt at the prospect. 'When would you like to move in?'

'How about tomorrow?' asked Percy.

'Tomorrow it is then.' Molly felt as light as air. 'I'll just get that front room ready.'

* * *

The women were still finishing the cleaning as dawn was breaking and the ship sailed out of port and up the river. When it reached the Mersey bar, the women were told they were being taken off the ship and onto a fire tender.

Peggy looked over the side of the ship and saw a small rope ladder swinging precariously in the wind. 'Jesus wept!' she exclaimed, never having stepped foot on such a contraption, let alone forty feet in the air from the deck of a ship.

'Don't be scared,' said Winnie, who was behind her, and if Peggy was expecting words of encouragement, she was sadly disappointed. 'If you fall in the water, we'll throw you a lifebelt.'

'I've got no bloody intentions of falling in,' said Peggy through gritted teeth. 'Here, hold onto my bucket while I get my foot on the first rung.'

'I 'ave to do everything 'round 'ere.' Winnie mimicked the voice of a petulant child, and the rest of the women laughed uproariously, including Peggy as the remark eased her fear.

'Have you done this before?' shouted Violet from above and Peggy thought it best to wait until she was on a firmer footing before she answered.

'The 'ardest part is when you 'ave to jump off,' called Winnie, 'so mind you don't jump in the water.'

Peggy clamped her lips between her teeth to stop herself calling back something most unladylike.

'Just hold steady and you'll be fine. 'Ere's your bucket,' Winnie shouted above the wind as the bucket hit Peggy on the head. She was so shocked she didn't even think of the consequences of what could happen if she lost her grip, and grabbed the handle of the bucket, slipping it onto her arm. The wind caught at her coat, and it flapped in all directions, covering her head and face.

'Sod this for a lark,' exclaimed Peggy, 'this is a nothing but a bloody nuisance.' As she spoke, she slipped her arms out of the coat and threw it down onto the quay, praying that it landed and didn't sail off into the Irish Sea.

The other women did likewise when they saw how fierce the wind had become, and they stuffed their coats into their buckets.

'My skirt's blowing all over the place, giving the men below a right eyeful.'

'Don't you worry about that, our Peg,' called Winnie, tucking her skirt into the waistband of her knee-length bloomers, 'false modesty's never been one o' my strongest points.'

Moments later, Peggy heard a chorus of shouts and screams and then a splash of water.

'She's fell in the drink!' the waiting women called, peering over the side of the ship, and Peggy's heart was in her mouth!

'Someone help her!' she cried to a huddle of dockers standing near the blazing brazier, warming their hands. A moment later, Peggy saw a figure jump from the ship's rail into the dark water below. For a moment, there was nothing to see, the swirling waters of the river Mersey took no prisoners, she knew that. She remembered Dar telling her that the narrows in the river estuary between Dingle Point on the Liverpool banks to New Brighton on the Wirral forced the water to flow faster, creating a perilously deep channel along this section of the river. The tide was ferociously strong and could drag a body under in the blink of an eye.

For a while, there was no sound and Peggy's heart pumped in her throat. Poor Winnie, she thought. Praying to every saint she could think of for her friend's safe return to dry land. Then a thought struck her, what if the sailor who had jumped into the water was dragged under, too. He would need to be a strong swimmer to get out alive. Time went so slow, she began to feel sick.

Soon a bright lantern shone on the quayside. The harbour master threw a lifebelt into the river and scanned the water with his powerful light from side to side in the hope of picking up the two bodies. Hopefully still alive.

Then the light caught the reflection of someone diving back down into the murky water.

'Winnie!' Peggy could barely whisper.

The remaining women made their way down the rope ladder, too concerned about Winnie to worry about themselves. Peggy did not know what she would do if Winnie did not come back up again.

'I've found her!' the sailor called and the women watched as he brought Winnie, coughing and spluttering, up onto the dockside.

'You'd better not tell anybody I peed meself,' Winnie told the matelot, who rolled his eyes. The woman had nearly lost her life and all she was worried about was people finding out she had wet her knickers!

The women were dropped off at the pier head, just as the first tram was about to pull out.

'You dare!' Winnie shouted, dressed in a pair of sailor's corduroy trousers and a thick plaid shirt. 'Just you bloody dare,' she shouted to the tram driver, 'and I'll have your guts for stitches!'

Peggy led the advance on the slowing tram, knowing the driver must have had second thoughts about continuing his journey when he saw the tired-looking gaggle of women in turbaned headscarves, all carrying their own buckets, making their way home at this ungodly hour of the morning after a full night's work.

* * *

'Mam! You look shattered,' cried Millie as her mother all but crawled up the narrow hallway into the kitchen.

'I'm fine, queen,' answered Peggy. She would tell Millie about poor Winnie's dive into the drink tomorrow, her eyes already starting to close.

'You go up, Mam. I've put the oven shelf inside a pillowcase to take the chill off the bed and I'll bring you a cup of tea.'

'You're a good girl, our Millie.'

Millie smiled as she watched her mother drag herself up the stairs, thankful today was Saturday and Mam had the day off. Even as she poured the fresh tea into her mother's cup, Millie doubted her mother would be awake long enough to drink it.

27

'Hiya, Ellie love,' said Peggy when she nipped in to the apothecary just before it closed for the night, 'I've just called in for Ma's liniment. I'd forget my head if it wasn't stuck to me neck,' she laughed.

'Your sister called in earlier,' Ellie informed her, and Peggy's eyes widened in surprise.

'Well, I never did,' she said. 'Fancy our Vi coming all this way, things must be bad if she came for Mam's linctus.'

'She didn't seem anxious in any way.'

'Don't let that *all-is-well* front fool you. Our Violet can hide anything under a broad smile.' Peggy had got to know her sister much better since they had been working together. There was a softer side to Violet she had rarely seen before.

Peggy began to realise that her older sister had been as much under her mother's thumb as she had for all these years. Ma had a way of getting what she wanted by having her offspring battle for her affection.

'I heard something today that will no doubt be of interest to you.' Ellie lowered her voice even though the shop was empty except for the two of them. 'Miles Houseman has been jailed for breaking into your house.'

'Let's hope it teaches him a lesson,' said Peggy, knowing the incident had unsettled her for weeks after the break-in, not having Dar's usual support. However, the incident had made a man of her son Jack, when he took on his father's role of family protector.

Wishing Ellie a good night, Peggy made her way out of the shop and up the street towards No. 3, glad Dar would be home on Christmas Eve. His arrival, which she was keeping as a surprise from her young ones, would make this the best Christmas they ever had.

'Peggy! Peggy, wait for me.'

Peggy turned to see Violet huffing and puffing her way up Beamer Street. In the hazy light of the gas lamp, a misty fog was meandering up from the river, but there was no mistaking her sister's piercing call.

'I'm glad I caught you.'

'Is it about the overtime? Because Dar's coming home soon and...' Peggy intended to give her notice. Knowing Dar's fees had been paid, she no longer needed to leave her children to fend for themselves. Dar would need her to take care of him.

'No, it's not about the overtime,' said Violet, her voice low and softer than Peggy had heard it for years. 'But don't you worry about that, queen.' Violet's voice dropped almost to a whisper.

'What's the matter?' Peggy instinctively knew something was wrong. 'You don't seem your usual self, Vi.' Her brows pleated in concern.

'It's Mam...' Violet said in hushed tones, 'she died just after I got back from work.'

Peggy gasped. The shock of the news hit her like a slap in the face. 'But I only saw her yesterday. She seemed...' Peggy was going to say her mother seemed fine, but, if truth be told, she had not been fine for a long time. But she would not listen to the pleading of her daughters to go into the infirmary.

'She'd had a letter off me father this week, but told nobody,' Violet's voice was flat and lifeless. 'I found it in the sideboard drawer...'

Rooting already, Peggy thought, then silently scolded herself for being bad-minded. Violet was the eldest girl in the O'Day clan. She would be expected to sort out the arrangements for the funeral, go to collect the death certificate, cash in the insurance, even though Peggy had paid the premium for many years. But none of that mattered now.

'Poor Mam,' said Peggy, 'she never had it easy.' Then she paused before saying, 'You mentioned a letter.'

'If I got my hands around his scrawny bloody neck, I'd throttle me father,' said Violet, with all the intense feeling she could muster. 'He wrote and told her he was never coming home again. He had another family in Newcastle.'

'Newcastle?' Peggy took a moment to think about this added information. 'Bloody old womaniser, he sent our mam to an early grave.' Peggy was surprised at her own reaction. She did not burst into tears, instead she felt distanced from the news somehow. For some strange reason, she felt sorry for Violet.

'Poor Mam.' Violet sniffed, and took out a handkerchief, blowing her nose and wiping her eyes.

'She didn't deserve what he put her through, I suppose,' said Peggy.

'None of us deserved what he put us through.' Violet's bitter tone was edged with rage. 'But I'll leave that for another day. I just thought I'd better come along and tell you myself.'

'That's good of you, Vi. If you need me to help with anything, you know where I am,' said Peggy. She rested her hand on Violet's arm. 'Come in and have a cup of tea before you make your way back.'

'I won't if you don't mind,' said Violet, 'I've got to tell the rest of them. I wanted you to be the first to know.'

'Are you sure you don't want me to come with you?' Peggy felt bad for letting her sister do the donkey work.

'Everything is going to be fine. I just need to think.'

'I don't know what you mean,' said Peggy.

'Don't fret, Peg, it'll all come out in the wash.' For the first time since she was a little girl, she felt Violet's loving arms around her shoulders. 'I'll see you tomorrow. Try to get some sleep.'

'I will,' Peggy said. Violet's hug made her feel warm, and wanted, and part of something she hadn't felt for years.

* * *

During the eulogy, in which her older brother paid tribute to their mother, Peggy's thoughts wandered to the untold tales he hinted at. What did he mean when he said their mother was a canny soul who would take her secrets to her grave? What secrets?

It was only later, in a quiet conversation with her sister, that Violet said she had something particularly important to tell Peggy, who assumed it had something to do with their father and the reason he had never came home for so long.

'He told Ma in the letter,' said Peggy, 'he said he had another family now.'

'It's not just that,' said Violet, 'but I will tell you tomorrow.'

* * *

Violet strode with her head held high through the dockside streets the next morning, intending to fling open Henry Hutton's office door and tell him exactly what she thought of him. She was not inclined to keep her voice down, nor did she care who heard her. In fact, the more people who heard what she had to say, the better. Her Peggy had been treated badly by Hutton and his jumped-up prig of a nephew. She had never asked him for a penny, but now he was going to pay.

Peggy was married to Hutton's best worker, who had undergone months of painful, expensive treatment, and had been offered a mere five pounds. Nor had she been offered the sick money, to which Dar thought he had been contributing. It was a disgrace!

Violet knew the time had come to put the record straight. All she had to do was hold her nerve. Stand her ground and make Hutton understand that he had wriggled his way out of his responsibility for long enough. Her mind strayed to that prohibitive place her own mother had forbidden her to acknowledge for the past thirty years. But she needed to face her demons. Put her fears behind her and put right the wrongs of the past.

She could see it now, as if watching a story unfold on the big screen at the picture house. Her father had been bouncing Peggy on his knee, teaching her a lively sea shanty. The kitchen was full of lively chatter and song, the table heaving with the tasty food he'd brought home. Ma, laughing, was enjoying her husband's company once again and neighbours popped in to greet the merchant seaman who had been gone for over two years.

Nothing had changed in that regard, thought Violet. Her father would come home only rarely with his pockets bulging, Ma would wait on him hand and foot, trying to persuade him to stay a day or two longer. But he'd soon be off when the money ran out and beer friends dwindled.

Sometimes he didn't even take the time to say goodbye, Violet knew. He just upped and left without a word before any of them woke. He was free as a bird. Leaving Ma to struggle and try to make ends meet. Feast or famine. There was never a happy medium.

But it was that one day, all those years ago, that changed their lives forever. The day before her wedding. Violet was expecting her father to give her hand in marriage to Fred when Henry Hutton came to their door. He had come to claim his daughter.

Her father was beside himself with rage when he discovered Peggy was not his child. His fury knew no bounds as the secret of Peggy's true heritage was revealed. And even now Violet cringed when she relived that day of flying fists and raging tempers.

Ma got Peggy out of the house and hid the child under the stone steps that led to the front door. Shielding her from the unholy brawl inside, where furniture was smashed, food scattered and blood splattered up the walls. Her father, roaring with rage, did not hold his disgust at Henry Hutton. Violet's one true love was remorselessly beaten and thrown onto the street.

'You took your bloody time to claim your own child, Hutton!' her father had yelled from the top step. 'You rotten bastard!' He then grabbed Violet by the collar of her dress and threatened to take her down to the river Mersey and throw her in, until her mother came to her rescue and hurried her into the house next door. 'A child I've paid for from the minute your mother told me she was one o' mine... And you... You are nothing but a whore,' he roared, 'and deserve no better than that work-shy Fred Oldshaw, who thinks he's marrying an unspoiled girl. A nice girl. A well-brought up girl. He doesn't deserve one, though, he's never worked a full week in his life.'

Violet had listened behind the door of Aunt Biddy's house, which her father broke down with two hefty kicks to get to her. Even now, Violet could feel the searing backhander that sent her flying across the room and would never forget the molten anger in his eyes as Aunt Biddy tried in vain to stop him. His nostrils flaring, the sweat ran down his face as foam gathered in the corner of his lips, like a wild animal, the image enforced by his guttural threats that bounced off every wall of the house.

Violet took one hell of a beating after Henry Hutton had been run out of the courts. She had no choice but to accept her penance, with the threat of more to come if she told the child the truth. Only her mother's interruption, standing firm between father and daughter, saved Violet from the pounding that, if continued, could very well have killed her.

'In truth,' her father gasped, his anger spent, 'he's marrying a ruined wretch of a girl. And if you tell him, I will kill you.' He hated Fred only marginally more than he hated her that day. Before slamming out of his sister's house, her father told Violet, 'You and that lazy, no-good, waste of God's good air deserve each other. I hope you live to regret what you did, until the end of your days.'

Violet had lived to regret her impetuous decision to marry. Life was never meant to be easy. Her mother had drummed that much into her. Peggy had been her father's darling child. Violet had bought her the most beautiful sunshine yellow dress, with a silk sash bow, to wear to her wedding, but he ribboned it to shreds before he took off back to sea, never to return. After that day, her mother made sure Violet no longer deserved Peggy's love and childlike devotion.

Forced to harden her heart to Peggy's love was Violet's own private punishment. Her shame hidden from so many by her mam. The secret disgrace all but swallowed her. After that day, Violet was no longer allowed to show her own daughter the love and security she so desperately deserved, and Ma never let her forget she was the reason her father left all those years ago.

But, after all this time, Violet knew she could do something to help Peg. She should have done it years ago, but she was afraid of her mother's spiteful tongue.

'You must allow me to help her,' Hutton begged.

'Oh you'll help her. There is no doubt about that,' Violet told him. 'You can pay her husband the six months' sick money you owe him for a start.' Violet leaned forward to make sure he got the message. He wasn't getting off so lightly this time.

But something stopped her dead in her tracks when Hutton said, 'I will pay Dar Tenant's hospital fees, all of it.' Hutton told Violet. 'If I bring you the money, will you make sure she gets it?'

'Every single penny,' said Violet, who knew better than to tell him the fees had already been paid.

'I will have it by close of banking this afternoon.'

When she left Hutton's office, Violet did so with the promise Peggy would be looked after. If she wasn't, Violet told him, his wife was going to find out the truth, and she was sure he didn't want his shareholders to hear that.

Later, when she returned to his office, he handed Violet the large envelope, filled with crisp white five-pound notes. She took it without ceremony or appreciation.

'I wish things had been different,' he said, and Violet lowered her head. If truth be told, so did she.

'Well, what will be will be.' Violet threw the words over her shoulder as she opened the door. 'And if I were you, I'd think on about getting a cleaner in. This place is filthy.'

'Now I know where Peggy gets that straight talking from.'

'Aye, she never licked what she learned from me off the floor. Ta-ra, well.' She deliberately spoke in that sloppy way she knew he abhorred as she felt the weight of the brown paper package in her hand. The envelope was stuffed to bursting. *My girl can do a lot with this money*, Violet thought.

* * *

'Can I come in?' Violet asked Peggy when she answered the knock on the vestibule door.

'You look dead beat, come and sit down, I've just made a fresh pot of tea.'

Violet was glad of the rest, to take the weight off her feet.

Peggy shook her head in amazement when Violet took the large envelope out of her bag and told her to look inside.

'It's all there, every penny that Hutton owes Dar, and more.'

'But... how? Why? What...? How did you...?'

'You know,' said Violet, 'you don't half ask a lot of questions.' She smiled, knowing for the first time she was able to do something for her daughter. 'Just go with me on this one and don't say a word until I've finished.'

Over the next hour, Violet told her daughter everything.

'Henry Hutton is your father,' said Violet, then with the black humour of the dockside, she let out a raucous laugh. 'I bet you're glad it's not Fred!'

'I can't take it in.' Peg felt like she'd been hit with a sledgehammer as she tried to absorb the enormity of the revelation.

'Henry told me he is changing his will. You, not Miles, will be sole heir to his money, his business, the lot.'

'Behave yourself, woman!' Peggy gasped. 'I only wanted to be able to buy this house.'

'Well, now's your chance,' said Violet, thrilled her daughter was able to do just that.

'But what about Dar, he's not here to buy the deeds,' Peggy said.

'He doesn't need to be,' said Violet. 'Don't you know women have been emancipated?'

'What does that mean?' Peggy had never been interested in politics and rarely read the newspapers, unless there was a big murder trial in Saint George's Hall.

'It means women have as much right as their husband to keep

their wages, inherit and hold property. The suffragists campaigning brought about the Married Women's Property Act of 1882.'

'I didn't know you were so clever,' Peggy said, her eyes widened.

'There's a lot you don't know,' said Violet, 'but all that is going to change.'

28

Daisy lowered her head and pressed her lips tightly together in a straight line lest she say something she might later regret. It was only three weeks to Christmas and Max had told her he was off to Harrogate, to work on an advertising campaign in aid of his aunt's ailing bed and breakfast.

'I'll be there and back before you know it, Dais.'

Given his track record, where he would disappear on a whim to chase a story, Daisy wasn't so sure about that.

'Don't hurry back on my account.' Daisy's tone was sharp with disappointment. 'I'll hardly know you've gone. I will be far too busy building my own catering empire to notice.' She was going to miss him so very much.

'Atta girl, Dais!' called Max, blowing her a kiss from the window of the moving train. 'See you soon!'

* * *

Max had been gone a week when Daisy opened the door just as the postman delivered a bundle of letters. Christmas cards, she supposed. Then she saw one addressed to her and recognised the handwriting at once. The paper boy handed her the morning newspaper, and she tucked it under her arm, eager to open the envelope, until Mam took the newspaper from under Daisy's arm and began to read aloud, about some famous author who had gone missing, presumed dead, and she wondered how much talking her mother and Percy could do on the subject.

'What I don't understand,' said Molly, 'is why she left a perfectly good fur coat in this weather?' The papers had reported the author's car was found on the edge of a cliff in Surrey. 'You don't suppose she's...' Molly silently mouthed the words, 'done herself a mischief?' By that, Daisy knew her mother meant the author had committed suicide but could not bring herself to voice the words.

And when the news reported that the author's husband was suspected of murder, it caused a sensation.

'Oh look Percy,' said Molly, outraged on behalf of the famous writer, 'the husband has left her for another woman!'

'What a cad,' said Percy, 'although, we don't know the full story yet, Moll, so we shouldn't judge.'

'That poor woman must have been devastated,' Molly said. 'I thought it was him, all along.' Molly nudged Percy's elbow as they sat around the table. 'Didn't I say, Perc?'

'You did, Moll,' said Percy, who agreed with everything her mother said, Daisy noticed. 'This sounds like a plot in one of her novels,' remarked Percy, who enjoyed reading of Agatha Christie's extraordinary disappearance. 'I went to buy her latest book, but every one of them were sold out.'

'Every cloud, hey, Perc.' Daisy smiled. 'It looks like her disap-pearance is good for business.' Daisy's tone, although light-hearted, hid a deep feeling of sympathy for the woman she had never heard of until she went missing.

'Every day there's a new development,' said Percy, tapping the newspaper.

'I've never known the likes,' said Molly, 'people can't get enough of these stories.'

'You can say that again, Moll,' Percy said, and Daisy watched her mother eagerly nod her head, while wondering if these two older people were anxiously waiting for the next exciting instalment.

'The news is very sad, though,' Daisy said, showing her mother and Percy a photograph of men dredging a pond, while other pictures showed searchers taking a break near a soft-topped chara-banc eating a packed lunch. 'They do look like they should be part of one of her stories,' said Daisy and Percy nodded.

'It's certainly caused a frenzy in the bakery,' said Percy. 'There's bloodhounds sniffing all over the place.'

'In the bakery?' asked Molly.

Percy shook his head and laughed. 'No, not in the bakery, at the site where Agatha went missing,' he explained. 'There's hundreds of volunteers out searching, even Sir Arthur Conan Doyle got involved and hired a psychic.'

'How can a woman, whose face is in every newspaper, suddenly disappear?' asked Molly. 'You can't go to the shops around here without everybody knowing about it.'

'It's a mystery and no mistake,' said Percy.

Molly had her opinion, and he had his, but usually he came around to Molly's way of thinking in the end, since she was a determined kind of woman who had a truly clear head on her shoulders, which he found wise not to contradict.

'Any news from Max on the matter?' Percy and Molly wanted to hear the latest news.

'Well, he's not in Surrey, that's for sure,' said Daisy, taking the envelope from her pocket.

'How do you know that?' asked Percy. 'I thought he'd be one of the first reporters on the trail.'

'He's gone to help his aunt in Harrogate,' said Molly. 'He'll be kicking himself, missing this.'

'The postmark says Harrogate—' Daisy frowned '—wherever that is.'

'It's in Yorkshire,' answered Percy. 'I served with a lad from Harrogate in the war; he lost an eye and got five kids, so it's not all doom and gloom.'

'Sorry to hear that, Percy,' said Daisy. 'Max is in Harrogate when every other reporter is in Surrey, he'll be missing out on a big story.'

'And they don't come much bigger than this one,' said Percy.

'Maybe you'd better open the letter and see what he's got to say on the matter, because as sure as eggs is eggs, he won't be happy,' Molly quipped as Daisy slipped her thumb under the flap of the envelope and quickly drew out the letter, her eyes zigzagging the page.

'Oh, you are never going to guess—' Daisy could not take her eyes off the letter '—he's only in the bed and breakfast next to a spa hotel.'

'Yes?' Molly's brows pleated in puzzlement, eager to hear the news.

'Max has only gone and found her.'

'Who? The novelist?' Percy was only half-joking and Daisy, dumbstruck, nodded.

'What!' Molly dropped the sugar spoon with a clatter onto her saucer, while Percy scraped his straight-backed chair and hurried to Daisy's side, reading the letter over her shoulder.

'Blimey! Excuse my language, but blimey!'

'I know!' Daisy exclaimed. 'Max says she's no idea how she got there because she's lost her memory.'

'That's a bit unfortunate when you're a writer,' said Percy. 'Mind you, with all those stories going round in her head, I can see how she'd forget some things.'

'Max says the hotel is waiting for her husband to come and identify her, because she's going by a different name.' Daisy folded the letter and slipped it back into the envelope.

'Maybe it's a ruse to get him back,' said Molly.

'Well, if my husband did that, I wouldn't want him back,' Daisy told them.

'Anyone in mind?' Percy grinned and Daisy rolled her eyes.

'I'm going to be like Mary Jane and have my own business.'

* * *

Daisy, secure in the knowledge they made a well-matched couple, agreed that Max was a very thorough journalist, and told him how much she admired the way he had got that detective novelist to tell him exactly why she had ended up in Harrogate when her car was found in Surrey. It was a scoop.

'Fancy leaving a fur coat in winter?' said Daisy, repeating her mother's question. 'How did you know Agatha was in Harrogate?' She had become accustomed to using first-name terms, what with her mother pestering Max to tell her every exciting detail of news when he came to the house to visit, while Percy was catching up with Max's story about his trip to his aunt's bed and breakfast in Harrogate and how he'd met the famous author.

'I didn't know she was in Harrogate,' said Max in all honesty, 'I was going to advise my aunt, about an advertising campaign she was thinking of doing to boost business, but now she has no need to advertise. She is booked to capacity for the foreseeable and beyond and has had to take on more staff to cope with the demand of the business.'

* * *

Daisy was telling Mary Jane about Max when she saw Peggy Tenant come into the shop. She could see Peggy did not look happy when she asked Mary Jane if she could have a word. Moving around to a quieter part of the shop, Daisy surmised Peggy had come about the money Mary Jane had given Millie earlier, and the free pies that weren't even stale.

'What's this money for?' Peggy asked, holding out her open palm. 'You know full well, I won't accept charity. Thank you for the pies. Millie told me they were going to the pigs, and much as I hate waste, my kids' bellies are just as important as any farm animal.'

'I'm glad to hear it.' Mary Jane smiled. Peggy's elasticated principles obviously didn't stretch to refusing free food. 'Your Millie looks like a good meal would pull her over.'

'She's small-boned, that's all...' Peggy's quick retort showed she resented the insinuation her daughter was half-starved, because she wasn't, not any more, and she was just about to say so when Mary Jane cut her off.

'Now look here, Peggy, I don't care what you and Dar do to manage, but I can't stand by and watch a poor kid go without. It's not in my nature, and I know it's certainly not in yours, so think on.' She wrapped bread as she spoke and served another customer. 'We can cope, us oldies, but the wee ones need something to help them grow and get this bloody country back on its feet.' She made the sign of the cross. 'God forgive me for swearing.'

Mary Jane's outburst left Peggy silent. Wouldn't they all be shocked when they found out she was the sole heir to Hutton's Logistics. But she wasn't going to say anything, because she would never besmirch Violet's name. Even though Oldshaw was not the most salubrious name she could have owned, but there you have it, thought Peggy.

'Thank you for your kindness,' Peggy said before turning to leave the shop when Mary Jane called her back.

'How old is your Millie? She must be nigh on leaving school?'

'She fourteen, leaving school this Christmas, why?' Peggy's brows knitted together in a quizzical frown.

'Do you think she could take to baking?' asked Mary Jane in a forthright tone, and Peggy nodded, telling Mary Jane her daughter would love it. 'Well, tell her to call in and see me. I think I've got a job for her.'

Peggy could hardly believe the recent turn of events. Jack had been offered an apprenticeship, Dar was coming home tomorrow and now Millie was being offered training. 'I'll send her along straight away.'

'Grand,' said Mary Jane. 'If it suits, we'll teach her all we know, me and Daisy.'

'It'll suit, all right,' said Peggy. 'You have my word on that.'

'She can start at eight o'clock, the same time as my other young apprentice.'

'An apprenticeship?' Even if the job was not well paid at first, Millie would have a trade, something to fall back on if times were hard.

'The job comes with a daily loaf, and a fruit pie at weekends.'

'Oh, my lor!' Peggy, not usually lost for words, certainly was now, thinking of the days when a fresh daily loaf and a fruit pie were luxuries she could ill afford.

'I'll see her this afternoon.' Mary Jane watched Peggy leave the shop and flit into the greengrocer's, saying to Daisy, 'I've never met such a stubborn woman as Peggy Tenant.'

'That'll be Mrs Pot calling Mrs Kettle, will it?' Daisy answered, knowing she had seen nobody with as much dogged determination as Mary Jane.

29

The Tenant family gathered in their cosy kitchen, adorned with new wallpaper and colourful Christmas paper chains, which the children had glued together with flour and water at the kitchen table, as it was too cold to play outside.

White gloss paint added to the fresh smell of polish and a crackling fire burned bright in the fireplace, while outside the sash windows a gentle snowfall transformed Beamer Street into a winter wonderland. The perfect backdrop to Dar's homecoming, thought Peggy.

The fruity tang of freshly baked mince pies filled the kitchen, mingling with the scent of pine disinfectant, which Peggy loved so much. Everything must be perfect when her beloved Dar came home. The sound of carol singers could be heard and the young ones, Eddy and Jane, hurried to the front door, while Peggy went to fetch her purse. There would be no scrimping and scraping this Christmas, she thought, as happy tears welled in her eyes.

Throughout the day, the little ones had been busy preparing for their supposed Christmas visit to Lavender Green, excited to see their beloved father, while Peggy set the table and prepared all of Dar's favourite food as the children settled to wrap little presents.

As the clock ticked closer to the expected hour, Peggy glanced anxiously towards the door, eagerly awaiting the sound of the ambulance that was going to deliver her husband home. There was so much she wanted to tell him, so much they had to catch up on in the privacy of their own home. Eager to give him the biggest Christmas present she could think of, knowing he was going to be so pleased.

'Dar!' Peggy heard the high-pitched delight in the voices of her youngest two and hurried out into the passageway. 'Mam, come quick, Dar's home for Christmas.'

'Dar's home for good,' Dar laughed. He had a noticeable limp, but at least he was able to walk up his own hallway and into the kitchen.

'Surprise!' called Jack and Millie, who had their own good news to tell him. There was so many voices talking at once, Dar had to hold up his hand and ask for silence.

'Listen, can you hear that?' he asked, and they all shook their heads.

'That's the sound of home,' he said.

* * *

The following morning, Eddy and Jane scrambled from their beds at an unearthly hour, before dawn. Clutching their stocking filled with apples, oranges and little gifts, their bare feet thundered along the landing to their sleepy parents' bedroom.

'Just another half an hour,' Peggy pleaded sleepily, enjoying once more the warmth of her loving husband beside her. Although her youngest two had other thoughts.

'Wake up, Mam, he's been!'

Peggy quickly realised she would get no more sleep this morning when, in the light of the gas mantle, she saw the loving glint in Dar's eyes. After the children emptied their stockings on their parents' bed, they then excitedly refilled them.

'Go back to bed,' said Dar, 'it's warm in your bed. And don't eat everything in your stocking before breakfast.'

'We won't,' the young ones promised. Giggling, they raced back to their own room.

'They will,' said Peggy, snuggling into Dar's loving arms. Then, unable to hold onto her news much longer, she whispered, 'I've got a surprise gift for you.'

'Later.' Dar gently pulled his wife closer and drew her under the covers.

* * *

'And this is the proof we own every brick and roof tile,' Peggy said as they sat down to breakfast. She handed over the deeds to the house. Dar swallowed hard as he opened the official document. His heart, a fist pounding the inside of his chest.

'You clever woman,' he said, not surprised, elated. 'You did this?'

'Yes, all by myself,' Peggy laughed. She had told him the whole story about Violet being her mother and Henry Hutton her father after the children had gone back to bed earlier that morning. She had even told Dar she was heir to Hutton's business, which made them both howl with laughter. A sound that had been sorely missed over the last months.

'You have changed beyond recognition,' Dar told her. 'I didn't think I would, but I love the new independent woman you have become.'

'Why thank you, kind sir.' Peggy's eyes danced with pleasure. 'We are a team, you and me.'

'Ready to do our best for our family.'

'We have so much to look forward to,' said Dar, 'long may it last.'

'Did I tell you our Violet's moving in next door?' Peggy said, her eyes twinkling. She had loved being able to tell Violet that Percy and his sister were moving, enabling her to move out of the courts and into Beamer Street. 'She can't wait.'

Dar smiled. Violet had never been as caustic as her mother, and he felt she would never have been so sombre, had life dealt her a different hand. Peggy agreed.

Dar offered Peggy his sympathy at Maggie's passing once more. But only for his wife's sake. There was no love lost between him and the woman who held her secrets close, like a suit of armour.

'I am so glad you're home,' said Peggy as he slipped his arm around her waist and felt the nearness of the woman he had longed to hold for months.

'What would I do without you all.'

EPILOGUE

Jack kept his father updated on his progress as an apprentice engineer, informing Dar he had been invited to the opening of the new Gladstone dock, when it would be officially opened by King George V next September.

'Mister Everdine says the new dock will be the biggest in the world.' Jack was so proud of his small part in its construction. 'The dock is over one thousand feet long, and over a hundred feet wide.'

'How deep?' Dar tested his eldest son, unable to keep the proud smile from his face.

'Forty-two feet,' said Jack, 'wider, longer and deeper than the Panama Canal!'

'That's some dock,' said Dar, glad his son had followed him to work on the waterfront, but in a much more exalted ability when he'd served his time. 'We have a lot to be thankful for,' Dar told Peggy, slipping his hand around her waist. 'Our son has a brand-new apprenticeship that will see him through the rest of his days. Thanks to you, we have our own house, all bought and paid for. Our Millie is in training.'

'Aye, but you know what brings me the most pleasure,' said

Peggy, 'a lot of questions were answered for me. Violet put my demons to rest and made me realise something stronger than bricks and mortar bind us together, when she told me the truth about being my mother.' Peggy felt secure in the knowledge her family was on the right track. 'Family is what holds us all together and makes us strong.'

'I know.' Dar gave Peggy a kiss and the two youngest giggled behind their hands. 'And I'll be back in work in the New Year.' Cal Everdine had given Dar a well-paid job managing his properties. 'First thing I'm going to do is paint the front door of every house,' Dar said. 'I'm taking on Molly's lad, young Freddy Haywood, he's just left school and I'm taking him on as my apprentice.'

'There will always be family ties in Beamer Street,' said Peggy, 'and I wouldn't want to live anywhere else.'

ACKNOWLEDGEMENTS

Once again, my thanks go to my wonderful editors Caroline Ridding, Jade and Sandra – patience personified. The editorial team at Boldwood is second to none. I want to thank everybody at Team Boldwood for their unfailing dedication to getting it right. Each one of you deserve the plaudits and recognition for which you work so diligently.

I would also like to thank my agent, Caroline Sheldon, one of the nicest women I have met, a true pioneer of her chosen profession. I salute you.

To my many friends in the writing world, past and present, who have offered encouragement, expertise and unfailing support. Long may we keep on going.

And last, but by no means least, I thank my readers, without whom this sometimes-crazy pursuit of living inside my own head to create the stories you love would be a solitary journey.

Lots of love and hugs,
Sheila xx

ABOUT THE AUTHOR

Sheila Riley wrote four #1 bestselling novels under the pseudonym Annie Groves and is now writing the second of two saga trilogies under her own name. She has set her series around the River Mersey and its docklands near to where she spent her early years.

Sign up to Sheila Riley's mailing list for news, competitions and updates on future books.

Visit Sheila's website: http://my-writing-ladder.blogspot.com/

Follow Sheila on social media:

facebook.com/SheilaRileyAuthor

x.com/1sheilariley

instagram.com/sheilarileynovelist

bookbub.com/authors/sheila-riley

ALSO BY SHEILA RILEY

Reckoner's Row Series

The Mersey Orphan

The Mersey Girls

The Mersey Mothers

Beamer Street Series

Finding Friends on Beamer Street

A Safe Haven on Beamer Street

Family Ties on Beamer Street

The Dockside Sagas

The Mersey Mistress

The Mersey Angels

Sixpence Stories

Introducing Sixpence Stories!

Discover page-turning historical novels from your favourite authors, meet new friends and be transported back in time.

Join our book club Facebook group

https://bit.ly/SixpenceGroup

Sign up to our newsletter

https://bit.ly/SixpenceNews

Boldw⦿⦿d

Boldwood Books is an award-winning fiction publishing company seeking out the best stories from around the world.

Find out more at www.boldwoodbooks.com

Join our reader community for brilliant books, competitions and offers!

Follow us
@BoldwoodBooks
@TheBoldBookClub

Sign up to our weekly deals newsletter

https://bit.ly/BoldwoodBNewsletter

Printed in Great Britain
by Amazon